Praise for *Hex*

One of Goodreads's Best New Horror Recommendations

"*Hex Education* is a magically spiked pumpkin spice latte of a fall read. I drank it right up!"

—K. J. Dell'Antonia, *New York Times* bestselling author of *The Chicken Sisters*

"A breath of fresh air . . . an absolute delight . . . If you're looking for a witchy book that is solidly cemented in the real world, you need to read *Hex Education*. It's fun and magical and will draw you in from page one."

—*Culturess*

"Kilmer spins a highly enjoyable narrative that often hints at something darker. . . . *Hex Education*, witty and entertaining, will beguile fans of *Charmed* or *Bewitched*, but it also asks deeper questions about magic, friendship, responsibility, and truth-telling."

—*Shelf Awareness*

"Sarah's domestic use of magic in her day-to-day life is delightful [and] laugh-out-loud funny. . . . A lighthearted witchy romp."

—*Kirkus Reviews*

"This amusing [tale] of magic gone awry is a solid choice for collections where stories of modern-day witches are popular."

—*Booklist*

"Kilmer enchants with this cozy fantasy novel that follows a disbanded coven who reunite to prevent magic from upending their lives. . . . The magical hijinks, pop culture references, and colorful cast (including a sassy talking cat) are sure to entertain. Fans of contemporary fantasy will find much to appreciate."

—*Publishers Weekly*

Praise for *Suburban Hell*

One of *Bustle*'s Most Anticipated Books of August 2022
One of *BuzzFeed*'s New Books You Won't Be Able to Put Down

"A cheerfully campy take on the usual concerns—conformity, boredom, demonic possession." —*Chicago Tribune*

"This delightful fiction debut is the hell-arious *Desperate Housewives*–esque novel that dreams are made of." —*BuzzFeed*

"A delightful, fun, spooky, scary story. At its core it's about friendship and the bonds of love for these four women. Maureen has hit a home run with her first novel." —*Red Carpet Crash*

"This novel about the horrors of suburbia—both supernatural and terrestrial in origin—has plenty of genuinely funny moments. . . . A good fit for fans of Grady Hendrix's *My Best Friend's Exorcism*, Rachel Harrison's *The Return*, or Junji Ito's horror manga *Uzumaki*." —*Booklist*

"A savvy, wildly relatable horror-comedy about suburban angst and the bonds of friendship that serves chilling scares and genuine laughs. Massively entertaining and fun as hell!"

—Rachel Harrison, author of *Such Sharp Teeth*

"Maureen Kilmer strikes the perfect balance in *Suburban Hell*. This is a scary, thrilling, and funny ride through a neighborhood nightmare. The pages turn themselves, you can't stop reading this one."

—Samantha Downing, author of *For Your Own Good*

NIGHTMARE
of a Trip

Also by Maureen Kilmer

Hex Education

Suburban Hell

Nightmare of a Trip

A NOVEL

Maureen Kilmer

G. P. Putnam's Sons
New York

PUTNAM
— EST. 1838 —

G. P. Putnam's Sons
Publishers Since 1838
An imprint of Penguin Random House LLC
penguinrandomhouse.com

Library of Congress Cataloging-in-Publication Data

Names: Kilmer, Maureen, author.
Title: Nightmare of a trip: a novel / Maureen Kilmer.
Description: New York: G. P. Putnam's Sons, 2024
Identifiers: LCCN 2023058015 (print) | LCCN 2023058016 (ebook) |
ISBN 9780593718599 (trade paperback) | ISBN 9780593718605 (epub)
Subjects: LCSH: Family vacations—Fiction. | LCGFT: Novels.
Classification: LCC PS3612.I635 N54 2024 (print) | LCC PS3612.I635 (ebook) |
DDC 813/.6—dc23/eng/20230102
LC record available at https://lccn.loc.gov/2023058015
LC ebook record available at https://lccn.loc.gov/2023058016

Printed in the United States of America
1st Printing

Book design by Nancy Resnick
Title page illustration by Anton Fomenok/Shutterstock.com

For Lucy

NIGHTMARE
of a Trip

Chapter 1

If the road to hell is paved with good intentions, then Satan himself planned our family trip.

One thousand two hundred and seventy miles, driving from our Milwaukee, Wisconsin, suburb to Magic Land in Orlando, Florida. It was supposed to bond us, bring us closer together.

We thought the only horror would be sharing a data plan. Long country routes, no Wi-Fi, spotty cellular service—annoyances, but ones we would conquer like the middle-class suburban pioneers that we were.

We were wrong.

"It's a road trip, not the apocalypse. I don't think we need ten boxes of mini muffins and cheese crackers." My sixteen-year-old daughter, Piper, stood with her hands on her hips as she peered into the backseat of our family's tan Honda Odyssey minivan.

I raised my eyebrows at her but said nothing. She wouldn't be complaining when we were in the middle of cornfield territory and her siblings started going feral from imagined starvation.

Piper turned and pulled her phone out of the back pocket of her jean shorts, lifting it toward the rear gate of the minivan. I heard the click of a photo and then she studied the screen, tapping at it, before she nodded and stuck it into her pocket.

"You doing it for the 'gram? Want to film a reel as I awkwardly pack the car? Sure to go viral," I said as I threw my body toward a blue duffel bag, trying to shove it into the space between the two captain's chairs in the second row of the car.

"No thank you." She leaned a hand against the van's exterior and then quickly withdrew it. "Ow. Too hot." She shook her wavy brown hair out of her eyes and squarely faced me. "Mom. This whole road trip will go down in social media history, since I'm documenting it all. Hashtags include: 'nightmare fuel,' 'gas station hot dogs,' 'are we there yet,' and 'hostage crisis.'"

"You don't even eat hot dogs," I said. I gave the duffel bag one last shove and then slid the door closed. Every inch of the interior was stacked with suitcases, snacks, electronic devices, headphones, and DVDs.

I turned to face my daughter. "I'm so glad you've decided not to be melodramatic. And I'm sure your followers will love it all. Hey, and maybe a cute guy will slide into my DMs—isn't that what you youths call it?"

She grimaced and then turned to walk back inside our house. "Gross."

As intended. If she was going to disparage our fun family road trip, the least I could do was horrify her. Although secretly I was worried I would be the one horrified by the end of the trip. I was looking forward to the vacation time with my family, just not how we were getting to our destination. It felt like a test to see if we would all like each other by the end, and I didn't know if we would pass.

"Oh. I named our van Tammy the Tan Squirrel," Piper called over her shoulder.

"What? Why?" I said. Our Honda did not look like a Tammy. Or a squirrel.

"Because," she said slowly, like she was explaining quantum physics to a toddler, "it makes sense." She perked up and smiled. "Can I drive Tammy through Illinois? Please?"

I shook my head and rolled my eyes. "For the hundredth time: no. Your dad and I will be driving on this trip. This isn't the time to test your driving skills."

My husband, Nick, opened the door to the garage as Piper walked through. "Almost ready?" He clapped his hands together as Piper walked past him, gaze fixed back on her phone. "Someone looks ready."

He walked toward the car, peering through the front windshield, brow furrowed, before his face broke out into a smile. "I hope that's everything, because nothing else is fitting in there."

I gave him a half smile before rolling my eyes. He put an arm around my shoulders and squeezed me to his chest.

"Leigh, it'll be great. I promise," he said. "Nothing will go wrong."

It was mid-June, a time when Nick's optimism always hit a peak. He was the vice principal of Hubert Middle School, and summer break had started the week before. Mid-June was a time when his days off stretched before him, endless possibilities and limitless adventures. It usually held firm until the end of the month. But once the Fourth of July hit, he would begin a slow emotional decline of realizing the summer wouldn't last forever.

I figured his good attitude—before any work stress began to percolate, before thoughts of parent-teacher conferences, curriculum night, and school board meetings began to loom—could fuel us through the Midwest and at least through part of the upper South. And maybe we would even enjoy the hours together. Maybe.

"Is it time to go?" My eleven-year-old son, Leo, called from across the street, where he was in a highly competitive game of yard soccer with the other fifth-grade neighbors; they'd run and push and argue until a parent inevitably got irritated enough to try to play referee. It was like a game of parenting chicken, and I always won. Mostly because my home office was in the back of the house, out of earshot.

"Just about. C'mon back, buddy," Nick called to Leo, waving his hand toward the car.

"I'll go get Sophie inside," I said. The last time I'd seen our seven-year-old daughter, she was shoving Squishmallows into a rolling suitcase, certain she could fit her impressive collection inside.

Twenty minutes later, after double-checking the security straps on the turtle top storage on the minivan's roof, throwing a few more snacks into a reusable cloth grocery bag, and packing more charging cords than could be used by an entire fleet of IT professionals, we were in the car and ready to back out of the driveway.

Leo and Sophie were in the captain's chairs, headphones on, as the movie *Rio* started on the car's DVD player. Piper was in the third row, stretched out as far as the seat belt would allow, her phone on her lap and earbuds in.

We got as far as the end of our driveway before Sophie said, "I forgot to go to the bathroom."

Groaning, Nick stopped the car, making me shift forward in my seat, and hit the button for the garage door. "Can you make it fast, Soph? We have a schedule to stick to."

Sophie nodded and unbuckled herself and slid open the minivan's door before racing inside, her pigtails streaming behind her.

I put a foot up on the dashboard, looked over at Nick, and smiled. I held up both hands, fingers splayed. "Ten feet. We've made it ten feet. We won't make it to the Wisconsin-Illinois border before fall at this point."

"Good thing I know how to forage in the woods." Nick held up a finger and cocked his head to the side. "If we don't hit any traffic, we'll still be on track. And at least we have good music." He pecked at his phone until "Holiday Road," of *National Lampoon's Vacation* fame, came on.

"Seriously?" I said with a groan.

"Road trip playlist on Spotify," Nick said. He tapped his hand against the steering wheel. I could tell he was picturing himself as Clark Griswold, ready to journey to Walley World and take over the park—at gunpoint if necessary. I didn't think the security guards at Magic Land would go so quietly into the night.

Piper harrumphed in the way back and opened a bag of Takis, her snack version of a weighted blanket, while Leo slowly closed his eyes and drifted off as we waited for Sophie. He was always the first to fall asleep in the car as a baby, something that had thankfully continued throughout childhood.

Once Sophie was back inside the car, we once again reversed out of the driveway. I waved for Nick to stop in front of our mailbox on the street, so I could check one more time to make sure we had collected all of the mail before the postal hold.

Empty.

Our trusty minivan—Tammy, apparently—made it to the end of the street just as Nick's phone interrupted "On the Road Again" to blare out that we should turn left on Orchard Road, before my good friend Kerry ran out of her front door. She waved, still dressed in her blue scrubs from her overnight shift in the emergency room at Germantown Memorial Hospital.

Nick put the car in Park in the middle of our street, and I opened the door as Piper groaned from the backseat.

"Hashtag hold on," I singsonged to her as I hopped out of our car.

"I caught you!" Kerry said as she lifted her palms toward the cloudless June sky. Her strawberry blond hair was wound in a bun on top of her head with a few loose strands collapsing downward. She still had indentations on either side of her cheeks from her medical mask.

I laughed and leaned forward, giving her a quick hug. "You already said goodbye, last night before you went to work. Remember?" Kerry had stopped by as I was trying to shove an extra pair of joggers into my already-stuffed suitcase. She'd plopped down on top of the plastic shell and I quickly closed it before it could open up again like a tube of Pillsbury biscuits.

She nodded and folded her arms across her chest, the hospital's logo stitched on the pocket. "Yeah, but as my shift was ending, I had this weird feeling that I needed to say goodbye one more time."

I twisted my mouth to the side and shielded my eyes from the sunlight. "That's sweet but weird."

"That's why we're friends," Kerry said. Her smile dimmed for a moment before she straightened up, gazing over my left shoulder with a wave. "Speaking of friends—look, M.J. is pulling up."

I turned and saw a large navy Sprinter van, nearly the size of the Amazon delivery vans that patrolled the neighborhood, coming to a stop behind us in the middle of the road.

My friend M.J. jumped down from the driver's side, hair twisted in her signature topknot, wearing her uniform of capri high-waisted leggings, a matching tank top, and athletic shoes. She gave us a vigorous wave before she jogged the few paces over to where we stood. Her eyes briefly slid to the blue ribbon tied around an aging elm tree on the parkway, a leftover from two summers ago.

"Hey! About to hit the road?" she said after she gave Kerry and me each a quick hug. She squinted in the sunlight, looking at our minivan and then back to me. "I thought you guys were supposed to leave hours ago."

I lifted my palms. M.J., if anyone did, should have understood chaos. I peered inside her Sprinter van. I could make out three shapes—a trio of her kids, of which there were two more somewhere else. Three boys and two girls, and about fifty-seven youth sports teams between all of them. M.J. had played soccer at Ohio State, and her husband, Tony, had been on the tennis team, so being shuttled to activities was almost a birthright for their menagerie of children. Meanwhile, the thought of having more than my current three children was nothing short of terrifying.

"I'm taking Mason to agility training," M.J. said. "And then it's the soccer club team meeting about next season." She looked at me. "I'll get the forms for you and Leo like I promised."

I gave her a grateful look. Leo and her son Ryan were on the Germantown travel soccer team together—another stick of dynamite to lay at the feet of my calendar. Leo was a defender and Ryan played goalie, and together they were an unstoppable force. It was a feel-good neighborhood story since Ryan had battled non-Hodgkin's lymphoma a couple of years ago, hence the summer of blue ribbons wrapped around the trees.

"See? We got you covered. She's got your sports, and I'll water your gardens. I'll make sure your garden is lush and full and—Wait, this is sounding dirty." She shook her head and winked as M.J. snorted. "Anyway, they will be kept hydrated per the highly detailed map you gave me."

"If I come back and my hydrangeas are burned to a crisp, I—" I stopped as I heard shouts from the neighborhood boys. Their soccer ball was rolling into the street in front of our car. As they ran to get it, the rear door of my minivan slid open and Leo hopped out, running toward the ball to kick it back to his friends.

From M.J.'s faux FedEx truck, Ryan jumped out to join in the game. His hair was cropped short in a buzz cut.

"That's my cue, ladies. If we don't get out of here now, we never will. This is like a space shuttle launch," I said as I waved for Leo to come back.

"Well, Sally Ride, be careful." M.J. laughed and linked arms with Kerry.

"One small step for the Somerset family, one giant leap for mankind. Or something like that," I said as I ushered my son back into the car and turned to wave again at my friends.

"You'll never guess what happened at work today." Kerry turned to M.J., arms crossed.

I didn't hear the rest of the story as I closed the passenger-side door. Kerry always had the weirdest stories from working in the emergency room, like the time a patient stole a car waiting out front, or the time when a visitor accused her of stealing her doll-head collection.

Ringleader of a medical circus, as she often described it. *P. T. Barnum can blow me.*

A pang of sadness ran through my shoulders as I saw my two closest friends huddling together, M.J.'s car still idling in the street. I figured they would probably make plans to hang out later together, once all of M.J.'s many children were finished with their daily sporting events. Normally, I would be with them, sitting around M.J.'s pool with Kerry, laughing and drinking wine.

"I'm not even going to ask if we're ready this time," Nick said as he waved to Kerry and M.J.

"Please don't. One more hiccup and I'm walking back home and you all can go to Florida without me." The thought of my house, alone, for two weeks, sounded more enticing than ever. I glanced longingly at the flower beds Kerry had promised to water for me. I'd spent nearly every summer for the past couple of years ripping out the old evergreen yew shrubs and planting new ones, slowly bringing the exterior of our Colonial from the 1980s to the present. Leo and I had planted a shade garden the summer before, and now they would be under Kerry's care.

If we ever actually were able to leave.

Eyes trained forward on the road, Tammy forged ahead, our modern-day Oregon Trail adventure beginning—thirty minutes from the first time we closed our garage door, and a mere half block from our house.

At least, I figured, none of us would have to hunt buffalo or fight off dysentery.

Chapter 2

After four hours in the car with my family, I had come to two very distinct conclusions: the first was that I-80/94 through northern Illinois to Indiana had never seen a construction opportunity it didn't like, and the second was that my family would definitely perish in the first wave of an apocalyptic scenario, as soon as the chips and Goldfish crackers ran out.

By the time we survived Illinois—and the Chicagoland drivers who only occasionally used turn signals—and reached Indiana, the sun was beginning to inch down the horizon, illuminating the cornfields and farmland along I-65. I eyed another billboard for a personal injury attorney. Jim Worniak and his legal team were definitely still on call to fight for us, just as prevalent as the radio commercial that urged us to donate our car to charity. Every ten minutes. And that was all before we hit the ubiquitous fireworks advertisements in Indiana.

As we had crossed the border into Indiana, the kids cheered from the back, waiting for their "state line presents." It was an idea I had, more of a bribe than anything, when we were planning the trip. A small present for each child every time we crossed into a new state, the presents increasing in desirability as we got closer to Florida. For Illinois, it was a Taylor Swift decal for Piper, a soccer key chain for Leo, and a small sticker book for Sophie.

It was an evolved version of what I had done for Nick when we took a road trip to the Outer Banks before we had kids. New state, new prize. Of course, back then it was things like a new CD for the car and a *Sports Illustrated* magazine. While he was appreciative of those prizes, he had a few other suggestions in mind to celebrate each state. And they weren't exactly kid-appropriate.

"Gross. What smells?" Piper moaned from the third row. She tossed a gray zip-up sweatshirt over her head, giving her a ghostly terry cloth appearance.

"Same answer as before: pig farms," I said.

Sophie had fallen asleep, her pink headphones sliding down to her neck and her mouth gaping open like a fish's during a rainstorm. Her loose front tooth dangled out of her mouth, and I nearly had to sit on my hands to keep from yanking it out.

"You still doing okay, Leo?" I said.

Leo looked up from the book in his lap, an old Christopher Pike book I had found at a library sale.

"Are we stopping soon?" he asked as he reached for his water bottle from the cupholder of the van's door.

I nodded and smiled. "Soon."

"We're almost to Lafayette, bud," Nick said as he spoke to Leo in the rearview mirror. "We're staying at a hotel there."

Leo's eyes narrowed suspiciously. "Does it have a pool like you promised?"

"Of course it does." I laughed. "Just hang tight a bit longer." I turned around and looked at Nick out of the corner of my eye. "They finished construction on it, right?" I whispered.

Nick nodded a bit too confidently. "That's what the nice lady Janelle said when I called the hotel last week."

"God help Janelle if she's wrong. God help all of us," I said.

I picked up my phone from my lap and resumed reading my work emails, as I had been for most of the state of Indiana so far.

It hadn't been easy to take the two weeks off for the road trip, especially since I was agreeing to spend half of that time in the car. I had only taken two consecutive weeks off once before, for our honeymoon when we went to Hawaii. I had just graduated with my Juris Doctor from the University of Wisconsin, where Nick and I met during our sophomore year. After seven years of intense schoolwork, my brain was so fried that I barely remembered how to go out to dinner with him without talking about a paper I had to write or which professor was rumored to frequent karaoke bars.

I still had the bar exam in front of me and months of studying for that after we returned from Maui, but I promised Nick—and myself—that I would lean into the trip. And I did.

This time, though, we weren't spending the two weeks filling ourselves with frozen drinks during the day and gorging on fresh fish at night. No, this was more gas station food and scary rest-stop bathrooms.

The beginnings of a horror movie.

I swiped down on my email to refresh it, and seven new client messages came through. I scanned each one, panic beginning to poke me in the ribs. I was a family law attorney, which meant I saw the worst things family members could possibly do to each other. Messy divorces, child custody cases, alimony settlements . . . everything. When I first started out, shiny and new, I believed that I would be the calm in the middle of my clients' emotional storms, helping them navigate their way through the legal system to benefit themselves and their families. That I would be an advocate for my clients, as I had seen firsthand how much family could hurt each other. Epic, disastrous levels of pain.

Nearly two decades later, I knew a better analogy was that I was like a second-class passenger on the *Titanic*, watching the first-class guests load their jewelry and luggage into the lifeboats.

My most time-consuming case at that moment was a client, Michelle Black, whose husband had left her for a younger woman he met at the gym (standard), but who was trying to kick her out of the house they shared with two small children. All of this was after she'd had a miscarriage and her plastic surgeon husband saw it as an opening to end the marriage. I was sure the demons were decorating his room down in a special place in hell, awaiting his arrival.

The husband, Lenny, had become quite the Instagrammer with the new girlfriend, harassing my client and sending threatening private messages. We were compiling all of it as evidence for the settlement hearing the next month.

I scanned the rest of the emails to make sure none were urgent—they weren't; just the garden-variety communications from other lawyers threatening to ruin my life and murder my children if my client didn't agree to whatever they had offered—and put my phone back, face down, in my lap.

"Look!" I said as I pointed to a green and white street sign. "Lafayette, next four exits. Guys, we've almost made it to the first stop. And we are all alive."

➡

"What do you mean the pool is closed?" Nick said as he rubbed his forehead, staring in confusion at the check-in clerk for the Traveler Inn and Suites.

David, the reception clerk, gave my husband a withering look. "Sir, as I already said, the pool has been closed for repairs for two months."

"Is Janelle working?" Nick asked. David snorted and shook his head. Janelle's whereabouts remained sealed in the vault of hotel employment secrets.

Nick looked helplessly at me, and I looked down to hide a smile. Of course it was closed. A problem, but not one we couldn't work around. If this was the worst thing that happened to us, we would survive.

"How are we going to tell Leo?" Nick whispered to me as he eyed our kids splayed out around the hotel's lobby, terrorizing the red and purple couches with the debris from our car.

"We can tell him and remind him that he's on his way to the most magical place on the planet. Maybe this is our tithe before we get to explode with joy," I said with a wry smile.

Twenty minutes later, after a few tears and shrieks of despair, we were in our adjoining rooms, bags of gas station candy spread out on the bed. It was the best we could do at short notice.

Nick went into the room with the king bed and flopped back

down on it, arms splayed out to the sides. I lay down next to him, propped up with an elbow.

"They're good, see? And please, if this is 'the worst thing that's ever happened' to Leo, we should all be so lucky," I said.

He nodded and closed his eyes, breathing deeply, the exhaustion of the first day on the road overtaking him quickly. I was about to curl up and lie next to him for a moment when I heard Leo scream.

Vision blurred, I shot up as Nick did too, crashing into my shoulder. We tore through the adjoining door as Leo continued to scream from inside the bathroom.

I wrenched open the bathroom door and found him huddled under the floating sink, arms around his bent knees.

"What? What's wrong?" I said as I knelt down on the yellow tile floor.

He stopped screaming and pointed across the bathroom to the closed shower curtain around the bathtub.

Piper shrieked behind me, and she quickly stepped back, thudding her back against the hotel room's entry corridor. "No. No. No. No."

Nick turned to her, his hand out. His other hand was gently placed on Sophie's shoulder. "It's okay. Everyone—it's okay." He looked back at me.

I guessed it was up to me to investigate whatever was behind that curtain. I stood up, putting a hand on my knee as my forty-two-year-old body creaked in protest.

I swiftly pulled back the curtain, breath held, waiting for the ax murderer.

Nothing. An empty, aging shower was behind the curtain.

"See?" Nick said from behind me.

I turned to Leo, who was still huddled under the sink. "All clear. What happened?"

A black movement caught my eye. I turned back and jumped as I saw a large hairy spider scurry across the white plastic bottom of the tub.

I started laughing. "Oh, man. Okay, I get it." I turned to my family in the doorway. "Giant spider."

Nick's shoulders relaxed and he patted Sophie's shoulder. "Just a bug."

Piper shook her head. "Nope. I've seen *Arachnophobia*. I'm not showering here." She stepped forward and snapped a picture of the spider as it disappeared down the drain. "Scene of the crime," she muttered to herself, turning away.

I held a hand out to Leo, whose eyes were the size of dinner plates. "C'mon. All gone."

He tightened his grip around his legs. "I didn't see a spider," he whispered. "It was a person."

Okay, creepy, I thought as I exchanged a glance with Nick. My husband stepped forward, and I turned to let him into the small bathroom. I moved out, toward Sophie.

"Let's go see if there's any more Skittles," I said to her.

She brightened and turned, demonic spider/fake ghost forgotten. "Leo is such a wedrio," she said.

I laughed. The term *wedrio* had become a family inside joke. A couple of years ago, Sophie had a school project called "All About Me," and in one of the sections she had to write adjectives to describe herself. She had meant to write *weirdo* (a source of pride for her, and for all the first graders) but misspelled it as *wedrio.* When we gently pointed out her mistake, she shrugged and said, "Maybe I'm just a wedrio."

You had to admire that kind of doubling down. Truth was, we were all a bunch of wedrios.

In the bathroom, I heard Nick whispering to Leo, and they emerged a few moments later, my son back to looking like himself. He was eleven, but in moments like this, he always seemed younger. A sensitive soul, on guard from the rest of the world, dangers lurking. His fears had somewhat abated as he'd grown, and I hadn't been reminded of how afraid he was of everything when he was little for a long time.

Piper caught wind of Leo's claiming to see a person in the bathroom and started laughing. "Was it your imaginary friend from when you were little? What was his name—Houdini? After *Magically Pawesome Pets*?"

I shot her a threatening look as Leo yelled at her to shut up. I had forgotten about Houdini, his invisible playmate from kindergarten. Leo used to watch the television show based on Magic Land characters every day after school. We had the figurines, the pet mansion, and the underwater submarine—why magical pets needed to explore the Mariana Trench was beyond me, but boy, did he love it.

To honor his favorite show, he dubbed his imaginary friend Houdini, although he told us Houdini was dead and had come back to life as a ghost to play with him. Creepy, yes, but on the spectrum of normal child behavior. Houdini had faded away, as imaginary friends often do, although sometimes I wondered if Leo just did a better job hiding him as he got older.

"Mom, there really was someone in there," Leo said before he flopped down on his bed.

"Yeah, I saw her, too, now that you mention it. She was looking for the pool," Piper scoffed. She harrumphed after I dialed up my glare from stern to threatening. "Sorry. I'm PMSing."

I forced a laugh. "Doesn't make it okay to torment your brother, Piper. Guys, it's been a long day, and there's no one in the bathroom, understand? And the spider is gone, so we're all good."

After the kids were settled back down in the bed, Piper in one, and Sophie and Leo in the other, and after I triple-checked the bathroom for any more insect infestations, Nick and I collapsed down on our bed.

"Did Houdini find the pool?" Nick said as he closed his eyes.

"No, he's on a date with Janelle," I said to the ceiling. Leo's claim that there was someone else in the room couldn't possibly be true, but it still pricked at me, one of those stories that I would recount later to my friends, and they would shudder. "Are you thinking an airplane sounds nice right now, like I am?"

Nick rolled over and put an arm around my stomach. "No. Because we are bonding. It's an adventure."

I grunted, staring at the stained ceiling pattern in our room. My own family, growing up, hadn't had much of a taste for adventure.

When Nick had first pitched the road trip idea to all of us, I was skeptical and unsure if we would last that long together in the car. But I put aside my hesitation and embraced visions of wholesome family fun. Of license plate games and inside jokes. Nick and I had road-tripped together before, and those trips had been some of our favorite memories. That was all I wanted for my family.

We were barely twenty-four hours in, and I just hoped we hadn't made a huge mistake.

Chapter 3

In preparation for our road trip, Nick had taken Tammy the Tan Squirrel into the shop for the once-over. They topped off the wiper fluid, checked the tires, and did whatever else was necessary to make sure our van didn't fall apart the second we left the state, lest we risk a reboot of *Planes, Trains and Automobiles*.

We had Tammy thoroughly vacuumed, even though we knew that was an exercise in futility. When the Thule turtle top carrier for the roof arrived, Nick spent hours studying the manual and watching YouTube videos on how to best install it, and tips and tricks for making sure it was secure.

We Amazon Primed six extra car charging cords for our phones and a pack of extra AA batteries for the DVD player's headphones. I brought packs of paper towels and garbage bags for any possible spills or unfortunate car sickness incidents.

After a thorough oil change, the employees at Firestone gave Tammy a clean bill of health, deeming her roadworthy.

We were an hour past Indianapolis, heading south on I-65, when the low tire pressure light came on. It dinged, almost proud, telling us the right front tire was slowly deflating.

"What the hell?" Nick whispered under his breath as he tapped at the information button on the steering wheel.

"Jesus. Already? Is it a mistake?" I said as I leaned over, trying to peer at the numbers scrolling across the dash display.

"Shit," he said as the display stopped on the pressure gauge for each tire. Three of the tires had whatever the appropriate amount of pounds per square inch was—thirty-five, according to the dash—while the right front tire had seventeen. I didn't know anything about cars—in college, I didn't realize that cars required oil changes and drove my Chevy Cavalier for two years before it started smoking when I drove it on the highway—but I figured that probably didn't bode well.

"What's wrong?" Behind me, Leo's tone held the faintest note of panic.

"Oh, nothing. We just need to check something," I said, keeping my voice light. I turned around and caught Piper's gaze. I widened my eyes, and she shook her head.

"I knew that car place was sketchy," she said as she peered out the window and sighed, the weight of knowing more than everyone on her sixteen-year-old shoulders.

"Well, let's just pull off at the next exit and see what's going on," I said. I scanned the horizon, looking for anything other than a cornfield or billboard proclaiming that the rapture was coming. On either side of us, the gold from the farmlands beamed back at us like sunlight, stretching toward the blue horizon. It felt like we were the only people in the world, save for the long-hauler trucks that barreled past us every now and then.

"Ah! Rest area!" Nick said triumphantly at the sign announcing the pull-off in five miles.

"Great," I said, although five miles felt like an eternity.

And it was, with neither of us saying what we feared: that if there wasn't so much as a gas station nearby, there weren't going to be any automotive repair places.

We pulled off into the rest area, dust kicking up on either side of our car, making it look like we were pulling in for a Tombstone-style shootout. I would not have been surprised to see a tumble-weed blow by.

I hopped out of the passenger seat as Nick parked, trying to convince myself that it wouldn't be that bad, despite the down-ward tick of the PSI as we drove.

"Shit," I said, echoing Nick.

The tire was halfway flat, sinking down toward the gravel like it was slowly frowning, expressing its displeasure at Indiana.

Anger flared in my midsection as I remembered paying the bill at the mechanic, the technician enthusiastically smiling at me as she told me specifically that the tires were in great shape and not to worry about the front right tire that randomly alerted to low pressure. She told me it was a sensor malfunction and that they had fixed it. What if it had blown out on the highway? One of my partners had made his fortune primarily from tire malfunction lawsuits. If this wasn't easily fixable, I had half a mind to ask for his advice.

Nick got out of the driver's side and knelt down, pushing on the tire. His forefinger sank into the rubber.

"Yeah: shit." He rubbed his hands on his shorts and stood up.

"No, it's *bull*shit. I can't believe they said everything was fine. 'Couldn't be safer,' was the quote, I think. I'm going to call them *right* now and . . ." I started to fume when Nick held up his palm and I stopped. I took a breath and caught myself. Lawyer mode was not appropriate right then and wouldn't help anything except to increase my blood pressure as well as scare the kids.

Nick gave me a slow nod, as if to say, *Welcome back, Leigh*, and then glanced around. "There has to be a service station somewhere, right?"

I didn't have to turn around and sweep my hand at the nothingness surrounding us. I pulled out my phone to search, just as Piper put down the window in the second row, leaning over Sophie.

"No signal," she shouted to us.

"Fantastic," I said as I held my phone up, one pitiful bar blinking in and out. I looked at Nick, who shook his head. No signal for him either. "This is when Jason Voorhees comes out of the woods, right?"

Nick frowned. "No, we're nowhere near Camp Crystal Lake." He chuckled, but I could see in his eyes that he was already mentally shuffling the tight schedule of our journey.

This was his dream trip, his final boss on the quest for family bonding. I patted his arm sympathetically and felt him relax.

A minor problem, I tried to telepathically convey.

I just hoped it would be an easy fix.

With modern technology failing us, we attempted to find a gas or service station the old-fashioned way: by driving around and looking for one.

We made the choice to drive Tammy around CR-47, which ran parallel to I-65, figuring at worst, we could stop at a farmhouse and see if anyone was there to ask for the closest service station.

Not that that particular scenario sounded any less ill-advised than visiting Camp Crystal Lake, but desperate times and all that.

Sophie remained oblivious to the issues as she colored in a book with her Color Wonder markers, watching pinks and purples appear on Magic Land princesses. Leo was quiet, looking out the window intensely but insisting he was fine. Piper took videos, saying that she would post a reel about farm life later that day when the signal returned.

"It's like we're camping," she said.

"You've never been camping," Nick and I said at the same time.

"Now I have," she retorted.

He rolled his eyes. His family owned their own camper, using it nearly every weekend in the summer. He grew up near Green Bay, home to the Packers and frostbite. His family was, to put it mildly, "outdoorsy." Ice fishing in the winter, deer hunting in the fall, and beer drinking year-round. My in-laws were something out of central casting for a Midwestern sitcom, fish trophies on the wall and a garage fridge full of New Glarus beer.

Camping in their falling-apart pop-up camper each summer was a rite of passage for them. Activities included shuffling through a creek—"crick walking"—and counting mosquito bites. When I declined to participate in this famed Somerset family tradition when we were dating, I think Nick still held out hope that I would soften. I did not, and he had blinked first. Our kids had never been camping.

Nick picked up his phone, swiping at it with his thumb, holding it up to the windshield in an effort to get a signal.

"Damn it," he muttered. "If this piece of shit would connect, we could figure out the closest gas station."

I smirked. "Good thing you upgraded last month."

I picked up my phone, which was so old Piper joked that it was an iPhone 1. I waved it around, the "No Signal" notification glaring at me, admonishing me for needing the small luxury of a working phone.

Disappointment ran through my veins as I stared at the screen. It felt like we had intentionally rejected the safe, calm way of going on vacation and had conscripted each other into something stressful and scary.

I took a deep breath and turned around to the kids, a too-bright smile on my face. "Hey, let's all play a game, okay? That will get us in a better mood while we figure this out. How about I Spy?" Leo looked up with interest, Sophie nodded enthusiastically, and Piper gave me a half shrug.

"I'll start. I spy something . . ." I trailed off as I searched the landscape for something, anything, other than corn and trash. I glanced back down at my phone, thinking.

A small rectangle glimmered on the signal status.

"Wait!" I said as I shoved the phone against the window, desperate to boost the signal. "I think it's—"

Before I could finish, a flash caught the corner of my gaze, blue and white darting across the deserted country road.

"Nick!" I said as I dropped my phone and it bounced on the WeatherTech floor mats.

His gaze shot up from where he still looked at his phone. "Shit!" he shouted as he gripped the wheel and slammed on the brakes, his phone sliding from his hand and disappearing beneath his legs.

We were thrown forward, the tires squealing beneath the hot

pavement. My seat belt locked into place and nearly strangled me as the kids shouted in the back.

I whipped around. "Are you guys okay? Anyone hurt?" My voice was high, tense.

Piper's eyes were wide, and I could tell she was relieved we hadn't acquiesced and allowed her to drive. Sophie nodded and bent down to collect the markers that had spilled onto the floor. And Leo slowly pointed a finger out of the windshield.

I spy.

I slowly turned around and leaned forward to understand what we'd almost hit.

The blue and white flash continued across the road, and I clapped a hand to my mouth, breathing heavily.

"Oh no," I whispered, the sounds of my kids behind me like white noise.

It was a boy, probably around eight or nine, with dirty blond hair that reached his shoulders. He wore a blue and white striped short-sleeved shirt and blue shorts. His feet were bare, and his eyes were light blue in the sunlight. There was a red birthmark on his left cheek, the size of a small strawberry, which looked like an eyedropper from the heavens had scattered melanin on him.

He stood on the side of the road, facing us, his expression blank. He lifted a hand to wave before turning and darting into a row of trees on that side of the highway.

I put my hand to my heart and leaned back, taking a deep breath. It was just a rascally kid running around and playing outside, probably a group of them daring each other to run across the street and freak out motorists.

"That was close," I said. I shut my eyes and then opened them and looked over at Nick. He was ghost white, still gripping the steering wheel, sweat trickling down from his forehead.

"Hey." I put a hand on his shoulder and he jumped, before he relaxed his shoulders and shook his head. "He's okay. Probably trying to freak us out."

"We almost hit a *kid*?" Piper screeched.

I turned and saw her words were sinking in. She had her hands over her mouth, eyes like saucers, and Sophie's chin was trembling in fear. Leo's face was poker straight, his eyes fixed on where the boy had disappeared.

"He's okay," I repeated to my kids. "We didn't hit him."

"How do you know?" Leo said, eyes searching the tree line. "What if he's hurt?"

"We stopped in time," Nick said quietly, rubbing his forehead. He reached for the sweating bottle of water in the console and took a drink, and then took a deep breath. "We would have felt it."

White-hot fear shot through me at the thought.

He quickly understood how that sounded and added, "I mean . . . we would have . . ."

I put a shaking hand on Leo's knee and squeezed it. "Everyone is fine, including that boy." He finally turned to me, eyes shifting in worry. "We didn't hit him."

"But what if we had?" he whispered. He looked back to the thick tree line, mouth quivering. "He looked like he was about the same age as me."

I swallowed hard, panic beginning to rise. Helplessly, I glanced at Nick, who shook his head slightly.

We didn't hit him.

Right?

No, we hadn't. That was true. That was real. No matter how scary it felt. "He's probably already forgotten about us and is off playing." But my voice was weak, thin, unconvincing.

Leo's mouth continued to quiver, and Piper reached forward and patted him on the head.

"I love that you're so worried, but that boy is probably off building a tree house or something cool," she said. She looked at me, stuck out her bottom lip, and jerked her head slightly toward her brother.

There was a heavy pause in the car as we considered this uncharted territory.

Finally, someone had to make a decision. And it was me. Nick was so looking forward to this trip, and I didn't want this to derail everything. I would find the kid and make sure he was okay, before possibly giving him a stern lecture on the dangers of playing chicken with harried motorists. Maybe even walk him up to his front door and tell his parents.

I unbuckled my seat belt. "I'm going to go check on him and see. He won't have gotten far. I'm sure I won't see any sign of him, and I'll show you the coast is clear, and then we don't have to worry, okay?" My irritation was building, but I hoped I actually would find him to prove once and for all that it was some kind of prank.

Piper gave a bitter laugh behind me. "Mom, this is how *Children of the Corn* starts. Like, exactly. You know that, right?"

I rolled my eyes and preemptively shook off Nick's protest. "Gimme one second."

The last thing I heard before I closed the car door was Piper cackling. "She who walks between the rows."

Chapter 4

On the outside of the car, the heat from the road made the pavement shimmer like it was from another world. Despite my confidence with my family, my heartbeat quickened and my stomach turned over, a warning: *Get back in the car, this is crazy, that kid is fine.*

I reminded myself that I dealt with far more strange and spooky things every day—like cheating husbands and horrifying prenups—and walked toward the trees. I felt the sharp rocks of the road's shoulder under the thin rubber of my flip-flops, and my ankles wobbled as I tried to avoid piercing through my shoes.

I stepped into the prairie grass, the blades waving against my ankles, as the sun beat down on my neck. I had forgotten my sunglasses, and my eyes strained against the oppressive sunshine as I lifted a hand to shield my gaze and peered toward the tree line.

It was silent, save for a few birds chirping high up in the branches.

I looked back at the car, shook my head, and lifted my palms. *Nothing to see here.*

"Mom?" I heard a small, disembodied voice from the tree line, near where the little boy had run. I stopped, leaning toward the sound, trying to pull it to my ear.

"Hello? Are you all right?" I called toward the trees. The trunks were silent.

A breeze ran through them, carrying the sounds of a few squawking birds and the thrum of cicadas but no human voices.

I gave a half turn, jutting my ear toward the trees, waiting for any other noise, and when I didn't hear anything else, I jammed my hands into the back pockets of my shorts and walked toward the van, meeting my family's watchful eyes. I half-shrugged, shaking my head.

All clear.

I was nearly back to the car, already eyeing the rapidly flattening tire, my worry shifting from the boy to how we were going to fix it, when I heard the voice again.

"Help."

Four letters. The sequence of which can activate a mom like no other.

I whipped back around, hands out of my pockets, and rapidly walked toward the trees, heart beating in my chest.

"Hello? Do you need help? I can help you," I called out.

I heard rustling through the trees, and the voice again. "I'm over here."

I waved to Nick in the driver's seat, panic in my eyes, before I steadily power walked toward the voice, despite the warning shots twisting through my stomach. Anything could be in the woods. It could be a trap. A crazy Indiana farmer family with antique torture devices. Human traffickers (not a particularly likely scenario, despite what some of my second cousins continuously posted on Facebook). Leatherface and his ilk.

It did make me slow down enough to allow Nick to catch up with me.

"What's going on?" he said as he nervously glanced back at our car, where our kids were huddled around the passenger and driver's seats to watch their parents disappear into the forest.

"That boy—at least I think it's that boy—called for help from over there." I gestured in the general area where I thought I'd heard his voice. "He might be hurt."

Nick squinted at the trees and then looked back at me, eyes wide. "We didn't hit him." He stopped, and I saw the fear on his face. "We didn't hit him," he said more quietly, as though trying to convince himself.

"We have to be sure," I said, my voice wavering. I may have imagined it, my brain conjuring up a hallucination out of panic and fear, but I had to know. I couldn't imagine getting back in our car and driving around, wondering if the kid was okay. Or even real.

Nick and I walked toward the tree line, listening carefully, hearing the sounds of the leaves crunching beneath our feet and the crows squawking overhead. A broken, dirty Big Wheel bike hid among the tall plain grasses.

"Hello? Anyone there?" Nick called as he stepped over a downed branch. He held a hand out, and I grabbed it, the lip of my flip-flop catching on the sharp bark. "Hey, I had one of those," Nick said, pointing to the Big Wheel.

"Nick, focus," I said. "Hello? Is someone out there? Are you hurt?" I looked around, trying again to avoid thinking that it was a trap. That my kids were now being kidnapped.

We stopped, listening, and a line of sweat ran down my back.

Nothing.

I exhaled. "I'm hearing things, I think," I said with a laugh. "Let's get back to the car."

But Nick's gaze was on something to his left. I peered around his shoulder. "What?" I leaned forward and stared. "Oh jeez."

It was a small white farmhouse—at least what used to be a small white farmhouse. White wooden slats, half burned from a fire long ago, rotting with decay, ash all around. Broken glass lay around the pile of burned wood, either exploded in the fire or shattered due to age. The air smelled damp, earthy, and it felt like we had interrupted a dinner party for Mother Earth as she devoured the house.

Clearly, no one lived there, and hadn't for a very long time.

Certainly not a little boy with a birthmark.

I saw a few rusted beer cans and some old cigarette butts on the ground. No doubt a late-night party hangout for wayward teens.

"Whoa. Cool," Piper said from behind me.

I whipped around and my three kids stood, oldest to youngest, staring at the burned house. Piper pulled out her phone and began taking pictures, Sophie's mouth curled down in distaste, and Leo stared at the rubble, studying it, trying to understand.

"Can we get back in the car?" Sophie whined. "I don't like this place."

"Just a couple more pictures," Piper said as she took a step forward, eyes trained on her phone.

"Yes. Let's get back in the car," Nick said as he held a palm in front of Piper's phone, blocking her picture.

"What happened to that house?" Leo said, and looked up at me.

I shrugged. "I don't know, but it looks like a fire. From a really long time ago," I said. I took his shoulders, ready to steer him toward the tree line.

"I want to go," Sophie said.

Nick bent down and scooped her up, and she wrapped her legs around his waist. "C'mon, Piper," he said, his tone hardening.

I grabbed for Leo's hand, but he darted away, toward Piper.

"I want to see the cool house," he said.

"No!" I called, but he ignored me, hopping over a pile of rocks and a bigger mountain of beer cans proudly sporting the Champagne of Beers logo.

He had almost reached Piper, who was muttering to herself about the lighting in the trees, when he misjudged another pile of debris and tripped, falling forward.

"Are you—" I didn't get the question out before he started whimpering.

Nick and I hurried over to him, Piper already at his feet on the ground.

"Mom, look," she said as she clenched her jaw, teeth showing.

Leo cradled his hand, an angry red cut across his palm, blood dripping from it into his uninjured hand.

"Oh no," I said, and bent down. I lifted the edge of my T-shirt and wrapped it around his hand to stop the blood, red blooming on the front of it.

"Mom told you not to go over there," Sophie said, her voice high.

"Shut up, Sophie," Leo said as tears ran down his cheeks. He whimpered again.

"Everything's fine. This is . . . fine," Nick said.

The bleeding slowed quickly, and I carefully unwrapped my shirt from Leo's hand. The cut wasn't big and wasn't very deep. I scanned the ground for what had cut him and saw a particularly rusty, sharp-looking beer can.

Great. Now my child has tetanus from a rusty can of Natural Light.

A piece of metal glinted next to the beer can and I leaned forward, pulling a leaf off of the metal. It was a small locket, old and tarnished. It was an oval, with a small metal bump on the left side that looked like hinges that would open and allow for a picture to be placed inside. The silver metal was dark from age and exposure. The long chain indicated that it had likely belonged to an adult.

"Whoa. Whose necklace is that? It looks old," Leo said, his eyes fixed on it.

"I don't know. Let's focus on your hand," I said as I turned back to him.

"Can I see it?" His gaze was still on the necklace.

"No." I looked up to Piper and said to her, "Start walking back to the car." I stood up and faced Nick. "I'll take Sophie. You take Leo, and we'll find the first aid kit in the car."

I tried to remember where I'd packed it. In a bag . . . somewhere.

I held out my hands for Sophie and swung her up on my chest. "Ready?" She nodded into my neck.

I started walking, careful in my flip-flops not to step on any more rusty, sharp metal debris, and heard Nick talking to Leo, coaxing him up, and then following behind us through the clearing.

Back at the car, I finally located the first aid kit in the fourth bag I searched, and by that time, half of our careful, Tetris-worthy packing job was all over the country road. We put Neosporin on the cut, and then a Band-Aid, despite Leo's protesting and claiming he was fine. I suspected he would relay the story to his friends as a war wound by the way his eyes glinted.

When the kids were back in the car, Nick and I took to the task of repacking our bags into the back.

"We really should get him checked out. When was his last tetanus shot?" Nick asked as sweat dripped down his forehead while he shoved a black duffel bag into the back, his map of packed bags long forgotten.

"How am I supposed to remember?" I whispered, more angrily than I intended. "And how are we supposed to find a doctor when we can't even find a gas station?"

From the third row, Piper heard our conversation and held up her phone. "Mom? Dad? I have like a half bar. Want me to see if I can find a hospital or something?"

"What about—" Nick held up a finger and opened Tammy's console, rustling through the paper. "This?" He triumphantly held up a small booklet with a plastic coiled spine. It was the AAA TripTik sent to us through the mail by my in-laws. When they'd heard we were taking a road trip, their glee could not be overstated. Good old-fashioned family fun vacation, the Americana way.

My in-laws owned smartphones, but the concept of traveling without a paper map and route planning rubber-stamped by America's finest automobile association, was unheard of.

"Last resort," I said as I looked pointedly at Piper. "Let's use technology to find a doctor."

Precious bandwidth had to be used for the most urgent problem: Leo, not the flat tire. The signal blinked into existence long enough for us to locate an urgent care center ten minutes away.

The irony, of course, was that there was a gas station also ten minutes away, in the opposite direction.

But it would have to wait until we knew Leo would be okay.

As we drove to find the urgent care center, it occurred to me that we had never found out if the boy was safe. Or whether I had heard him calling for help.

Chapter 5

On the Bates Motel scale of cozy and welcoming, the Hoosier Roadway Inn was solidly subzero. A one-story white wooden rectangular structure with a peeling red roof, it proudly sported **FREE HBO** on the buzzing neon sign out front. The parking lot was white gravel littered with cigarette butts, vape pods, and various road trash. A few torn plastic lawn chairs sat outside the rooms. The only other car in the parking lot was a blue Honda sporting a police boot.

I could feel the horror reverberating off the kids behind me as Nick put the car into Park, so many things yet unsaid. I pointed to the buzzing sign emphatically.

"See that?" The most important words on the sign were not *Free HBO*. "Vacancy. It's the only place around here with a room."

A laugh bubbled out of Piper as I opened the passenger door and shot her a weary look. I was sure her Instagram followers would get a kick out of our night's accommodations, although they would have to wait. I had made her promise not to post the content from our trip until after we returned home. I may not have been an influencer, but even I knew that posting your exact location, in real time, not to mention advertising that your house was vacant for a couple of weeks, was not a particularly good idea.

Sophie was already asleep in her seat, so Nick carefully extracted her while I went inside to rent the aforementioned vacant room. Leo's eyes had been slowly closing as we approached the motel, exhaustion setting in from the eventful day.

A couple of hours before, we'd arrived at urgent care, thanks to the fleeting cell signal. The receptionist there seemed surprised when we walked through the door, looking over her shoulder a couple of times with an expression that clearly said, *I wasn't even supposed to be working today. I was told it would be a slow day.*

After some back-and-forth and more unpacking of the car to find the envelope where I had stashed our medical insurance cards, we were escorted to a room so someone could look at Leo's hand.

The Nerds candy that I had procured from the emergency snack stash chose to kick in at that moment, and Leo had what can only be described as verbal vomit for the next twenty minutes while the physician examined his cut.

In between his telling Dr. Dickemann that his favorite Xbox game was *Call of Duty*, and that his room was painted blue, she looked up, an alcohol pad in her hand.

"Where did you say you guys are traveling to?"

"Florida," Nick and I said at the same time.

She looked back down. "Fun! A family road trip."

I snorted before I could stop myself and then recovered when she looked up. "Fun, yes. Just not this part."

"Do you see people with a lot of birthmarks?" Leo said, his words running together like someone had fed him a month's supply of amphetamines.

"Sometimes," Dr. Dickemann said evenly as she wound gauze around his cut.

"We saw this boy with a birthmark on his face by the trees where I cut my hand and he ran near our car and then went into the trees and then we couldn't find him and then I started bleeding," he said.

"Okay, okay," Nick said as he patted Leo's shoulder, trying to tether him back to reality.

No more sugar for today. Or any day, I thought. *At least the ones where we are trapped in a car together.*

"We couldn't see him really good but he had a red birthmark on his face like paint and then there was that weird burned house that looked like a tornado hit it with fire and then I fell." He stopped, catching his breath, his chest rapidly moving up and down underneath his yellow Green Bay Packers T-shirt.

It was then that I noticed Dr. Dickemann had paused, gloved hands in the air.

After a moment, I looked at Nick, who shrugged.

"Everything still going smoothly?" Nick said when the doctor didn't move.

"What? Oh." She smiled and her hands relaxed. She looked at us and shook her head. "It's just . . ." She looked down at Leo. "Nothing."

Nick and I exchanged a glance.

He has tetanus, doesn't he? I thought, my brain desperately trying to recall, again, when his last tetanus booster was. I still couldn't remember. The doctor had already said that he would need a booster from his primary care physician when we got home, but it wasn't anything urgent. I wondered what had made her stop.

She finished winding the gauze around Leo's hand and smiled. "Good as new." She stood up and slowly took her gloves off, hesitating.

Here it comes. Tetanus. Leprosy. Rare amoeba or bacteria only found off CR-47 near rusty beer cans.

"I'm sorry—did you say a birthmark on his face?" she said, looking embarrassed.

"Yes," I said, my eyebrows lifting.

The doctor pressed her lips into a line, jaw tightening. She stiffened her arms at her sides, and for a reason I couldn't understand, the air in the room shifted.

"Carla will give you the discharge papers," she said curtly before she turned and walked out of the door.

"We say something wrong?" Nick whispered as we followed Leo out of the exam room.

I was too tired and confused to contemplate it. "Probably. But let's just go," I said.

As I walked behind Nick and Leo, who was now babbling about how he might have superpowers from the rusty beer can, I wanted to turn back and ask the doctor what had gotten her so upset.

Because she hadn't just looked irritated, she'd looked . . . spooked.

Like she had seen a ghost.

You're just keyed up from everything that's happened on the trip. Don't turn hysterical now. You still have hundreds of miles to morph into a banshee.

I tried to shake off the feeling that I was missing something, that we shouldn't leave, that the doctor had something we needed to hear, as we approached the reception desk. Sophie and Piper were slumped over in blue plastic waiting room chairs, looking as forlorn as pioneer ladies waiting for Jebediah to fix the axle on the covered wagon.

"C'mon, girls. Onward," I said to them as I waved them up.

"Mom, can I have them look at my loose tooth?" Sophie opened her mouth and pushed her loose tooth out, wiggling it back and forth with her tongue in a way that made my stomach turn.

Nick saw my expression and chuckled. He knew how much teeth grossed me out. "Sorry, Soph. It'll come out, I promise."

We left the urgent care center, armed with knowledge from Carla—who confirmed my suspicion that she was not supposed to work that day by telling me, "This is the last time I cover for Rayanne"—as to the nearest gas station for the tire, and also the closest room for the night. The station was able to quickly change the tire, and then we headed for the Hoosier Roadway Inn.

Despite outward appearances, the room at the inn was clean and didn't smell.

"Maybe it's like *Schitt's Creek*," Nick said as he tossed our overnight duffel bag onto the navy and yellow floral comforter.

"Like a formerly rich family is stuck here? If only Dan Levy could come and save us now." I cocked my head to the side and heard the cries of a toddler from two rooms over. "Ah, there it is. I knew there was a catch."

I should have brought earplugs. And sleeping pills.

My days of battling bedtimes, waking up in the middle of the night to fetch a glass of water, and arguing over what shape to cut a PB&J sandwich were thankfully over, but whoever was in room 140 clearly had a long night ahead of them.

I pulled out my phone, eternally grateful we were finally in an area with cell reception. I saw a text from Kerry to me and M.J.

It read: Just checking in on the road warrior. Give us a buzz when you can! Nothing is wrong.

After a tetanus scare, the nightmare farmhouse, the rattled employees at the urgent care, and the flat tire, I highly, highly doubted that nothing was wrong.

Chapter 6

M.J. and I just want to know if you've murdered any hitchhikers yet." Kerry's voice crackled through the shoddy cellular connection, and I stepped outside the motel room's door in hopes of boosting the signal. "You're on speaker, by the way."

"Not yet. That's on the agenda for tomorrow. Get it straight." I looked down and thought about sitting on the plastic lawn chair positioned outside of our door but saw the colony of black spiders guarding the webs that crisscrossed the back of it and remained standing.

I heard M.J.'s tinkling laugh. "Is that before or after you accidentally leave the kids at a rest stop? I almost did that once. Don't recommend."

"Before. Definitely before. And not accidental. We will need to get rid of them as witnesses."

"Well, we're always around if you need help burying a body." M.J. laughed again.

If I had to dispose of a dead body, I thought idly, *these two would be my first call*. Kerry never judged or questioned, even after one night months ago when I had too many glasses of wine and wound up talking about my family. I suspected she knew all of the heavy stuff already—my maiden name had been in the local press for years—but she just listened. And M.J. was so used to project-managing the schedules for her five kids that she would organize the corpse cover-up with the assembly-line precision of a multi-child soccer-practice carpool.

"So, friends, how's everything back there at home? Not that we're that far away yet." The sounds of the highway in the distance floated across the prairie grass field littered with fast-food wrappers and newspaper circulars.

"It's fine. Normal. I watered your hydrangeas last night before I left for work," Kerry said. I heard her stifle a yawn. "Long shift. Busy ER. I had a guy on drugs repeatedly ask me on a date, so at least I've still got it." Kerry had been divorced for two years, keeping the house and primary custody of her two boys. It wasn't hard to get a favorable divorce settlement after the lawyers saw all of the evidence she had compiled into folders—including pictures of her ex making out with a bartender at an all-inclusive resort they'd stayed at for a family vacation a few years before. Her five Irish Catholic brothers had to be literally held back from roughing up her ex-husband after the final court date. My colleague had represented her at a deep discount, a personal favor to me, and made sure she came out on top.

"Of course you've still got it," I said. She did, in fact, still have it. She'd turned forty the year before and had never looked better. I suspected her ex had been an energy vampire, slowly draining away her youth and optimism when he lived there. Now that he was gone, she was regenerating like a starfish, although instead of limbs she was regrowing her soul.

"We're headed to silks right now," M.J. said. In a lower tone she added, "You were supposed to turn back there."

"I know, I know. I still have objections and think I might syncopize during this," Kerry said.

"Stop using medical terms," I heard M.J. retort.

When M.J. had first presented the idea of an aerial yoga class, Kerry and I could not have said no faster. I guess Kerry had been worn down by the fact that I was gone. In that moment, I wanted nothing more than to be back at home with my two closest friends, even if it meant hanging upside down from fabric.

"Kerry had the weirdest dream about you and she woke up half freaked out, so that's why we wanted to check in on you," M.J. said.

"Do tell." I kicked a few of the sharp white gravel rocks in the parking lot of the motel, watching them skitter away in puffs of dust. I heard my family either arguing or having a lively discussion inside the room. I'd have put money on arguing.

"I had a dream that your car broke down in the middle of nowhere and you guys had to walk all the way to Florida—you insisted that you guys just walk instead of waiting for a tow truck—and one by one your family disappeared, but you were like, nope, I'm going to Florida. You were on some kind of quest. I don't know if you ever got there or not, but it freaked me out for some reason. It just felt so . . . real," Kerry said, her voice low. There was a slight crackle and then she laughed. "Stress dream on your behalf, I guess."

I eyed the new tire on our car and thought of our trip to urgent care. "Well, we aren't walking, but it hasn't been the smoothest experience." I quickly filled them in.

M.J. gave a little squeak "Wow, only two states over and you've already unlocked some new level of road trip hell. Congrats. I don't think anything close to that has ever happened on my family trips. We never saw any ghost kids."

"No kidding, I—"

I stopped as Sophie came tearing out of the room and ran toward me in the parking lot, one hand held up, her pointer finger and thumb pinched together.

"Mom Mom Mom Mom. I lost it—the tooth!" She thrust her hand forward and I saw a small white tooth in her hand. She smiled, and I saw a gaping, bloody hole in her mouth.

My stomach turned as I forced a smile. "That's great, honey! We knew it would happen, didn't we," I said as I ran a hand along her cheek.

"Tooth fairy time!" M.J., who had overheard, called from the phone.

"Does the tooth fairy come to motels?" Kerry added.

"I guess we'll find out," I muttered, and then smiled again at Sophie.

Before I walked back into the motel room, I stopped and glanced at the sky. It was a brilliant sunset display of creamy oranges and fiery reds. I thought back to one of Nick's sayings from his parents: *Red sky at night, sailor's delight. Red sky in morning, sailors take warning.*

According to a completely nonscientific pithy saying, our weather the next day should be favorable. I smiled, allowing myself to wrestle back some optimism. I just needed to let everything go, try to remember why we were doing this, and embrace our family adventure.

I wasn't one foot inside the motel room before Piper yelled, "Mom, I need more tampons tomorrow."

Sophie's tooth carefully cupped in my hand, I nodded. "We can stop at a drugstore in the morning," I said, and turned away when I saw her look of annoyance. I walked into the small, pea-green bathroom and carefully placed the tooth in the soap dish. I was about to rummage through my toiletries bag for a container for the tooth when I froze, trying to remember when I'd had my period last.

A couple of years ago, my cycles started to get weird, like they were in their rebel phase. Sometimes three weeks apart, sometimes six. I asked my doctor about it and she shrugged with a sympathetic smile, telling me that women's cycles become unpredictable as they get closer to menopause.

Menopause. What a terrible word. Visions of decaying spinsters and old women in rocking chairs on a front porch, waiting for death, had dramatically entered my mind. Not to mention, the preamble was getting to be wary of light-colored pants no matter the week and feel trepidation at pool parties. (Not that I had ever been that thrilled with them.)

Before I had talked to my doctor, I'd spent a few months mired in anxiety, taking pregnancy tests over and over, wondering if the universe had decided to laugh at me in my apparent golden years. They were always thankfully negative. After my appointment, I realized it was a pointless endeavor, especially when my doctor told me that a woman of my age has something like a 5 percent chance of getting pregnant, and that was when she was actively trying to have a baby.

I was not. So 95 percent sounded pretty good to me.

Still, it has to have been almost two months. That is the longest cycle I've ever had, right?

I carefully placed my phone on the vanity and took a deep breath. No, being pregnant was not something to even consider. I was miserable when my kids were newborns. No sleep, continuous feelings of inadequacy, the sense that my body would never be mine again as I nursed at three in the morning. It wasn't until each of them got into a regular sleep schedule that I started to feel like myself again. Sophie was the hardest of the three, with colic for three months and naps that lasted for a maximum of twenty minutes. It was an extended hostage situation, and I was ready to give up all the national secrets just for a moment of rest.

I felt like a terrible mother during those first few months, second-guessing everything, trying to find joy in small moments, though it always seemed so fleeting. I never wanted to feel like that again. Once that part of my life was safely behind me, it became time to enjoy my kids growing up into actual people.

Don't spiral. This is the last thing you need to worry about. Focus on the giant spiders, urgent care visit, and possible ghost.

I shook my head, forcefully pushing away any thoughts or worries about what my body was doing. I needed to focus on the trip. Besides, there was no chance I was pregnant.

The minutes of the clock ticked by slowly that night. I stared at the red numbers next to the side of the bed, watching as they mutated. I alternated between slight panic over the insomnia and mentally beating down any worries about my body, about our future.

I slowly got up, tiptoeing across the room, and slid into the kids' room after I grabbed a dollar bill from the tooth fairy off of our dresser. I held my breath as I carefully lifted up Sophie's pillow, feeling around for the tooth. She sighed and I stopped, waiting for her to wake up. But her eyes fluttered and she exhaled, going deeper into her dream.

I slid my hand around the sheet, feeling for any bumps. It was smooth as glass. I moved her head a bit higher on the pillow, reaching further back, but still nothing. I paused, my eyes flicking around in the darkness. I had seen her put it under her pillow—hadn't I? I remembered watching as she carefully placed it on the sheet, my attention laser focused so I could easily switch it out for the money later.

The parking lot lights cast a glow across the room, creating long shadows that stretched the expanse of the worn carpeting. They looked like they were reaching for me. They looked like they had reached for Sophie's tooth, wanting a keepsake.

I shivered and blinked a few times, asking my rational mind to come through.

It must have fallen off the side or against the wall. We can search tomorrow. We'll find it easily in the sunlight.

I carefully placed the dollar under the pillow. *We'll find it*, I silently repeated.

And we would. Just not how we expected.

Chapter 7

"Mommy! The tooth fairy came back and gave me a dollar!"

Before I opened my eyes, I felt something placed on the bridge of my nose.

"Look!"

I slowly opened my eyes and sat up, the dollar I had left under Sophie's pillow fluttering down off of my face. She stood proudly next to my bed, jack-o'-lantern smile wide.

"See?" She grabbed the worn dollar off of the bed and pressed it to her chest. "She came back," she repeated.

"Came back?" I said with a laugh as I stretched my arms over my head. Nick still snored lightly next to me, pillow over his head. "What do you mean?" I swung my legs over the side and carefully slid my feet into the tan slippers next to the bed. No way was I walking around on that motel carpet with bare feet.

A wave of nausea hit me in the face as I moved to stand up. "Ohhh," I sighed as I rubbed my forehead. It felt like a gremlin was inside my midsection, gently blowing hot air upward, surging up my esophagus.

"She came back," Sophie said impatiently. She brushed a stray lock of messy red hair out of her face. "I saw her come in and take the tooth and she didn't leave anything. But then she must have come back to leave me this money."

"That sounds strange," I murmured as I slowly inhaled and exhaled, trying to put mind over matter. Thankfully, my stomach listened and the nausea lessened to the point where I could stand without fear of biological consequences.

I walked toward the mirror over the dresser and swiped at the stray mascara under my eyes—I had fallen asleep before taking my makeup off the night before. "Maybe she forgot," I said. I wondered if she'd had a dream about the tooth fairy before I was able to sneak in.

"You don't believe me? That I saw her?" Sophie said quietly. She looked down at the dollar bill and ran her finger around the edge of it. "I did see her." She lifted her chin, determined.

"I believe you. But maybe you were dreaming. I thought the tooth fairy was invisible." Or wearing an old University of Wisconsin Law T-shirt.

"She's not. I saw her. She was a brown cloud that came in with some weird smoke above her. She looked around the room until she saw me. Her eyes were black holes but still were kind of glowing. She didn't have a mouth, either. So I just held out my tooth for her and she took it. Then she told me what she does with the teeth." Sophie said all of it so matter-of-factly, I nearly stepped back in surprise. I guessed her imagination was more active than we had thought.

"So . . . what does she do with the teeth?" I finally said, eyeing a sleeping Nick.

"She makes new people," Sophie said with a smile. "She told me her set for our family is almost completed."

Okay, not creepy at all. I frowned and shook my head. "How did she tell you this if she didn't have a mouth?" Not the most important question, but it was all I could think to ask.

Sophie rolled her eyes and shrugged. "I don't know. She just told me. In my head."

"That's . . . crazy," I finally said. Telepathic tooth fairies were a new one. And I was too frayed to continue asking questions.

Sophie didn't seem freaked out about her story, and I was certain it was just a strange dream or kid hallucination, so I figured I should end the conversation there instead of letting Piper hear it. She would undoubtedly end up crafting an Instagram post about it that would probably go viral, and soon Jason Blum would be shooting *The Fang Fairy.*

I followed my daughter into the kids' motel room. Piper was face down in one of the double beds, her hair splayed around her, and Leo was still on his side of the bed that he shared with Sophie. When he saw me walk into the room, he quickly pulled the covers up and his eyes darted around.

"All right, what are you hiding?" I said as I stood on the edge of the bed.

He shook his head. "Nothing." *Wrong.*

"I told you no Roblox first thing in the morning," I said. I assumed the iPad was hidden somewhere under the covers, his avatar slowly swaying, waiting to enter a virtual theme park or town.

"I wasn't . . . Okay," he said finally. His eyes darted around again as he tried to will me to leave the room.

I gave him a stern look and put my hands on my hips, before slowly shuffling over to Piper and scooting into the bed next to her.

"Good morning, sunshine," I sang into her ear.

She flung an arm over her head. "Mom, stop. It's too early."

I rolled over and whispered in her ear. "No it's not. You better get up before the Fang Fairy comes back."

"What?" she said as she turned over and opened her eyes.

"Exactly. Rise and shine," I said triumphantly as I stood up. "Time to—" I stopped when my gaze landed on the alarm clock next to Piper's bed. It had stopped at eleven fifteen. "Huh." I walked over to the clock and picked it up. It was still plugged into the wall, and the numbers weren't flashing as though there had been a power outage.

"Weird." I slowly put the clock back down and walked into our room, feeling an uneasy sense settling over my shoulder. I hadn't looked at the alarm clock since I'd checked the time on my phone. I stopped suddenly and put a hand on the doorway when I saw the clock in our room.

Eleven fifteen.

Not flashing. Still plugged in.

I walked over to the nightstand and felt around behind it, and yanked the power cord out of the wall. The alarm clock slowly died and the face turned black.

I reasoned it was some kind of electrical disturbance. After all, it was an old motel, and lots of quirky things could happen . . . yes?

I didn't want to waste time contemplating the source of the occurrence. I turned and called out to my family, "Time to move.

We have lots more cornfields and morally instructive billboards to see."

Nick's head popped up off the pillow. "We have to stay on schedule, guys."

An hour later, everyone had packed again. Nick and the kids were outside of the rooms, arguing about what movie to put on in the minivan as we started our next travel day. I was in the bathroom, praying that I would finally get my period.

Not yet.

It's just hormones and stress.

I washed my hands and then leaned over to grab the towel. As I did, a shape on the floor caught my eye. I stopped, hands dripping on my shirt, and turned. The marks on the linoleum, which I had dismissed as random patterns in the material, were clustered on one of the tiles. The brown markings on the yellow linoleum had formed together, like pieces of metal drawn to a magnet, into the shape of a person. Not just any person, but a woman. She had large eyes, with deep creases under them and a mouth pressed into a thin line with sunken cheeks. The bottom half of her face looked like it lacked structure.

It looked like she didn't have any teeth.

My skin pricked with the beginnings of fear as I stared at the design, telling myself it was just a trick of the eye. Yet her mouth mesmerized me, like she was holding in so much that she could not say, would not say. Like her teeth had rotted away.

Sophie's tooth.

I pushed off the vanity and ran into the adjoining kids' motel room to search for the tooth. I ripped off the covers and took the pillowcases off the pillows. I moved the bed frame from the wall to check behind, frantically throwing blankets around.

Nothing.

Her tooth was gone, or wedged into some microscopic crack somewhere, forever a part of the motel.

Or maybe the Fang Fairy really had come.

Chapter 8

WELCOME TO KENTUCKY!

I'd never been happier to see three words written. I sighed in relief as we crossed under the blue and white state line sign on the highway. I craned my neck around and watched it pass from the back window of the minivan, behind the heads of my three sleeping children. If they were awake, I planned to give them their "Kentucky prizes," all sourced from the Dollar Store.

I had volunteered to take the first leg of that day's trip, welcoming the opportunity to drive and focus on the road, rather than the kids and the chaos.

"We did it. We actually made it out of Wisconsin, Illinois, and Indiana. The Midwest is behind us. No stopping us now."

Nick laughed and punched at the radio, trying to find a station that wasn't a preacher spouting the Book of Revelation, warbling country, or static. After a few turns, he gave up. His Spotify road trip playlist had cycled through three times before we all started twitching and begged him to find something else.

"We had an interesting start to the trip, but smooth sailing today," Nick said. He leaned forward, squinting. "Did I just jinx us?"

I pulled the minivan to a complete stop, a line of cars stretching far ahead of us into the horizon. I saw the faint flicker of police lights up ahead.

"Must be an accident. Can you see if we can route around it?" I said to Nick.

Fifteen minutes later, we were cruising along a wooded back road that ran parallel to the highway. To our left we could see the line of cars stretching, the view hazy from the road exhaust. The kids were still asleep in the back, blissfully unaware of any of the traffic.

I slowed as we approached a town, just one main street with a few shops.

WELCOME TO JASPER, announced a sign that was half falling, the metal hooks on one side rusted and left for dead some time ago.

"I feel so welcome," I whispered as I took in the overgrown yards, boarded-up shops, and cars long abandoned in parking spaces. It looked like the zombie apocalypse had rolled through Jasper and long ago found another destination to ravage.

"Where is everyone?" Nick said as he peered out the window into what was left of the glass of a hardware store front.

I looked out the driver's-side window, glancing at Breck's Hardware. As I did, I saw a flash of something from behind the glass.

Startled, I slammed on the brakes, throwing our bodies forward. As the car stopped, we heard a loud crash and the sound of something falling off the roof. We watched as the turtle top carrier slid down the windshield and fell onto the road.

"Oh shit," I said as I turned to Nick.

"Oh shit is right," Nick said as he wrenched open his door.

I heard the stream of four-letter words wafting through the minivan's windows, a litany worthy of the father in *A Christmas Story*.

The kids were all awake then, murmuring concerns and alarm.

"We're good. Just hang on," I said as I opened my own door.

Strewn around the zombified streets of Jasper, Kentucky, were all of our belongings. The turtle top had become unattached, tumbled down, and split open. Our stuff was all over Main Street. My underwear, Nick's self-regenerating collection of black Nike socks, Sophie's emoji pajama pants, and an electric-yellow athletic shirt of Leo's were all splayed on the asphalt like they were being autopsied. I spotted Piper's red bra blowing across the street.

"Sorry. This is . . . fixable, isn't it?" I said hopefully.

Nick grumbled something like *yes*, and I began to bend down to collect our clothing.

"Dad, I can drive. I promise. I won't break anything like you guys did," I heard Piper call from the car.

"It was an accident. And no," he called back as he grabbed an errant sock off the road, shaking out the gravel.

An hour later, the turtle top was back on the car. I refused to relinquish my driving position to Nick or Piper, not wanting to feel like a kid in time-out. As I drove away, I stole another glance at the hardware store, searching for any sign of what I thought I'd seen earlier.

Get your shit together, Leigh.

I chewed on my bottom lip as we left Jasper, a twinge at the center of my stomach even though I told it to screw off.

Because what I thought I'd seen in that abandoned hardware store was the little boy with the birthmark on his face.

I spy . . .

➡

"So you're seeing the tetanus boy now?" Piper asked from the third row while we were parked at a gas station, waiting for the car to fill up. She had just returned from going inside to buy tampons.

I turned around and rolled my eyes. "I'm sorry for even telling you, okay? It was just a weird trick of the light."

"Or you're losing it," she said.

"I believe you," Leo said from the seat in front of his sister. His hands were braided in his lap, a serious look on his face.

I leaned back and squeezed his knee. "Thanks, buddy. But I was just being silly. Maybe I need my glasses." My voice was too high, too singsong. Because even though I deserved Piper's ribbing, part of me still knew what I had seen and told me not to discount it.

"Is that boy a ghost?" Sophie said with a wide smile. "Ghosts are fun."

I hung my head and then shot Piper a scathing look. She held her hands up in surrender, her phone in her hand as Nick put Tammy into Drive after she was filled with gas.

"No, honey," I said.

Piper held a finger in the air. "Well, there's only one way to find out." She stuck her tongue out the side of her mouth as she stared at her phone's screen. "There," she said with a final tap, and then looked up.

"Why am I afraid?" Nick said, his eyes on the road. We had gotten back to I-65 quickly and entered the hills of Kentucky, which seemed to be all twisty roads and irresponsible truckers.

Her phone began to ding, back to back, and she smiled. "Ha. Hmmm." She muttered to herself as she scrolled. Then her head snapped up.

"Got it. Oh, this is good. Maybe you did see a ghost," she said coyly.

When she saw my expression—my *I technically own your phone and data plan, so the mom giveth and the mom taketh away* look—she raced to continue.

"I posted a picture of the creepy house on my Instagram stories just now, asking if anyone knew of any urban legends or weirdness about it. And"—she paused, relishing her moment of attention—"two people already messaged me that there are stories about supernatural things happening in that area, and that there may have been a mom with kids that lived there, the Vickerys. The dad was already dead or something. There was a fire a really long time ago, in the eighties—what?"

"The eighties were 'a really long time ago'?" Nick said with a bemused expression.

Piper rolled her eyes and continued. "There was a fire back in the olden days, and after that, they disappeared, and then people used to party in those woods and they said haunted things happened."

There was a moment of silence as I absorbed this information. Nick was the first to speak.

"Weird things happened? Sounds like a 'friend of a friend of someone's cousin's former roommate' thing. Game of telephone—that's how ghost stories endure," he said.

"So there was a ghost?" Sophie said, clapping. She balled up her hands into fists and pumped them in the air. "I knew it!"

I shook my head. "No. There is no ghost," I said firmly.

Yet as I turned back around, the pit of my stomach twinged again. There was something about what Piper had said that was true; I felt it. Something was there. Something had seen us. Something was there now.

"Well, this one girl says that the Vickerys are still at the house and like to haunt people," she said.

"There's no such thing as ghosts," I said, a bit too loudly.

Nick negotiated around an aggressive semitruck and added, "Your mom is right. There's nothing to those stories."

I swallowed hard. *It must be stress. There's a lot going on with this trip, leaving work, clients in crisis.*

It was stress. This was worldly, not otherworldly, bullshit.

I closed my eyes.

"Mom?" Leo's voice came out small, silvery, from the back.

"Yeah?" When he didn't answer, I opened my eyes and looked back.

He had his hands still in his lap, pressed together. His gaze was down, his mouth trembling.

"Leo? What's wrong?" I looked at Nick with alarm and hoisted a leg onto the seat so I could fully face him. "Honey?"

"What's wrong, Leo?" Nick said, looking at him in the rearview mirror.

I reached forward and touched his knee, which seemed to bring him out of it. He slowly looked up, eyes wide with fear. Then he looked down to his hands.

I realized he wasn't braiding his fingers together, he was holding something tightly in his lap. I held my breath, and the twinge in my midsection grew to a throb. Something was off. I knew it. Mother's instinct.

Leo slowly unfurled his fingers, turning his palms over.

A tarnished silver object was in his left hand, coiled like a snake. The locket from the abandoned house.

I exhaled quickly. He had taken the jewelry after we had asked him not to, but it wasn't like he had robbed a 7-Eleven or stolen pain pills from the pharmacy.

He extended his hand, and I leaned forward. I carefully, slowly, took the locket from his palm. It was heavier than it looked, made of real silver. The chain was worn and tarnished, and flaked a little in my hand.

In the center of the chain was a circle with a hinge on one side, for opening the locket. I slowly clicked it open and saw it was—thankfully—empty. I shut it with a satisfying click. As I did, I felt an engraving on the front.

I brushed away at the dirt and squinted, trying to make out the embellishment.

When I saw what it was, I nearly dropped the locket.

In the center of the locket, a letter was engraved, presumably the initials of whoever owned it.

"What was the name of the family from that haunted house?" I asked Piper without looking up.

"Um, Vickery," she said. "Why?"

Because the engraving at the center of the locket was the letter *V*. For *Vickery*.

The inaugural souvenir of our family vacation was not the fridge magnet or gas station key chain I had expected.

Instead, it was fuel for our nightmares.

Chapter 9

"Mom! Hold that right there, up to the light so I can see the V," Piper shouted from the third row. "I need to post that."

I clamped my fingers around the metal, feeling it warm in my palm. "Not a chance." I tightened my hand around the circle, feeling the metal chain dig into my skin. I looked over at Nick, who rubbed his face and shook his head slightly.

I turned to Leo. "Why did you take this?" My tone was angrier than I intended.

His eyes were downcast, and he wove his fingers together in his lap again, pressing his lips together.

"Hey," Nick said gently, and patted my leg. I shot him an irritated look. He almost always played good cop, and like most times, I had to be the bad cop.

"You stole a necklace?" Sophie said, eyes wide. She looked from him to me and then back to her brother. "You could go to jail."

"Creepy ghost jail," Piper muttered as she angled her phone toward me, trying to zoom in on the necklace in my hand.

Leo's head snapped up and he looked at me, tears rimming his blue eyes. "Really?"

Nick looked at him in the rearview mirror. "No one is going to jail. Piper, quit it."

"What are you going to do with it?" Piper said with a sigh as she dropped her phone and reached into her bag. She pulled out a bright pink spray bottle adorned with gold flowers. She aimed it toward her body, ready to press the nozzle.

I held up a finger. "No. You will not spray that in the car."

Memories of instant headaches as I walked upstairs in our house, after Piper had left for the night, flooded my brain. She and her friends wore cloyingly sweet body spray, like lilies or a Frankenstein-esque combination of brown sugar and roses.

I certainly didn't want to be trapped in Tammy with a cumulus cloud of teenager scents.

"Leo, we told you not to take the necklace. I don't know whose it is, but it isn't ours. And we specifically told you to leave it at the house," I said, my voice tight. I didn't really care that he had taken the jewelry, but it was one more thing that I had to deal with. One more hassle.

One more secret.

"Are you going to keep it?" Leo said, his voice small. He frowned and his eyes moved from the locket to me.

"I don't know what I'm going to do with it. But we told you not to take it, so I'm going to hang on to it," I said as I reached forward to put the necklace into the backpack at my feet. I supposed it belonged to me now.

I shifted the necklace to my left hand as my right unzipped the inside pocket. I felt the metal grow warm, softening my skin. As I yanked at the backpack's zipper, the metal continued to increase in temperature, warmer and warmer.

"Ow!" I hissed as I opened my palm and let the necklace fall out. It bounced on the rubber floor mat and disappeared under the passenger seat.

I looked at my palm, and where the necklace had been were the faint pink lines of the chain and a circle. I held my hand up to the window, my palm throbbing and stinging.

It looked like a burn.

"What happened?" Nick said as he glanced down at my hand. "Jesus."

"Mom—" I heard Sophie say from the backseat.

"Nothing. It's nothing. It just felt hot all of a sudden," I said quickly. I wrapped my hand around the cold can of Diet Coke from the console cupholder. I winced as my skin protested and then finally relaxed when the cold sensation began to overtake the burning.

My hand still on the pop can, I reached forward with my right hand, groping around blindly under the seat until I felt the metal. I extracted it with two fingers, dangling it in front of me before dropping it into the backpack and zippering it with a flourish.

The car was silent, waiting for my assessment.

"Must have gotten hot from the sunlight," I muttered. I took my hand away from the pop can and flexed it a few times; a long red line with a circle in the middle of it was starting to form on my palm. I put my hand back on the cold can, wincing again at the sting.

It was cloudy outside, gray tufts lazily drifting around the horizon. I kept my gaze trained outside the car's window, unable to look at my family. I didn't know how to tell them that I couldn't explain what had just happened.

The sounds of Nick's road trip Spotify playlist wafted through the car again, but this time, no one had the energy to stop him.

I barely heard the music as I felt a pressure begin to build in my chest. My breath quickened and it felt like something heavy was sitting on my shoulders. My fingers itched to reach back into the backpack and pull the locket back out, to study it and understand why I wanted, badly, to hold it.

A whispering began to fill my head, small rustling noises like pieces of loose-leaf paper slowly crumpling next to my ear. It was a woman's voice, the edges of her words blending together, like in an unknown language.

But I understood—I felt—that she was trying to tell me something but couldn't figure out how.

I had experienced this feeling before, at work. Sometimes I had a client come into my office and sit across from my desk, a thick file of information sitting on their lap, as they tried to tell me what was going on and why they needed me. Usually they would make an appointment and give a brief overview of what they were looking for—help with a divorce, renegotiating a custody settlement, assistance with dividing up marital property—but when they actually walked through the doors to my office building and sat down and faced me, there was an undercurrent below their words.

Not just a divorce, but a heartbreak.

He shouldn't get shared custody because he never cared about the kids before.

She had an affair, so she needs to be the one who moves out.

I had to ask a lot of carefully crafted questions to really sort through the noise, to figure out what the client was really looking for. It wasn't ever just a piece of paper. It was so much more than that.

I want a divorce to be free, to really start my life the way I should have.

I'm worried that he will treat the kids the same way that he treated me in our marriage—with ambivalence.

I want to hit her where it hurts.

Only once I truly understood what they wanted could I devise a legal strategy to get it. Or at least try to. But the understanding had to come first.

My eyes slid down to the backpack, where it rested against the car door, the zipper closed, the necklace safely inside.

The locket whispered to me, trying to tell me something, trying to show me what it needed.

I closed my eyes tightly and took a deep breath, telling myself that none of it was real, that a piece of jewelry wasn't trying to give me a message from the great beyond.

I swallowed hard and opened my eyes, watching the mile markers as they passed, hoping the distance we put between us and the Vickery house would be enough to quiet the whispers.

Chapter 10

"Here, this looks like a nice spot," I said as I pointed to a sunny patch in the expansive green lawn of the park just off the exit.

My kids grumbled behind me but followed. Nick was a few paces behind, clutching the takeout bags from the place we had stopped for lunch. Harry's Hot Dog Stand at first seemed like an odd choice, but no one wanted to sit down in a restaurant, and we were already sick of fast food.

So cheese fries it was.

Well, not for Sophie. She refused to eat french fries—always had, even as a toddler who had no frame of reference for refusing them. So she'd gotten an order of chicken nuggets that looked like they had been fried for about ten minutes too long.

The hot dog stand had a large grassy picnic area behind it that, surprisingly, wasn't filled with debris and old car parts.

I plopped down at a picnic table and motioned for my kids to join me. Piper inspected the table carefully and I held my breath, waiting for her to find some flaw in my location choice. But after a moment, she silently sat down and Sophie and Leo did the same.

Nick passed out the food and sat across from me. "So, family." He wiped his mouth with a napkin and leaned forward to peer down the table at the kids. "What is everyone most excited to do when we get to Magic Land?"

"Mystic Twister, for sure. That's the first thing we're doing when we get there," Piper said, a gleam in her eye. Mystic Twister was the largest roller coaster in the park, an enormous wooden monstrosity that appeared to have an almost completely vertical first drop. From birth, she was my adventurous child. No theme park ride was too steep or too fast for her, no town carnival attraction too dangerous looking. The year she finally hit fifty-three inches tall was a banner year, because it meant that she could finally ride everything offered at Six Flags.

"Flight of the Dragon," Leo said with a smile. He seemed to have forgotten the exchange over the necklace, his eleven-year-old brain not stopping on unpleasant things for too long. Flight of the Dragon was an interactive ride with 3D glasses and video screens.

"Unicorn magic brunch!" Sophie shrieked, and clapped her hands.

"Dumb," her brother said, and she frowned.

Piper smiled and leaned over and tapped Sophie on the hand. "Well, I'm excited for it. Are you going to wear a fairy princess costume?"

Sophie nodded happily and then held up a chicken nugget, frowning at the dark brown, overfried color before setting it back down.

Nick leaned across the picnic table. "You made the reservations for that brunch, right?"

I widened my eyes and nodded solemnly. From my online

research and, unfortunately, the Magic Land vacationers social media group I had felt obligated to join (well, pushed to join by M.J., a classic Magic Land superfan), reservations to the unicorn magic brunch were more valuable than toilet paper during a pandemic. I had been carefully instructed to log on to the reservation website right at midnight the day they were released to ensure a spot.

I had fortified myself with a cup of coffee as Nick went to bed and sat in front of my laptop, waiting for the reservations to be released. It was like Christmas morning, except I was receiving something I didn't really want. I had an early court appearance the next morning for a child custody case, but the power of the unicorns prevailed.

We got the reservations, and I got three hours of sleep. But when I told Sophie the next morning, her excitement fueled me through lunch. It was another solid reminder that the trip was about our collective family, about being together, about seeing the kids overjoyed. I could swallow any discomfort for that.

I took a sip of my Diet Coke and looked at the park around us. The grassy picnic area was delineated by a hedge of dappled willow shrubs. Their variegated white and pink tips reached toward us, waving in the gentle breeze. I had planted a couple of the shrubs a few summers ago after I saw them on sale at Home Depot. After a year, I quickly regretted it, because they grew to radioactive plant levels along our fence line in the backyard, and I had to move them before they became self-aware and started communicating.

Gardening had become a hobby that I never thought I would

have. People who were into plants were dorky suburban grandma types, or at least so I'd thought. I'd never imagined myself having an entire Pinterest board full of porch planter "inspo" or that I would perseverate over finding the perfect thriller to put in the center of my containers.

For the record, I went with pink snapdragons.

So while we were gone, Kerry had the very important job of watering my hydrangeas. I thought about texting her again to remind her to water today—according to my phone, the temperature at home would reach ninety-one degrees. And to remind her to water the roots, not from the top, or else the leaves would burn in the sun.

But I was self-aware enough to know to hide my crazy. Or at least try to.

I had a secret way to check on my plants: the Ring camera. I flipped over to the app for our doorbell camera and hit *Live View.* A video from our front door popped up and I peered at the screen, trying to see my hydrangeas, but they were just out of the frame and all I could see were a few leaves at the end. But they looked happy and healthy based on that glimpse, so I smiled.

A wave of homesickness washed over me as I scanned the rest of the yard. The ancient pine tree at the front corner of the yard waved slowly in the breeze. Poor tree—we would have to remove it at some point, because it was infected with needle blight, like most of the evergreens in our neighborhood.

My porch planters—pink snapdragons and all—seemed like they'd exploded with color ever since we left. A stray soccer ball was in the middle of our front yard, probably kicked there last night and left until the neighborhood kids made an appearance this afternoon. I suspected that they were probably using our front yard for their games since we were gone.

But I wanted, more than anything, in that moment, to be back home, sitting on my porch, surrounded by the garden that I had carefully tended, watching my kids play.

Where they're safe.

The thought came to me from out of vapor, almost as though it had been whispered in my ear. Despite the warm sun on my shoulders, I shivered, and looked down the table at my kids, who were arguing over what ride to go on second. Everyone was here; we were together. What could be safer than that?

We're in danger.

Again, the whisper came as though telepathically.

I shook my head and stood up. Nick looked at me in surprise.

"Already done?" he said as his gaze shifted down to my uneaten meal.

I gave him a wavy half smile. "Just want to stretch my legs a bit."

My head felt filled with cotton—the rough, plastic-y variety that was jammed into stuffed animals from the town fair. I tried to tamp down the warning bells going off in my head, telling myself that I was just anxious about the potential disasters that waited ahead, but they persisted.

Trying to get back to equilibrium, I walked from the picnic table over to the row of dappled willow hedges. I smiled as I reached them, the shoots pointing toward me, as though they were waving me over and wanting to show off.

I extended a finger toward the end of one of the shoots and lightly stroked it, the delicate leaves gently moving against my touch. Palm up, I held a branch in my hand, my thumb moving along the veins. The branch stiffened, tightening up like mac and cheese being reheated in the microwave.

In one quick motion, it moved out of my palm.

Weird.

Undeterred, I reached forward to grab another branch, but it did the same thing, like it was avoiding my touch.

I frowned and leaned forward, peering at the plant, trying to see if a critter was hidden in the branches to make them move like that. Nothing.

My heart beating faster, I pressed my mouth into a line and reached forward quickly, roughly grasping a branch and clutching it in my palm.

I smiled, victorious.

I felt the branch in my hand move, begin to contract. I looked down and saw the leaves turning from pinkish white to brown. They grew smaller and more brittle as they aged in the span of two seconds. Two seconds to move from summer to the dead of winter.

Then the plant released the branch in my hand, like a lizard shedding its tail in a predator's grasp. The piece in my hand, dead and brown, separated from the plant, and I was left standing holding a twig with a few desiccated leaves still attached.

"Mom! I have to go to the bathroom." Sophie's voice floated across the grassy picnic area to the edge, where I stood.

I slowly turned, the branch still in my hand, my legs unable to move. Had I imagined what just happened? Had the branch actually been dead already, hanging on to the plant and only appearing to be alive?

I opened my fingers and let the twig fall to the ground, where it lightly bounced before resting in a bed of crabgrass. I had reached forward to touch another branch, just to prove that I had imagined what happened, when I heard Sophie shouting.

"Mom! I said—"

I turned and held a palm up, letting her know that I'd heard her. I had just glanced at the dappled willow one last time, ready to jog over to Sophie, when a burning pain twisted through my stomach, running up to my shoulders and settling at the back of my throat. Before I could acknowledge what was happening, I leaned forward and threw up, next to the plant I had possibly half-murdered.

If whatever I'd done first didn't seal its fate, the undigested fries would certainly finish it off.

Thankfully, my back was to my family, and all they saw was me bent over, leaning closer to the center of the plant.

"Mom! I have to *go*," shouted Sophie as I discreetly wiped my mouth with my shirtsleeve.

As I waited outside the bathroom of Harry's Hot Dog Stand, breathing deeply as the nausea dissipated, I tried to make sense of what had just happened. It had to be the lack of sleep, the stress from the trip, the anxiety over not getting my period . . . *Yet*, I reminded myself.

It was nothing. An already sick plant and too much grease from the fries.

As I walked Sophie back to the picnic table, where Nick was throwing away trash while Piper stared at her phone and Leo ran around in the grass, I stole a glance at the willow hedge. The one I had touched looked robust, healthy, no sign of decay.

"Ready to get back on the road?" Nick said with a smile as he crumpled up paper napkins and shoved them into the white take-out bag.

I nodded and leaned over to scoop up the rest of the trash as Sophie bent down to pick dandelions from the grass. Then I stopped. Maybe I couldn't control much of what had happened or what was going to happen, but I could at least stop feeling strange about the willow.

I turned and jogged back toward the dappled willows, determination in every footfall.

"What are you doing?" Nick called after me.

"Mom's running away from the family," Piper laughed.

Breath quickening, I averted my gaze from where I'd left my lunch, jerked forward, and grabbed a branch on a different dappled willow, smiling as it remained alive and healthy in my palm after a few seconds.

See? Stop driving yourself batty.

But then I felt the branch twitch in my palm, as the other had. My head felt light and my vision clouded as it began to shake, like a toddler was grabbing on to the base and rocking it back and forth. I clutched harder, mostly out of fear and confusion.

A loud ripping sound came from the base of the tree as the entire front side of it pulled away and fell to my feet. I let go as it came crashing down around me, dried leaves decorating the green grass.

Down the center of the shrub was a large gash where it had willingly cut half of itself off. At my feet was the branch it had expelled to get away from my touch, already brown and wilting.

"Mom, you killed that plant!" Sophie's shriek wafted across the field, light and airy in the breeze.

I backed away from the dead branch on the ground, looking from it to the green willow.

Could that really have been my fault?

"Leigh?" Nick called from his spot halfway to Tammy. Piper and Leo were already at the car, negotiating their road trip nests in the backseats. "C'mon. We don't want to get any more off schedule than we already are. I'm going to have to go ten miles over the speed limit to keep us on track."

"Must have been a sick branch," I said brightly to Sophie, whose gaze moved between me and the plant. "Ready?"

She slowly nodded and turned to walk back to the car.

"What just happened?" Nick whispered as we followed our daughter.

"I wish I knew," I said. I resisted the urge to look back to the willow, try to find a rational explanation for what had just happened, but words escaped me. So I was left with the option of disassociating. "I'll drive this leg," I said to Nick. "I'll go ten miles over the speed limit. Eleven, maybe, if I feel crazy," I added when I saw he was about to protest.

Key fob in hand, I started up the car and waited as it revved up while everyone else piled in. As the clock blinked on, the time made my hand freeze in the air.

Eleven fifteen.

It had to be wrong. We'd arrived at the hot dog stand after one, Nick commenting that it was a late lunch.

The white numbers stared back at me like a challenge.

"What the . . ." I grabbed my phone from the center console and checked the time: 1:47. I looked back at the clock, still frozen at 11:15. The back of my neck grew hot and prickly as I looked down at my phone again, then back up to Tammy's clock.

"Nick, I—" I started to say when the numbers blinked out and then displayed 1:48.

"What's wrong?" Nick said from the passenger seat, turning his head to see what I was looking at.

I shook my head and closed my eyes for a moment. "Nothing." I swallowed and pulled the car out of the parking lot and onto the highway.

So many things had already happened that I couldn't explain, didn't know how to begin to explain, but I did know one thing for certain: this road trip was not going how any of us expected.

Magic Land waited for us, but what would it take to get there?

Chapter 11

We drove further through Kentucky, leaving the areas populated with strip malls and rest areas, leaving the half-dead dappled willow behind. The landscape changed from areas where you could tell people lived and went to school, to bright rolling hills that increased in size, to rocky peaks and taller trees. We had officially entered Appalachia.

Nick directed me to the Blue Ridge Motel, our stop for the evening. I don't think any of us had the strength to argue or complain about the HVAC system, which had two settings: eternal hellfire and Siberian wasteland.

The next morning we left the motel before the sunrise, to get back on track and try to get a bit ahead of Nick's schedule. I feared if we got too far behind, I'd end up going thirty miles over the speed limit, and receiving a traffic violation wasn't really a core memory I was hoping to make.

But we didn't leave the motel before I had to throw up again, the nausea intensifying as soon as I lifted my head off the pillow. I managed to discreetly slip into the bathroom while Nick was still asleep, turn the faucet on, and do my business. After splashing some cold water on my face, I felt slightly human again.

I wondered if I had developed some kind of food allergy, like I was suddenly sensitive to gluten or dairy, even though I knew how ridiculous that sounded. But it was more comforting than the alternative. Having a baby in my forties was not something in my carefully constructed life plan. Not at all.

Denial was powerful, and I intended to use every ounce of that power.

Nick took the first shift, and I watched as the sun rose over the mountains, casting a golden glow on the rolling fields below, looking as though it were illuminating a particular treasure in the fields, like Indiana Jones using a special crystal staff to find the Ark of the Covenant.

It was breathtaking.

"Damn, Mother Nature is showing off," Nick said from next to me, looking out the passenger window. All three kids were asleep in the back, slumped over various pieces of luggage and stuffed animals. They'd tried to watch movies and use electronics, but they each succumbed to the movement of the car and the white noise of the trucks around us in the morning haze.

"So, Magellan, are we on track according to your calculations?" I said as I took a sip of motel coffee that could've doubled as motor oil. I set it down when my stomach protested again.

Nick reached down and picked up the TripTik, paging through it and referencing the mile markers we passed as he kept one eye on the road. He gave me a quick nod.

"I knew you could do it."

"Well, yesterday I went twelve miles over the speed limit just to make sure. I didn't want to find out what would happen if we had to detour again."

Looking at the orange and pink sunrise on the horizon, the rays of light slowly lifting, the sun peeking its head out to start another day, it was easy to hope that all the trouble was behind us.

I caught a glimpse of my reflection in the passenger-side window and quickly looked away, the same reaction as when I accidentally caught a glimpse of myself in the Target self-checkout camera.

"Oof," I said.

"Why don't you try to doze off for a little while? The kids are all asleep anyway," Nick said, confirming my thought that I looked like a Victorian woman with a laudanum addiction wasting away on a fainting couch.

"Nah. I'm good. I might try and sleep a little later, though." Optimistic words, even though I knew Highway 40 loomed ahead, the dreaded leg of our trip. Highway 40 ran through Tennessee, winding through the Smoky Mountains with hairpin turns, rock formations on either side, and trucks barreling through, ignoring the white-knuckled parents behind the wheel.

I had heard about that particular highway from everyone who had made a road trip south. It was usually mentioned with an offhand smile and widened eyes, like someone recounting, when you're pregnant, how their baby had colic for three years and they still haven't slept for longer than an hour at a time. Horror stories.

"You okay? You seem like something is on your mind," Nick said quietly, almost whispering.

I paused and considered my coffee. I could tell him, share my worries about the possible pregnancy. Or I could tell him that I was unsettled by everything that had happened on our trip so far—the necklace, urgent care, the willow bush . . . everything. But I thought of how excited he had been to plan the trip, of all the research he had done—up late at night to look up different stops and the exact right turtle top. This was his dad Super Bowl, and I didn't want to take that away from him.

Besides, I could get my period that day, and the rest of the trip could be easy, enjoyable, even. And we would forget all about the bizarre things that had happened. Or they would become family lore. Like the time M.J. had taken her boys to a water park and one of her son's diapers exploded in the lazy river.

Those thoughts were all reasonable, but they weren't the whole truth. There was a part of me that I didn't want to acknowledge, though. I was wary for another reason: I was afraid Nick would be delighted at the idea of having another child, and I would be the only one with any negative feelings.

And once again, he would be the perfect dad, the exemplary husband, the excited parent. And I would be the one who only thought of the struggles and uphill battles, brought all the negativity. I didn't want to be that person. At least not right then, with the beautiful sunrise happening in front of us, whispering promises that good things were right around the corner, but we just had to keep going.

A warmth filled my chest and I looked over at Nick, gratitude pulsing through my body. We were together. The kids were safe. Everything was good, at least in that moment.

I reached a hand over to place it on his shoulder, and as I made contact, his form changed. His shoulder underneath my hand disintegrated into sharp bones, his U2 T-shirt balling up in my hand as the flesh and meat melted away. His face sank inward, lines forming on his graying skin. A hole began to appear at the center of the front of his T-shirt, obscuring Bono's face, right where Nick's heart would be.

I yanked my hand away, prepared to scream, and he changed back.

"What? What's wrong?" Nick said, his eyes rapidly going back and forth between me and the road. "What's wrong?"

"I—" I looked down at my hand and then back to him. I tentatively reached forward and poked his shoulder with one hand, terror building inside me, waiting for him to turn decayed again. But this time, nothing. I clutched his shoulder a few times, feeling the relief that it felt like him again. Human, alive Nick.

"Ow. What are you doing?" His eyes were narrowed, his mouth turned down. Confusion moved across his face, morphing into concern as he looked at me like I had decided to root for the Bears over the Packers.

"You looked . . . different for a second." My voice came out cracked, unsteady. I wiped my eyes, pressing the heels of my hands to my face, not caring if my contacts popped out. "I think I'm seeing things."

Nick didn't know how to respond to that; they didn't cover spousal hallucinations at Green Bay Middle School.

I pressed my lips together and inhaled deeply, the car settling into silence again. I glanced over at the clock slowly.

Please let it be the right time. Please.

It read 7:20 a.m.

"Oh, thank God," I whispered as my shoulders sagged. Not 11:15 again. Not anything weird or unexplainable. The vision of Nick was just that: a trick of the light, a hallucination brought on by stress. It was the road trip's fault. Apparently, I was able to bully opposing counsel or sweet-talk a judge, but I turned into a fragile woman on the road. But I could walk through hell to get to the Magic Land prize at the end, for my family.

"'Hell is real!' Wow, they don't mess around with that message," Nick muttered next to me.

I didn't respond, watching the billboard move past the car. The kids, who had woken up, turned in their seats to read it, too.

"Is hell real?" Leo asked from the backseat.

Nick and I exchanged a glance—not exactly a light conversation. And here I was hoping we would just play I Spy or the license plate game to pass the time before we stopped for lunch.

I half-shrugged to Nick, unsure of how to answer. We weren't exactly a religious family, more spiritual if anything. We went to church on Christmas and Easter—Christers, Kerry called us—but I had no idea if hell was real. I suspected no, but it wasn't like I had any actual proof. The priest hadn't covered that topic last Easter.

"Mom, where's my Nintendo Switch?" Leo asked, the question on hell forgotten and unanswered.

Grateful for a question I could answer, I eagerly reached forward into the backpack at my feet to retrieve the gaming system. As I did, another billboard caught my eye.

Instead of proclaiming the existence of an afterlife full of torture, this one espoused the wonders of hell on earth: personal injury attorneys. *Injured at work? Want a happy ending (legally)?*

I rolled my eyes a little as I continued to reach forward to rifle through the backpack to find the Switch. My eyes were on the billboard as I fumbled around in the backpack, feeling for the long oval case to the gaming system.

My finger brushed against it, and I had just reached forward to pull the whole thing out when I froze. My hand was still in the backpack, fingers half curled. My gaze was frozen on the billboard as it moved closer to us.

The lawyer's shiny black hair, tanned skin, and too-white teeth loomed closer to us, like a spoon reflection. As the billboard approached, the lawyer's face began to change. His eyes darkened into two small holes, and his hair flattened against the sides of his head. His teeth went from blue-white to brown and decaying, stretching the limits of his lips. Chunks of skin hung from his lips, blood dripping from the corners.

"What the fuck," I whispered. As it came closer to us, his eyes on the billboard shifted to look directly at me.

I jumped back, slamming against the passenger seat.

"What's wrong?" Nick said, his eyes searching for whatever had made me startle.

"I—" I craned my neck back as the billboard passed us and the black and gray scaffolding on the back side moved further into the distance. "Nothing."

I looked down at the backpack, Switch peeking out from the top. I quickly reached forward for the gaming system, thrusting it to Leo in a gesture more aggressive than I intended.

"You sure you're okay?" Nick said quietly as we heard the sounds of Mario Kart start up.

Lawyer Leigh took over, and anger rose in my chest. "You know what? No. I'm not, so stop asking that," I snapped, and then instantly regretted it when I saw his face. "Sorry. I just . . ." I couldn't finish the sentence. I didn't know how.

There was no way he would think I was mentally stable if I told him what I had seen—what I *thought* I had seen. Between feeling his bones under my hand and the billboard, I was left questioning everything. What was real anymore?

I became a lawyer because the law made sense. While certainly subject to interpretation (always for the benefit of my clients), it was at least a guidebook, laid out in black and white.

"You know, I think I am going to try to take that quick nap before we stop for lunch," I said, mostly to myself, and then balled up the hoodie from my lap and placed it next to the window. I leaned over, ignoring the strains and creaks in my neck and shoulders. I pulled my baseball cap down over my brows and closed my eyes.

Chapter 12

Sleep came quickly. I dreamed I was back home, in my garden, lovingly tending to my hydrangeas. Their blooms were just beginning to turn a creamy white, and I watched proudly as honeybees and bumblebees buzzed around the flowers. I had just reached a hand out to touch one of the leaves when I heard a voice.

"Leigh? We're here."

I heard Nick's disembodied voice float through my consciousness like a pebble disrupting a stream. I felt a shake on my shoulder.

"Leigh, wake up."

I slowly opened my eyes and squinted at the sunlight streaming through Tammy's windshield. I straightened my body, my neck protesting at the angle. I rubbed my shoulder and looked around, the disorientation of sleep still clouding my vision.

Through the windshield, I could see we were in the parking lot of what looked like a log cabin. A bright yellow sign with brown lettering was displayed at the entrance to the parking lot.

CRACKER BARREL

Streams of people headed toward the entrance like they were giving away free biscuits.

Nick saw my expression and chuckled. "The kids insisted. It won't be that bad. And it's better than fast food again."

I shook my head. "It's not that. Look." I pointed to the never-ending groups of patrons marching toward the door, regenerating every time it looked like they were going to slow down. It was like a zombie horde that was compelled to buy tchotchkes before they ordered a number six, the Old Timer's Breakfast, with a side of freshly cooked brains.

Good thing I also liked the Old Timer's Breakfast, neurological material excluded.

"We can sit outside while we wait." Nick's tone was upbeat, but he gave a small sigh as we exited the car, as though he was preparing himself for a long, arduous battle.

"Hour wait," Nick said as he exited Cracker Barrel and came to where I sat in a red rocking chair on the porch. "Not as bad as I thought."

Piper gave a harrumph as she tucked her feet up on her rocking chair, phone in her hand. Sophie whined and laid her head on one of the chair's arms.

"Mom, can I go look at that pond?" Leo pointed to a small body of water flanking the porch. I saw orange and white fish swimming under the surface, mouths wide for any leftovers.

I smiled and nodded as Nick took Leo's chair, edging out a woman who had been hawking our spots ever since we rushed them when the Newman family's name was called. She gave me dagger eyes as Nick sat down. I smiled sweetly and gave her a wave. She reeled back and harrumphed away. That worked about 99.9 percent of the time, in the courtroom or not. First, you come in strong, make your point, mark your territory. Then, when they're all worked up, you smile. Correct or not, it worked.

The smell of bacon wafted through the porch as another family opened the door to go put their names down on the wait list. My stomach rumbled, and I crossed my arms over my midsection. Finally, I was hungry and didn't feel like I wanted to puke.

"I didn't think Cracker Barrels were still this popular," Nick said as he slumped down in his rocking chair.

He had a faraway look on his face, and I knew he was recalculating how far we would get that day on the road.

"Are we going to make it to the world's largest ball of twine?" I said with a laugh. I stopped when I saw his sheepish expression. "Oh no. That's really a thing?"

He smiled, and his shoulders relaxed. "No, no. I just thought the kids would want to see more of the scenery before it got dark. But we can always take a more leisurely route on the way home."

"Nope. I'm good. We should stick to the original plan of driving home quickly, especially if you let me drive," Piper said as she put her phone down on the arm of the chair. "I just want to eat."

I leaned forward and looked around Nick, putting my forearms on my thighs and clasping my hands together. "You know, growing up, I used to wait two hours—on vacation—to eat at a Cracker Barrel."

Piper's eyes widened and she scoffed. "Probably because they barely had food back in colonial times."

Nick laughed, and I rolled my eyes. "Yes, and our covered wagon took us there quite speedily."

It was true, though. Every year my parents would take me on vacation to Hilton Head Island, South Carolina. My dad would usually spend the vacation going through documents at the condo's kitchen island or leaving to take a client call. Even as a child, I'd found it odd that most of his client calls were after nine p.m. So most of the time, it was just my mom and me, and she had no interest in actually parenting. The frozen daiquiris and bartenders at the beach bar were far more interesting.

But on the Sunday morning of vacation, she stepped up. She instituted a tradition of going out to a quaint little diner we had never heard of called Cracker Barrel.

We, along with seemingly every other vacationer, would wait to eat there on Sunday mornings. The waits were usually two hours, sometimes more. We would pass the time by watching the fish in the pond outside, hawking the rocking chairs on the porch, and wandering around the prodigious gift shop. It became an essential part of our vacations, a destination within a destination.

This was before the restaurant went through a rapid franchise expansion, before it was on the edge of every highway exit. Before it slotted into the restaurant category right next to Denny's.

I'd been delighted when a few started popping up closer to us. One year, I saw one open in Baraboo, forty-five minutes away, and begged my mom to take me there for my birthday. She declined.

And then, several years ago, the restaurants were everywhere and they didn't seem quite so charming.

So, waiting over an hour to eat at one with my family struck me as a full-circle life moment. I settled back into the rocking chair, putting a foot on the seat and wrapping my arms around my shin. I looked over at Piper.

"Anything new in the high school news that I should be aware of?"

She looked up from her phone and put it on the arm of her rocking chair with a sigh, as though the world were crumbling around her and all she could do was watch from the Cracker Barrel waiting porch.

"Well, Hope decided to break up with Will, and now he's been asking Delaney out, even though she's Hope's enemy, just to get back at her." Piper shook her head, her long hair tousling around her shoulders. "I'm honestly kinda glad I'm not at home to deal with all of it."

"Attagirl," I said with a nod. I reached over and patted her on the knee, which she accepted. I couldn't push too much with her, or get too warm and fuzzy, or else she would dismiss it all. The fact that she was seemingly happy and somewhat well-adjusted gave me more peace than she could comprehend.

The knowledge that we only had a couple more years before she went away to college was another file in my denial box. I couldn't imagine not hearing her complain about the brand of bagels I bought or not finding the endless empty bottles of Propel and protein bar wrappers scattered around the house. Or her coming into my bedroom every night to hug me good night, no matter how late it was or how irate she had been about the Wi-Fi signal earlier in the day.

It was another reason I had agreed to the road trip: to dig into the time we still had and force it to slow down. Even if it tortured us.

Sophie picked her head up from the arm of the rocking chair. "I have to go to the bathroom."

I sighed and looked at Nick, who'd started to rise from his chair. "No, I'll take her."

I held Sophie's hand as we walked into the restaurant through the famed gift shop. We had to pause behind a family arguing in the vestibule about whether they were going to stay until a table was ready. Apparently, the wait had grown to ninety minutes. Surprisingly, they decided to stick around, even though the mom looked like she wanted to run away and live off the grid. I understood.

"Stay close," I said to Sophie as I tightened my grip on her hand. The gift shop was packed with people, standing nearly shoulder to shoulder and looking increasingly panicked and hungry. The air held a certain feeling of desperation, like the parents of the kid who wailed on the floor were about thirty seconds away from buying pounds of rock candy as a salve.

I steered Sophie around a table of aggressively patriotic garden flags and a tower of books on tape, and we wound our way back to the bathrooms. I stopped when I saw a long line of women looking fidgety.

"Guess the line starts here. I'm sure it will move quickly," I said brightly, even though I did not see anyone heading toward the bathroom.

"Mom, can I look at those toys?" She pointed to a large display of plushies against the back wall.

"Sure. Just stay where I can see you while I wait in line," I said.

She walked over to the shelves, and I eyed a garden décor display that was all religious items and butterfly trellises. There was even a gazing ball with a Bible quote etched into the center. My mother-in-law would have happily furnished her entire house, as well as the exterior, with Cracker Barrel chic.

A woman pushed through toward the end of the line, knocking over a bin of umbrellas, and loudly sighed as she saw all of us waiting. Her hair was styled around her head in frosted tips and looked like the kind of hairstyle set in foam rollers and covered in a sleep bonnet each night. She looked like Abby Lee Miller, the formerly incarcerated star of *Dance Moms*.

She put her hands on her hips, which were swathed in stretch jeggings with bedazzled back pockets, and groaned.

"Is this the line?" she said, tapping her coral-pink fingernails against a wood table displaying pinwheels.

I confirmed and she groaned again, louder this time. I smiled apologetically at her, but that only seemed to infuriate her more.

"This is ridiculous. It's so hot in here, and there aren't enough bathrooms for everyone. I don't know how they can do business like this." Every word increased in intensity, her voice breaking off as she got more heated.

Then she said the words that I knew she would—that I secretly hoped she would, just to confirm my impression of her.

"I'm going to speak to the manager."

I saw people jump out of the way as she barreled toward the hostess stand. I couldn't make out what she was saying over the din of the crowd, but I could certainly feel the fallout. The patrons in line in front of me began to murmur, their discomfort palpable.

I craned my neck and located Sophie, who was happily

examining a pink octopus plushie, and then looked back toward the bathroom door. We hadn't moved at all, and soon she would forget about the toys and really have to go.

I recalled that Nick had broached the idea of packing a travel porta-potty. I have never said no to anything more quickly in my life. Now it seemed as though karma was going to teach me a lesson about hubris in the Cracker Barrel gift shop.

My anxiety and frustration started to spike as I remained in line, unmoving, still staring at the Jesus gazing ball. I felt a trickle of sweat move down my neck and rubbed my forehead roughly, craning my neck toward the bathroom, as though that would do anything.

The muffled sounds of an altercation at the hostess stand grew stronger across the rows of wax-bottle candies, and my ears started to ring. All of the conversation around me mixed into one gray substance with spiky edges.

I took a couple of deep breaths, but the panic in my chest continued to rise. I tried to remember the yoga breathing from a class I'd taken with M.J., but the sensory overload was too strong to tamp down.

The pressure in my chest built and built until I was ready to start screaming, too. I quickly understood why that woman was beginning to freak out. (I did not, however, understand her hairstyle.)

A child knocked over a table of souvenir marbles, hundreds clattering onto the floor. She started to wail, and her parents rushed over and began to hastily collect the marbles spinning out of control.

I started to see black spots in my vision and felt like I was going to pass out. I pulled out my phone to text Nick and Piper to come inside to take my place so I could get some fresh air and calm the hell down.

But before I could type out the text, the overhead lights brightened, and there was more screaming. This time, it wasn't from a bathroom emergency or the hostess assaulter.

I knew that sound. That was my Sophie, invisible to me, hidden somewhere behind the tchotchkes.

Chapter 13

I snapped my head up, and my phone tumbled from my hand as my whole body locked up, trying to process what I saw.

All around the Cracker Barrel, tchotchkes were launching off the shelves, hurling from their places against the wall, through the air. I watched as a bag of caramels sailed over my head before hitting the fridge magnets, then dropping to the ground. A decorative candle flew just past my face, and I leaned back, narrowly missing getting clipped by a maniacally spinning pinwheel.

"Sophie!" I screamed across the store, and I saw her peek out from around a display of bedazzled sweatshirts and then run to me. I put an arm around her shoulders, and she buried her face in my stomach. I covered her head with my other hand, holding her close.

All around me, people began screaming and panicking, ducking down to avoid the items as they flew through the air and across the gift shop. A revolving display rack of postcards began spinning, the force flinging the postcards out like razor blades through the air. A can of Silly String exploded, raining Silly String down on the head of the manager seeker. She stood there, stunned, hot-pink string dripping down from her hair helmet.

It felt like the restaurant's whole building was shaking, like the walls were about to crumble around us.

I grabbed Sophie's hand so tight that she yelped.

"We have to get out of here," I shouted. Sweat began to drip down into my eyes as I frantically looked around, checking to see if the path to the exit door was clear. Pieces of candy and fridge magnets were still slashing through the air in a crosswise pattern. We would have to time our escape to avoid the debris.

I pulled Sophie forward and then stopped abruptly as we were in a clear lane, between a stream of flying Jolly Ranchers and another lane of wax bottles that danced back and forth.

I waited for another wax bottle to fly past us and then yanked Sophie forward, stopping again to assess our path.

I looked up and saw Nick, Piper, and Leo standing on the porch, frantically slapping the window, shouting something I couldn't hear over the chaos of the flying tchotchkes.

I lowered my chin and made eye contact with Nick, my mouth pressed into a line.

I will get us out of here. I will keep our daughter safe. The words flashed through my eyes and Nick nodded, understanding.

"Get ready," I said to Sophie as I timed the next lane, dodging tea candles in the shape of miniature roses. Those would hurt—the candles were encased in small glass vases.

I gripped Sophie's hand and rushed forward. To my right, I saw a man collapse as he was hit from behind by one of the candles.

The shouting around me reached a fever pitch.

I was about to pull Sophie through the candle lane when there was a loud buzzing sound. And then everything that was flying through the air halted, like someone had pressed pause on a remote control.

The items in the air—magnets, candy, maps, postcards, books on CD—quivered and then dropped to the ground. It was as though contact had been lost.

The lights in the restaurant dimmed back to normal, and the faint sounds of a country music soundtrack returned to the speakers. I slowly looked around, Sophie's hand still in mine. On every side of me, patrons were uncovering their heads, standing, looking at each other and trying to figure out what the hell had just happened.

I took the opportunity to tug Sophie forward and run out of the doors. A crowd had gathered on the porch, and Nick pushed through everyone to grab me and Sophie.

"Mom!" Leo shouted as he wrapped his arms around my waist. Nick picked up Sophie and held her, reverse piggyback style.

My hands shaking, I clung on to Leo, and Piper put her arms around both of us.

"What was that?" Leo said from my midsection.

My hands were shaking, and I pressed them to his back. "I don't know." My voice was wavering, my heart thudding in my chest. I looked up at Nick and saw the fear in his eyes, the questions that no one had answers to.

"Is she okay?" I said as I reached forward and rested a hand on Sophie's back. Her face was buried in Nick's shoulder.

He half-shrugged but then gave me a quick nod. We were all physically fine. It was the mental and emotional toll that would be paid later, once we could process what had just happened.

If we could even accept what had happened without explaining it away. I saw it all the time at work. In the face of glaring evidence of something like a gambling problem or an addiction or cheating, one of the spouses would twist themselves every which way to try to convince themselves that the truth wasn't true.

Strange, flirty texts sent in the middle of the night? Must be a wrong number.

Bank account slowly draining away? Must be all those subscriptions we need to cancel.

Work calls at ten p.m.? Must be a busy time at the office.

The human mind had an extraordinary ability to process away anything out of the normal range, to make it make sense.

"Did you feel that shaking? I didn't know they got earthquakes here," a woman with a long drawl said to her husband. He nodded profusely, content to have an explanation.

"Some kind of earthquake, yes," I heard another woman murmur.

"I think they're jackhammering up some concrete down the street. They must have hit some kind of underground line," a bearded man to my left wearing a University of Tennessee hat said.

"Mom, what happened?" Piper said. Her eyes were wide, full of worry, and she bit her bottom lip slightly, as though she was trying to hold back what she really wanted to say.

"I'm not sure," I said. I wasn't going to lie to her and make something up, but I sure as shit wasn't going to reveal what I really thought.

Her eyes flicked down to her phone and then back to our car, and I could read in them what she was thinking as though there were a closed caption.

But what about the ghost stories?

What about the locket that we have?

What about everything weird that has happened to us?

I squared my shoulders and was going to say something—anything—to get her thinking back on track. Less *Poltergeist* and more *National Lampoon's Vacation*. But a wave of burning pain seared through my midsection. It was a white-hot ball of agony that traveled up my esophagus, feeling like it was burning away my internal organs.

I put a hand on my stomach and took a deep breath, trying to calm down my body.

"You okay?" Piper said as she put her hands on my shoulders.

I nodded, unable to open my mouth. The burning surged again, upward, this time with more force. I broke away from my family on the porch and ran down the steps, barely making it away from everyone as I threw up into a rhododendron. Plants were apparently my go-to for getting sick.

The crowd gathered on the Cracker Barrel porch paused and watched me, and then went back to exclaiming over what had happened inside. A few other people looked queasy, especially the woman sitting in one of the rockers, fanning herself with her hand.

She looked over. "You shouldn't do that out here. It's disgusting," she said with a frown.

I slowly stood up. "Oh yeah? Where should I do it, then? In your lap?"

Nick jolted at my words and rushed over, standing next to me, as the woman in the rocking chair opened her mouth to retort.

"Sorry," he whispered to her.

I shot him an annoyed look and wiped my mouth with my sleeve slowly, making eye contact with her until she looked away, whatever retort she had fizzling out.

"Let's get out of here," Nick said, and pointed to the parking lot.

I marched toward Tammy, shaking my head, the anger and confusion at what had just happened slowly dissipating into something else: fear.

I put my hand on the driver's-side handle and held out my palm. "I'm driving."

"Are you sure?" Nick said, still looking at me like I was a live grenade. "Maybe I should drive."

"Oh, can I drive?" Piper said brightly.

"No," we said in unison, our voices raised.

A silent moment passed between Nick and me. I gave him a few slow blinks and relaxed my face into what I hoped resembled normal. He finally gave up and placed the key in my hand as we saw a Cracker Barrel manager emerge from the wooden door, looking shaken.

"Let me go see what he says," Nick said before he jogged over.

The rest of us loaded into the car and I stared at the clock, daring it to turn to eleven fifteen. But the ghostly activity was done for the moment, having cashed all of its chips in at the Cracker Barrel, and it read the correct time.

"That's right, asshole," I whispered. "This stops right now."

If only.

Chapter 14

No one spoke very much in the car after we got back in. The official word from the very young, very terrified-looking manager of the Cracker Barrel was there was underground digging a mile away, and they must have hit some kind of gas or electrical line, which caused the shaking and flying. Even as he was explaining, I could tell from my vantage point in the car that he didn't believe any of it. He had the air of someone ready to jump out of their skin. The willow shrub abandoning a dead branch.

But that was the official explanation, and we didn't have another one.

As we got back onto the highway, Nick silently passed snacks back to the kids since they hadn't gotten to eat breakfast at the Cracker Barrel from hell. Piper's eyes remained fixed on her phone as she chewed a Z Bar; Leo stared out of the window, an uneaten packet of cheese crackers in his lap; and Sophie gazed down at her doll.

Even Nick was quiet as we drove past flyspeck towns, mind

obviously on what had happened. I wondered if part of him was regretting the trip, if he finally saw what we all did, what we were all afraid of. If he was finally understanding his optimism might have been a little misguided and too aggressive.

I thought of his face when we were first planning the trip. His excitement, his emergency car kits, his hidden gems along the route. Now his cheeks were drawn, and his eyes flicked back and forth on the road, listless.

His dream family vacation was quickly becoming a nightmare. I had finally calmed down, my distress fizzling into a slight prickle, and now the softer emotions came through. A pang of sadness ran up my spine.

I leaned over and patted his shoulder, hesitating for the briefest of moments, the memory of his body wasting away in front of me still potent.

"Interesting morning, huh?" I said with a laugh, keeping my voice light. "Something to tell our grandchildren about, I suppose."

"Or something to tell my therapist," Piper grumbled from the third row.

I turned and gave her a death stare before looking back at Nick. I squeezed his forearm again. "Where's our next stop?"

Of course, I knew what our next stop was, but I figured it was good to get him talking. He loved discussing schedules and structure. Driving times and logistical plans. He thought in details, and I thought in big picture.

"Pigeon Forge, Tennessee. We should be there in about two hours if we don't hit any traffic or construction." His tone was light, but his words were flat, like a balloon slowly deflating.

I squeezed his arm again and mustered up the brightest smile I could. "The kids will love it."

He kept his gaze trained forward a bit longer and then looked at me, and finally his face broke into a small, grateful smile. He nodded. "I hope so."

"Mom?" Sophie said from the backseat.

I braced myself and turned around, ready for more questions I couldn't answer about what had just happened.

"Am I tall enough to go on all of the waterslides?" she said. Her eyes were wide with childlike hope.

I probably showed the adult version of that expression when I asked a judge to move a court date or for a continuance in a divorce case.

"I think so," I said brightly, pushing away any thoughts of long lines, interesting water park patrons, and the biohazards in the water.

"Sophie, you'll chicken out before you even get to a waterslide," Leo said.

"Mom! Leo's being mean," Sophie said. "I am too going on a waterslide. You're stupid."

Nick turned around. "Leo, Sophie will go on the waterslides. Sophie, apologize to your brother for calling him stupid."

"But he is stupid," she said firmly. I heard a wail and knew Leo had reached over and smacked her. I looked up into the rearview mirror and saw the two of them leaning as far over as their seat belts would allow, reaching to commit sibling assault.

"Hey. Hey. Hey. Guys, stop," Nick said as he put an arm between them.

"I hate her!" Leo shouted, and then lunged for his sister again.

"If you two don't stop it, we're going to skip the water park and stay at another motel, okay?" My tone was louder and harsher than I intended, but the stress of everything that had happened didn't allow for any restraint. "We're on this trip together to have fun. And we. Will. Have. Fun. *Got it?*"

The car was silent, my words sharp sticks pointed at everyone. Nick slowly withdrew his arm from the backseat, trusting the violence had stopped.

"Remember what I told you about this resort? The wave pool and slides and dump buckets? Let's all get along and look forward to that," Nick said evenly.

When Nick had planned our stops, he'd decided we should stay in the Smoky Mountains for a night, figuring it was a good midway point for our trip. And this stop would not be sans pool or working HVAC unit. No, he'd booked the Mountain Lodge Resort, the largest outdoor water park hotel in the Pigeon Forge, Tennessee, area. The kids were thrilled. I was less so, having been to a water park resort twice with our kids. Both times in the Wisconsin Dells, a seeming rite of passage for Midwesterners looking to spend hard-earned dollars but also be horrified. The first time, I watched a twentysomething chug a Mountain Dew mixed with what I suspected was some kind of moonshine and then throw up in the hot tub, and the second, we had to leave early due to a ringworm outbreak.

Of course, those were the things I remembered. Nick and the kids remembered the waterslides and the garbage food poolside and the black-light mini golf.

When I was in elementary school, I had seen commercials on

television for water park resorts and asked my mother why we couldn't visit there. She just laughed and shook her head, while I remained oblivious to why she had said no.

"We aren't water park people," she finally told me when I pressed the issue.

We weren't a lot of things. A family that hugged each other. One that laughed together. The idea of unconditional love after the divorce was one that involved writing checks to get out of whatever mess we encountered, my father buying me a car for my sixteenth birthday, and free rein with my mother's credit card number. I was the envy of everyone at my school, St. Michael's Academy. At least, until my senior year, when everything came crashing down when my father was arrested. Then I'm sure there were hushed conversations over family dinners in our town.

His "normalcy" was what first attracted me to Nick. When he was growing up in Green Bay, his family was focused on ice fishing, the Packers-game score, and cheese curds. They were water park people. And I wanted something else for my future, something that didn't involve newspaper articles or seeing my name in snarky internet comments.

I just wanted to be normal. And Nick's family was as quintessentially normal as I could have pictured. The Midwestern version of normal, anyway.

So with that, I made a deal with the devil: To do all of the things with my own kids that I thought I had missed out on. Water parks, amusement parks, town carnivals, roasting s'mores, water balloon fights in the front yard.

And now it was time to pay up.

➡

Two for one $10 all you can drink margaritas

The scrolling marquee outside the Mountain Lodge Resort flashed between the margarita advertisement and five dollars off the indoor ropes course after ten p.m., entirely on brand for everything I feared at a water park resort.

"I spy . . . a headache in a glass," I said with a quick laugh, trying to lighten the mood in the car after snapping at the kids. "You think they're making those with Don Julio?" I steered Tammy into the long, winding driveway.

I was relieved when Nick laughed. "Gasoline. We might need to try some, though."

I raised my eyebrows and kept my gaze trained on the windshield, watching as the tall pines on either side of the driveway canopied our car. I didn't want him to see my reaction to his words. A margarita sounded good—gasoline aside—but I couldn't drink one without knowing what was going on in my body. The question was a loaded gun, one that I couldn't face. Not yet. And maybe I wouldn't have to.

I pulled the car into the valet overhang and Nick went inside to check us in as the kids squealed with delight in the backseat. I turned around and smiled at Leo and Sophie, their faces bursting with joy. I looked behind them to Piper, who had also shed her usual teenage ennui.

This is for them. Not for you. Don't ruin it.

As I watched a group of twentysomething men wearing T-shirts that said **CALEB'S LAST HURRAH** with a picture of a ball and chain underneath, I rubbed my forehead. They pulled a luggage cart piled with Busch Light beer behind them. The one pulling the cart stopped before they walked in, and they circled around the luggage cart and ripped open one of the cases, each taking a beer and counting down before shotgunning them. They completed the ritual by crushing the cans against their foreheads.

I almost wished we were back at the Cracker Barrel.

Chapter 15

The Mountain Lodge Resort's theme was a mix of rustic log cabin charm (at $500 a night), Vegas-style advertising on every wall (two-for-one appetizers at Old Willie's Saloon), and excessive chlorine. The smell nearly knocked us over as we walked through the lobby. Overhead was an enormous chandelier made of antlers, casting dappled light on the red and brown carpet. The furniture all appeared to be carved from sturdy trees, although as I ran a hand along the arm of one of the Adirondack chairs in the lobby, I realized the smooth surface was plastic.

Just off the lobby was a candy store, the Sugar Canteen, with rows and rows of rainbow-colored treats hanging from self-dispensing containers, and plastic bags marked *$2 per pound.*

"Per pound?" I whispered to Piper. "How many pounds is necessary for a water park vacation?"

She turned to answer, a smirk on her lips, but before she could say anything, Sophie screeched, "Candy store! Can we go in?"

"No," Piper, Nick, and I all said in unison.

Sophie grumbled as we walked through the winding hallway to our room: L1408.

"Are you sure this is the right way?" Leo said as he pulled his roll-aboard bag behind him. "This hallway is only F."

"Yes. It's a big place," I said, half-turning around. I stopped and let him go ahead of me, putting my hand on my own roll-aboard's handle and stepping aside.

The front desk agent had slapped a map of the resort down on the ledge in front of us as we checked in. She pulled out a highlighter and smiled brightly as she traced it through no fewer than four hallways and an elevator bank. Then she took out a pink highlighter and traced the six hallways we would have to navigate to find an indoor water park numbered one out of three.

No wonder I saw so many parents dressed in swimsuits and coverups pulling rolling coolers and wagons behind them through the halls. They probably packed full meals inside to stop and have lunch in between hallways three and four.

As we stepped away from the check-in desk, walking around a family with twins all wearing Mountain Lodge Resort T-shirts—ten points for loyal customers—we were stopped by a far-too-friendly twentysomething guy sporting a polo shirt and a clipboard. He had the smell of a door-to-door lawn care service salesman.

"Hi, folks. Welcome!" he said as my shoulders stiffened, the words *no thank you* already on my lips. "If I could have just a minute of your time . . ."

Nick gave him his easy middle school principal smile. "Oh, we appreciate it, but we're going to head to our room to check in," he said, and gestured for us to follow.

We didn't even know what exactly he was selling, but I had never been more positive in my life that I did not want whatever it was.

"Do you kids like magic shows?" the happy salesman said, turning to Leo and Sophie.

Shots fired.

"Yes!" Leo said enthusiastically, letting go of his roll-aboard's handle, and it wobbled and toppled forward to the ground.

"Well then, come follow me, buddy!" the salesman said, gesturing for Leo to step inside the small office next to the check-in desk.

Nick and I each raised a hand in protest, strangling out reasons to stop, to no avail. Leo, followed close behind by Sophie, was already wandering around the office.

The inside of the office had three desks, each with a matching overeager salesman sitting at it. Two other couples were seated on the other sides of the desks, looking enraptured by whatever each recent college grad was pitching.

A quick glance at the walls around the office told me we were in the exact place I had feared: a time-share sales office.

"Nick," I hissed, and poked him in the ribs, my eyes certainly conveying my rising panic. As a general rule, I hated confined spaces where people were trying to sell me things. Car dealerships, furniture stores, even the high school kids coming to the door to sell coupons to raise money for their sports teams. I would stand there, listening to the sales pitch, wishing I could make my phone ring. Feign a fainting spell. Have our kids interrupt me. (No, that only happened when I was on a client phone call, like the time I was finally making headway on a divorce that'd dragged on for two years because the couple could not agree on a boarding facility for the two papillons they had joint custody of. In the end, I don't think the dogs, or anyone, won, because the breeder heard they'd split and asked for the dogs back.)

"We really should get going. The kids are looking forward to the water parks and we are only here for one night," Nick said apologetically, and hooked a thumb toward the exit.

I looked back at Piper, who had refused to enter the office. She was plopped down on one of the faux-wood Adirondack chairs, eating from a bag of Flamin' Hot Cheetos and scrolling through her phone.

Smart girl.

It again gave me hope that we had done something right when we raised her.

The time-share salesman was undeterred.

"One night only, huh? Well, then you have to see the magic show! It's a bucket list item for kids who love fun!" he said, practically shouting.

Sophie and Leo hopped up and down excitedly a little as he reached into his desk and pulled out a glossy brochure with a picture of Rick Stephenson, magician extraordinaire, on the front. He wore a black tuxedo, black spray-on hair thick enough to ignite in a strong sunbeam, and a tan that would have made a Boca Raton retiree blush.

"Now," the time-share salesman said, "you all are in luck, because the magic show for tonight is sold out. But"—he lifted a finger emphatically in the air—"I do happen to have some special tickets left, for a special family." He smiled and made eye contact with both of the kids before he reached below the desk and fanned out a stack of five tickets, each with a picture of the helmet-haired magician on it, holding a top hat and pulling a margarita out of it.

Leo and Sophie squealed, and I nervously glanced at Nick. I

took a step toward the exit. "Again, since we're only here for one night, I think we're going to have to pass. But thank you."

The salesman pretended not to hear us. He reached under the desk again and laid out a brochure in front of us. He opened it, smudging it with fingerprints. "And here's a coupon for a free photo package with Rick Stephenson after the show." He looked at Nick. "I'm sure you want a memory from your stay at Mountain Lodge."

Nick leaned forward and looked at the brochure, pretending to consider it. He was always too nice to people. Every brain cell of mine was screaming, *No, screw off*, but Nick at least gave the façade of contemplation. I found ripping the Band-Aid off much easier.

No, we will not agree to let your girlfriend spend the night when you have the kids.

No, my client will not pay your legal fees.

No, you cannot move the court date because it conflicts with your men's softball tournament.

No. A complete sentence.

As Nick studied the brochure and I saw Piper lift her hands outside of the office, saying, *What gives?* silently, I realized I was going to have to be the brute force. Again.

"No thank you," I said firmly, placing my hand over the brochure. I met his gaze, unblinking. "We are not interested." I spoke slowly, showing him that he would not rattle me.

The salesman's eyes seemed to gleam as he smiled at me, his mouth curling up at the corners like a piece of paper that had caught fire.

Something had changed. Something behind his eyes was

black, blacker than the results of a career in time-share sales. I felt a bead of sweat prick at my hairline as we stared.

"I think you and your family would enjoy the show tomorrow at eleven fifteen," he said, his voice barely above a whisper. His face held no emotion, save for his half-upturned mouth.

A whoosh of anxiety sounded through my ears as my shoulders squared, the blades twitching.

"I don't want to experience anything at eleven fifteen." My voice was a low rumble.

He chuckled, a tutting sound, but his eyes remained black. He leaned forward and I felt a nudge from Nick, who was still standing next to me.

"It's really something," the time-share salesman whispered. His lips had started to curl up again when the top half of his face changed. His eyes were no longer black, but a light brown with dark flecks in them. A look of confusion washed over him as he slowly leaned back, glancing from the desk to my face.

Nick elbowed me again, and I turned sharply toward him. "Water park time!" I said as cheerfully as I could before I walked out the door, toward Piper. Leo and Sophie groaned out protests as the time-share sales guy remained quiet, whatever he had just experienced a mystery.

"What was that about?" Piper asked as she raised an eyebrow at a toddler melting down on the lobby floor, screaming for more Goldfish crackers.

"The devil works hard, but people in time-share sales work harder," I whispered to her. I turned back to Nick and shot him an annoyed look for pretending to entertain the sales pitch and held out my hand for the room key cards.

I was trying to appear normal, my brain unlocking the mom instinct to pretend everything was fine.

Eleven fifteen?

I shook off the bad feeling.

Nick gave me a sheepish, apologetic look and silently passed the small white envelope with the two cards inside.

"You get to tap in as the bad guy next time," I said, ignoring Sophie's whines about wanting to see a margarita pulled out of a top hat.

He put an arm around my shoulders. "Done."

"But I want the souvenir cup," Leo said, sticking his bottom lip out.

I looked over at Nick, raising my eyebrows, silently reminding him that he had agreed to play bad cop next time. Nick stepped forward and began to deny, and then to negotiate with, our son about the twenty-five dollar souvenir cups with unlimited soft drink refills from the Frosty Moose concession stand next to the Wild West Water Park. (Indoor water park one of three.)

I left him with Leo and walked back over to the two chairs we had managed to snag. Piper had taken Sophie to the Tornado Slide, and I craned my neck until I saw them waiting in line, slowly making their way up the staircase to the front of the slide. A long line of guests snaked behind them, holding inflatable rafts and tubes.

I carefully navigated around the soggy Cheetos someone had dumped on the ground and sat down in one of the chairs, exhaling. The sounds of the water park around me melted together, a roar of white noise, punctuated by the smells of french fries and hot dogs (also sold at the Frosty Moose).

After we'd escaped the doomed time-share sales office and I'd successfully decided not to explore the option that the employee was some sort of demon, we found our room. Room L1408. As we walked through the endless hallways, stepping aside for the double strollers, wagons full of beer pulled by already drunk men, and throngs of children who looked like they had been paroled from kid jail, I felt like we were in an endless time loop.

The room itself was a pleasant surprise. Although decorated somewhat atrociously in cabin rustic, it was a relatively large suite. A bedroom held a king-size bed and a master bathroom, with a shower curtain depicting an owl scene. The main room had bunk beds (made of plastic "wood"), a kitchenette, and a pull-out couch. It wasn't exactly my taste, but it was enough space for all of us.

We had quickly changed into our bathing suits and packed a bag to bring into the water park. Even though there were increasingly threatening signs saying not to bring in our own snacks or food, I pretended not to see them. I'd be damned if I was going to pay ten dollars for an apple.

As I rifled through my backpack, digging beneath contraband snacks to locate a phone charger, my fingers clasped something small and metallic in the front pocket. I lifted my hand halfway out of the pocket, saw what it was, and quickly dropped it back down. The creepy locket.

I zipped up the front pocket, feeling a strange tingling in my fingertips. They inched toward the zipper, wanting to pull the pocket open again, bring the necklace out into the light. It felt like magnets were underneath my skin, begging to grasp on to the jewelry and hold it.

The echo of the din around me melted into a roar that moved through my brain and my body, a shock wave that rendered me immobile. My vision tunneled, small points of light forming so that everything was black on the periphery and all I saw in front of me was a blur of color. Unconsciously, I sat up straight, my spine a rod, and placed my hands on my kneecaps. I felt my body sway a bit, as though dancing to a tune no one else could hear.

A jolt moved through my arm and it shot out, not controlled by me. It reached into the backpack and grabbed the locket. I felt the metal dig into the skin of my palm but my fingers wrapped tighter around it until my entire hand felt numb.

And then the pinpoint image of the water park in front of me went black, and a new image appeared. It was as though someone had placed a movie reel on a projector and flipped it on. I was a mannequin in the seat, watching a scene I had no business observing.

I had to watch whatever the locket wanted me to see.

Chapter 16

My vision sharpened and the scene around me came into focus. As it did, I realized I stood in a 1970s-style kitchen. The cabinets were a light wood, maybe oak, with black tendrils for pulls. A small wooden table was just off of the sink, with barely enough room for someone to move between them. I flexed my hands and slowly looked around, body on edge and ready to protect myself from any jump scares.

I let out a yelp as I saw a woman standing next to me, washing her hands at the white kitchen sink. At least, I tried to let out a yelp as the stab of surprise hit me, but no sound came out. I was an observer, unable to speak or move. I just had to watch.

The woman looked in her midthirties, although it was difficult to pinpoint her age. She wore no makeup and her skin was tanned and lined, but her dark hair didn't have any streaks of gray. It was pulled into a low ponytail at the nape of her neck. She wore yellow shorts and a black and red striped white T-shirt. Her feet were bare. As she rinsed the soap off of her hands, she hummed a song: "You Are My Sunshine." I used to hum it to the kids when they were little and I spent endless hours in the rocking chair, eyes closed, praying for a nap.

She finished washing her hands and turned toward me, water dripping on the floor. She held her hands out and looked straight at me.

I held my breath and tried to cry out again as we locked eyes. Her eyes were the color of copper pennies, with yellow flecks around the pupils. She took a step forward. I cringed and tried to move out of the way, but she kept moving. I felt a whoosh go through me as she didn't stop.

She walked right through me.

A pressure in my chest, the smell of cinnamon. When she stepped back, I could breathe again and saw that she had reached through my midsection for a kitchen towel on the countertop and begun drying her hands.

I was panting, hyperventilating from the ghostly violation. As I tried to catch my breath, I noticed she wore the locket that Leo had found, with the V engraved in the center, around her neck.

The woman finished drying her hands and tossed the towel onto the countertop. She wiped her hands on her yellow shorts and turned away from me, walking into another room. Unthinkingly, I followed her. I floated, just scooting behind her, propelled by whatever had brought me inside the house.

As I followed her down the hallway, a ticking grandfather clock to my left on the wall caught my attention. Breath held, I slowly turned my head to check the time.

Ten fifty-nine a.m.

A whoosh ran through my chest as I exhaled. Not eleven fifteen a.m. Thank goodness.

In the other room were two small children, a boy and a girl, who looked about the same ages as Leo and Sophie. Their backs were to me, and their heads were bent down around papers scattered on a coffee table covered with half-used crayons, some of which had rolled off the table and onto the floor.

My body stopped abruptly in the doorway of the room.

The woman walked over to the television, a large monstrosity in a wooden surround, and pressed a button to turn it on before sitting down on the orange and brown floral couch across from it. Her children continued to draw in front of her.

She had a vacant look as she stared at the screen, which came to life with the familiar sounds of the theme song to *Days of Our Lives*. The famous hourglass appeared, and the deep voice of the announcer told us about the passage of time. I recognized it well, since in college my roommate Pam was obsessed with the show, organizing her class schedule around it. I unwittingly learned almost everything about the show, following every plot line I overheard as I was trying to study. It wasn't long before I was racing home from my classes to watch with Pam.

The woman on the couch reached for the combination lamp and coffee table next to her and grabbed a pack of Marlboro Lights, pulling one out of the soft pack and lighting it with a lighter next to a glass ashtray. She settled back onto the couch, the ashtray on her knees, eyes fixed on the television.

The first scene of the show included a familiar character. *Marlena*, my brain whispered from far away. Her clothes told me the scene I watched was sometime in the seventies or eighties, blue eyeshadow and bouffant hair. She was with John Black, the character that I had joked to Pam always looked like he was auditioning for a porno. As John and Marlena embraced, Stefano DiMera walked into the room with an evil grin.

On the couch, the woman leaned forward, cigarette in hand, intensely watching.

"Mom, I—" said the girl at the coffee table. She turned toward her mom, her back still to me. She had long red hair that looked like it hadn't been brushed in a few days.

"Shhhh," the woman said, waving her cigarette around.

The little girl harrumphed and turned back to her drawing, whispering something I couldn't catch to the little blond-haired boy. His face was bent down toward the paper, but he turned to listen to his sister.

A scream died in my throat. He had the same birthmark as the boy we'd almost hit with our car.

My eyes darted around the room: the garishly patterned couch, the coffee table, the television, the lamp/table combo, macramé doilies, complete with the smell of cigarettes.

"Mom, I'm leaving," came a teenage girl's voice from across the house. The woman didn't move or acknowledge the goodbye, and I heard a door slam shut and a car engine rev outside.

I turned to look out of the front windows at the engine's noise and saw the taillights of a blue sedan moving down a gravel driveway, dust kicking up around it, before it disappeared.

As I looked out the window, my gaze fixed on an old tree outside. The branches slowly swayed in the wind, the hot breeze moving through the house, offering no relief from cigarettes and summer. It was the same oak tree that was still standing so many years later. Next to it was the yet-to-be-broken Big Wheel, waiting for a rider to hop on. A laundry line dangled above it, one end connected to the tree and the other to somewhere on the house.

My eyes slid to the mantel above the fireplace, peppered with framed school pictures, one for each child. A wedding photo of the Vickerys—I assumed—bookended the row of frames. In front of it was a small prayer card with a picture of a handsome dark-haired man.

From across the room, I squinted to read the card.

GREGORY JAMES VICKERY

Born August 6, 1941, and entered into eternal life
on April 25, 1982

The recently deceased Mr. Vickery.

I realized I didn't even know Mrs. Vickery's name or the names of the children. I scanned the room and located a child's drawing pinned to the wall in the hallway. It was a scene of a mother with three children standing in front of a child's drawing of a house in crayon. On the bottom, it read: *Mom, Lyssa, Joey, and Annie.*

I smiled. Of course her name was *Mom*. I wasn't even sure if my own kids remembered my first name. I looked back to Mrs. Vickery, studying her, recognizing the exhausted hunch of her shoulders, the dark circles under her eyes, the living room strewn with toys, crayons, shoes. It could have been my house. It was my house, rewound several decades. And she was all alone.

I certainly didn't know everything, but I did know that I always thought of Nick as my lifeline. If I had to draw my own road map to being a good parent, when to yell and when to argue, when to hug and when to forgive, it would be a messy mosh pit of things I saw on television and examples I read in books. With Nick, it was organic.

The idea that, with a few more twists of fate, he wouldn't be there to help me raise the kids was my biggest fear.

And then the knowledge that something *did* happen to this family, that this mother *couldn't* keep them safe, left me feeling like I was a body without bones.

Before the scene fizzled away, I saw a magazine addressed to "Patty Vickery."

Patty.

I wanted to reach forward through time, space, and physics and grab her, tell her what was about to happen. Tell her that she wasn't alone and she could save her family.

"Leigh? Hello?"

Nick was saying my name and gently shaking my shoulder. I was again sitting in the Wild West Water Park of the hotel, in the same chair by the slides.

I slowly turned to look up at him, his face full of worry and concern.

"There you are. What happened? Are you okay? You weren't responding," he said. He moved around me and sat down in a PVC chair next to me, putting a hand on my leg.

My head began to hurt as I came back to reality, the sounds of the water park filling my ears, too loud, and the lights seemed too bright. I blinked quickly a few times and shifted my spine, and noticed my back begin to ache.

I relaxed my shoulders and my hands, and felt the locket slip through my fingers and fall to the wet concrete beneath my chair.

"What happened?" Nick said again. He frowned and slowly moved Piper's wet towel and hung it over the back of the chair.

I shook my head and looked down at my hands, which were on my knees, palms up. "I'm not sure."

I opened and closed my eyes a few times, feeling lightheaded and woozy, like I'd had too many glasses of wine. I took a few deep breaths, coming back to my body and back to the present.

"I had some kind of vision or daydream," I said, my voice cracking. I rubbed my forehead and pressed the heels of my hands into my eye sockets. When I pulled them away and looked around, my breathing began to slow and the feelings of disassociation were gone.

"About what?" he said as he leaned back in the chair, fingers fiddling with the room key on the table.

"That weird house in Indiana where Leo took the locket. It was like I was inside, watching the family that lived there. The Vickerys," I said quietly. "Patty, Lyssa, Joey, and Annie Vickery."

Nick cocked his head to the side, thinking. "What? Are you serious?"

I bent over and saw the locket coiled on the wet concrete beneath my chair. I nudged it with my foot and it splayed out.

"Yes, the Vickerys," I said finally, my gaze still on the jewelry. "I touched the locket and then I saw that scene or whatever it was."

Nick made a noise and widened his eyes. He bent forward, reaching to pick up the locket, and I gasped.

"No, what if—" I started to say as he picked up the locket in one quick grab and dangled it between us.

"You think it's haunted?" he said, a teasing tone behind his words. His eyes sparkled and a faint smile lifted his lips.

"Don't be weird. But something happened," I said, my eyes fixed on the swinging V in the center of the medallion.

"Only one way to find out," he said. He lifted his other hand and grasped the locket just as I had.

His eyes shut tightly and he began to sway back and forth. My blood pressure spiked again, and I shot an arm out to grab it from him but stopped, fear coursing through me.

Then he opened his eyes and laughed. "Just a locket. No ghosts." He gently tossed it in the air and caught it in the same hand. "Nothing exciting to see here."

I shook my head, feeling very foolish. "Hilarious," I muttered as I rolled my eyes. "Put it in there. I'm not touching that thing again." I pointed to the backpack, and Nick lightly tossed it into the front, a perfect shot, no net. I quickly zipped the pouch closed and nudged the backpack away from me, under the table.

"You're stressed," Nick said sympathetically, leaving unsaid his thought that I had imagined all of it.

And maybe I had. The power of suggestion, the information about the Vickerys rattling around in my subconscious, waiting to pop out when I wasn't paying attention.

I sighed and looked around the water park. I noted a woman who had a lower-back tattoo of the name *Darren* crossed out with *Joseph* written above it. I guessed tattoo removal was too much of a hassle.

I spotted Leo and Sophie waiting with a throng of overly excited kids. They were ankle-deep in the cold water, listening for the bell that would signal a countdown before an enormous bucket of water shaped like a miner's bowl would tip over, and water would come crashing down on whoever waited below. The group hopped up and down excitedly, glancing up at the contraption as it filled.

Okay, two of them are safe.

"Where's Piper?" I said, a tinge of annoyance in my voice. We had told her to stay with her siblings. I caught sight of her red bathing suit over by the hot tub, a half-indoor, half-outdoor structure surrounded by a plastic rock wall. She had her arms above the water line, stretched out on the concrete behind her. On the other side of the hot tub was a group of children, and despite the numerous signs clearly stating, **No Children Under the Age of 12 Without Parental Supervision Allowed in the Hot Tub**, they took turns dunking each other under the water. Next to Piper was a group of very hairy men chugging margaritas out of hurricane glasses. I could only imagine what was floating around in that soup.

All my children located, I settled back into my chair, trying to push my lingering hallucination or whatever it was out of my head.

"Welp, it's five o'clock somewhere," Nick announced, and then slapped his knees and stood up, the classic Midwest move for heading somewhere. "I'm getting a frozen drink. They're two for fifty dollars. I'll get you one."

Before I could think of a protest or excuse, he walked off, waving to the kids under the bucket. The alarm for the bucket sounded, and the kids underneath shrieked and screamed before thousands of gallons of water dumped on their heads.

My own head started to throb. The chaos was enough to make me want one of those two-for-fifty-dollars sugar-bomb concoctions, but I couldn't. Not until I knew what was going on with my body.

Chapter 17

As I sat at the water park, I felt like an oyster without a shell. My house was my safe zone, my cocoon. And now I was exposed.

I picked up my phone and tried Kerry to check on everything back home, but the call went to voicemail, so I called M.J. next.

"Leigh!" she shrieked as she answered the phone. "How's it going? You all still alive?" I could hear the muffled sounds of her children arguing in the background, then rustling as she called to them, "I told you two to stop shooting each other in the face with the hose." She sighed. "Sorry. Just another summer day."

I laughed as I leaned back to put my feet up on Nick's empty chair. I spied him waiting in line.

"We're at the water park resort now, so that should tell you what you need to know," I said.

"Oh, but those can be fun," she said. "Yes, interesting crowd at times, but my kids always have a blast. Have you gone down a slide yet?"

Out of the corner of my eye, I saw the two slides, one blue, one green, that twisted together before spitting the patron out into the plunge pool below.

"I love that you said 'yet,' as though it's something on my must-do list," I said.

"It's fun. You're missing out," she said in a singsong voice. "But really, how has it been? Any more ghostly kids?"

She laughed, but a cold feeling ran through my gut, and I could almost smell the cigarette smoke and grass from the Vickery house. The strains of *Days of Our Lives* tickled the back of my brain as overwhelming sadness washed over me, realizing Greg Vickery had passed away likely just a couple of years before.

"Leigh? You still there?"

I shook my head. "Yes. Sorry. This place is a little chaotic," I said.

"Try to have some fun, though. Just go with it," she said. "I'm sure Nick's been down every waterslide twice."

I rolled my eyes. "Maybe after his margarita—two-for-one special!"

Normally, I was grateful that Nick was like a giant kid, which made it all the more funny that he was actually in charge of groups of children.

But sometimes, like when I was sitting in a water park and hearing my friend say it, it irritated me that he could so easily do things I couldn't or wouldn't. The kids loved it, loved that they had the kind of dad who would ride the Hyper Loop with them at the town's rickety carnival, whereas I stood off to the side, silently evaluating all of the safety concerns. It wasn't fun to always be the stick in the mud. But one of us had to be. M.J.'s husband, Ron, filled that role in their family.

If M.J. and Nick had gotten married, they would probably be owner-operators of a go-kart park and a mini-golf course, and re-invigorate the entire Rainforest Cafe franchise. Maybe opposites attract for a reason.

M.J. was right, though. We were here, and strange occurrences aside, I should try to lean into it as much as possible.

"What else is going on?" she said.

I paused. I had called her because I needed to tell someone—anyone—about my strange vision. I needed a sounding board, someone to tell me what Nick had: that I was just tired, was just stressed, just had low blood sugar. A rational explanation, one that I wouldn't have to worry about.

But in that moment, I shoved it down. I didn't know how to explain or where to begin. So I went with "out of sight, out of mind."

Instead I told my friend about the pushy time-share salesman and how our carrier had crashed open. That was more than enough road trip fodder to shove any ghostly happenings straight to the edges of my thoughts.

I was cut off by a toddler having a screaming meltdown a few feet away. She was maybe three years old, her curly red hair in two pigtails on top of her head, sporting a *Frozen* swimsuit. In one hand she had a snack-size bag of Doritos. Her other hand pointed to the ground, where all of the Doritos had emptied into the zero-edge infinity pool, the orange triangles slowly floating away into the overchlorinated water.

"Aw, sounds like someone is having a rough day," M.J. chuckled. "Oddly enough, I miss that stage."

"That's because there's something wrong with you," I said as I shook my head. "I can't imagine ever—" A wave of terror ripped through me as I thought of finding out my body wasn't in perimenopause. I couldn't finish the sentence.

M.J. didn't seem to notice my abject horror. "It would be great! I could watch Ms. Rachel all day long and not have to hide it."

"You . . . what . . . really?" I shook my head, surprised but not. "Better you than Kerry."

Or me.

She laughed. "True. If it was Kerry, she'd find the nearest fire station. Or just give it to me to raise. You'd do the same."

I managed a chuckle, but I was sure my expression was more grimace than grin.

"So where are you all stopping next?" M.J. said.

Before I could answer, Piper came running over, her arms crossed over her stomach and a look of disgust on her face.

"Mom! Someone threw up in the wave pool, and they're making everyone get out so they can drain it," she screeched.

"Oh God," I said as I sat up straight, craning my neck around to look for the rest of my family. "Go find your brother and sister. The last thing we need is them swimming in . . . that."

She nodded and jogged off, stepping around the toddlers wailing on the side of the pool.

"I've gotta go, M.J. Water park disaster," I said.

"One every time we visit!" she said cheerfully. "Remember, Leigh, you can do hard things. You got this," she added before we hung up.

Nick walked over, carrying a drink the size of a fishbowl in each hand. They were electric blue and had *Mountain Lodge Water Park Resort* stenciled on the glass and twisty straws.

"Really?" I said as I eyed the drinks. "Now I see why they're twenty-five dollars each."

He held a fishbowl out and I took it, not knowing what else to do. It weighed about seven pounds. My stomach turned at the thought of what was in it. No doubt blue dye, juices not from any naturally occurring fruit, and watered-down bottom-shelf liquor. No way was I drinking it, possible delicate condition or not.

Nick, however, felt differently.

"It's not bad!" he said with a nod of appreciation, his tongue tinged a faint blue.

I set mine down on the PVC table next to my phone before putting my hands on my hips and scanning the crowd for my kids.

"Who were you talking to?" Nick said. He took a long sip of the drink, and his mouth puckered from the injection of sugar, followed by a look of disgust as the moonshine hit his palate.

"M.J. It should come as no surprise that she loves water parks." I watched as a family hurriedly wrapped their kids in beach towels and carried them out of the water park, grumbling about biohazards and calling the health department.

I thought about what she'd said: *You can do hard things*. I always thought of myself as someone who was tough, brave, confident. But maybe I was only those things in my own environment and in situations that I could control. M.J. and Kerry were both brave, but that was easy to see. Kerry had gone through a horrific, traumatizing divorce, and M.J. had parented a child battling cancer. They had proven themselves.

It felt like I couldn't even handle a few vivid daydreams on our road trip. Every mile that we had put between us and our home had led me further astray from the person whom I thought I was.

I took a deep breath and refocused on Nick before I allowed my thoughts and fears to pull me too far down. "Drink looks less than appetizing," I said as he took another sip, to the same effect.

He considered the neon-colored atrocity in his hand. "I'm hoping it gets better the more I drink it."

I arched an eyebrow. "Or your taste buds will just be obliterated, so you will become immune."

"Here's hoping," he said, and took another long sip.

I didn't want Nick to get halfway through the drink before we were able to escape the sanitation disaster that was the Wild West park, so I stood on my tiptoes until I spotted my kids, frantically waving them over.

"Time to go to the outdoor water park?" Leo said. "The Lost World. They have huge dinosaurs along the pool."

Nick, fueled by the few sips of his atomic drink, nodded furiously. "Sounds great!" he said, and turned toward the doors that led outside. He glanced back and saw my drink still sitting on the side table. "Don't forget that."

Of course not.

"Why are there dinosaurs if this place is supposed to be a mountain lodge?" Piper said from the pool chaise next to me.

I opened one eye and looked around the "adult pool," which was inexplicably adorned with concrete sculptures of brontosauruses and triceratops.

"Good question." I wondered if whoever designed it had had a few of those neon-colored drinks.

My frozen concoction was on the table next to me, melting in the hot Tennessee sun. Nick had taken Leo and Sophie to wait in line for the Tsunami slide, a four-person monstrosity with multiple twists and a giant swirling toilet bowl of water into which you were spit out at the end. Piper, wise girl, had chosen to stick with me.

I lifted a hand to pat my daughter's knee and then paused, retracting it. I wanted to tell her how I knew college was looming in the next few years and I couldn't fathom not having her around every day, how I was afraid that I wasn't a good mom to her for the first few years. Having not had a stable blueprint to follow when we had our firstborn, I'd felt like I was constantly failing or doing the wrong thing. Choosing the wrong door, the one with the tiger behind it, not the new car. But I tried. I kept opening doors and letting myself be mauled by tigers in the hope that one day, I would choose correctly. Or at least when she was old enough, I could tell her I had tried to do my best.

Yet I knew it wouldn't be fair to her to tell her all of that. I shouldn't put my emotional and maternal insecurities on her, ask her to validate me. And definitely not while we were at a water park.

Instead, I said, "I'm happy we get a quiet moment alone together."

She nodded and smiled, looking out over the crowd. That was enough for me.

From our vantage point, we could almost pretend we were at a normal resort, as long as I kept my gaze trained forward and the Jurassic decorations out of my sight line. I took the opportunity to check my work emails.

It had been forty-eight hours since I last looked at them, and I nearly chucked my phone into the splash pad as I watched them load, email after email, nearly all with the subject line *Urgent*.

I closed my eyes, took a deep breath, and then steadied myself to respond to as many as I could.

Ninety minutes later, I had worked through maybe half of the original emails, yet more kept coming through, some as responses. Immediate email after immediate email, all vying for my attention. I should have known taking two weeks off would sentence me to purgatory.

I focused on the Black case, the client whose husband had left her for an Instagram model a few months after she'd had a miscarriage and was trying to kick her and their kids out of their house so he could move said model in. The Blacks had just the year prior built a monstrosity in a suburb filled with major-league baseball players, executives, and a few politicians. Some of their wives had been my clients. The neighborhood was almost a kiss of death, an omen for a divorce as soon as a family moved in.

The husband, Lenny, had decided he wanted to cut Michelle's spousal support while the divorce was in process. He claimed she was overspending and using the money for herself and not the children. Typical.

His lawyer, Chester Iverson, had sent a condescending, overly aggressive email that bordered on insulting, to both me and my client. Amateur.

But they didn't have a leg to stand on. The spousal support

agreed upon was more than fair, and far less than the spending that had occurred during the marriage. Lenny was just being an asshole and wanted more money to spend on Miss Social Media.

The issue was that we also wanted to renegotiate her prenup, which left her with nearly nothing. In her defense, she had signed it when she was a twenty-two-year-old waitress who thought she had met Prince Charming.

"What's his is mine . . . that's what he said," she'd told me tearfully during our first meeting. "He always said he would take care of me, deal with the finances, and everything would be fine."

I nodded sympathetically, reading through the document and taking notes on how we could contest. But it unfortunately was a situation I had seen far too many times. A naïve woman getting married and then getting screwed, every which way, when her husband's options were suddenly limitless. The wife was usually either undereducated or underemployed, often both, having given up her independence for a dream of a perfect life. The white picket fence was intoxicating but a fallacy.

I wanted to tell these women that they could have built their own fence, grabbed that wood and erected it themselves, so that no one could take that away from them. But it was far too late for that kind of conversation.

Which is why I hammered it home to my kids every day: College, postgrad, career. Then you think about everything else. Protect yourself first. Being in love is great, but being financially and emotionally secure is even better.

If only my mother had had that kind of advice.

I typed an email back to Lenny's lawyer, Chester. Chester was straight out of central casting for a Martin Scorsese Mafia movie. Lots of gold rings, continuous gleam of sweat emanating from his forehead. Legal maneuvers dirtier than the hot tub at the Mountain Lodge Resort.

I responded that the spousal support was still legally binding and we would not be budging on any of it, reminding them that Judge Gerson had not seemed to be a fan of Lenny during the last court appearance. I also denied their request to push the court date out and took great pleasure in hitting Send, and a small bit of pride in knowing Chester would read it and turn into a cartoon character, face getting tomato red and steam shooting out of his ears. I hoped he had taken his blood pressure medicine that afternoon.

I slid my phone back into the backpack at my side, eyeing the front pocket, reminding myself of what was real and what was not. Chester Iverson was real. The Vickerys were not, at least not in the present.

Besides, I had more important things to worry about: keeping everyone safe and disease-free at the water park.

"What's new in the world, Piper?" I said as I settled back into my chaise longue, closing my eyes behind my sunglasses.

"So much, Mom," she said.

She launched into the latest scandal at Germantown High School: a party had gotten busted and people were accusing each other left and right of having been the ones to call the cops. Never mind that I was certain the sight of cars parked all along the street, with teens spilling out and sauntering toward the house holding cases of beer, was what had done all of them in.

"Harper said her parents have to get her a lawyer. Can you talk to them? Like, off the record?" Piper said, her tone lifting toward the end of the sentence.

I sighed. "I'll be happy to talk to them. But as a friend, not as their lawyer."

"Awesome. Thanks. I'll tell her," she said. I heard the clicking of her phone as she sent a text.

I closed my eyes and drifted off. The sun was warm, my kids were happy, and the shouts of the water park dulled into white noise. For a few moments, I was in bliss. But I was brought out of the tranquility by ice-cold water dripping on my arm.

"Mom? I'm hungry."

I opened one eye and saw Leo standing next to me, soaking wet. My reprieve was over. It was time to head back to the room.

"Leigh, did you take the TripTik out of the safe?" Nick asked. He stood in our room, in front of the closet that held the small wall safe.

"No. I don't even know what combination you chose," I said. I sat on the bottom bunk of the faux-wood bunk beds next to Sophie, one arm around her as we lounged against the wall. The television in front of us played an episode of *Camp Chronicles*, a Magic Land show about kids who go off to summer camp. Leo was on the top bunk, hair still wet, dressed in his pajamas. Piper was flopped out on my bed watching old episodes of *Dance Moms* on her phone.

We had left the water park soon after Leo's hunger declaration and come back to the room, where we changed out of our wet bathing suits and ordered a pizza. The kids were still trying to angle for a postdinner swim/slide excursion, but we had said, "We'll see," which meant "Please forget about this."

"It's gone," Nick said, scratching the back of his neck. "My wallet is there, but the TripTik is missing."

I untangled my arm from behind Sophie and hoisted myself up, feeling my stomach rumble. I had felt queasy since we began to pack up our things outside. Nick told me it was probably from the chemical-laden frozen drink. I didn't tell him that I hadn't even had a sip.

I padded over on the brown and orange carpeting to stand next to Nick. Inside the safe were his wallet, an iPad, and a laptop. I stuck my hand into it, thinking the TripTik was somewhere in the back and hidden in the shadows. I remembered he had put the loose cash inside, carefully setting it atop his wallet. I had rolled my eyes at the time but didn't say anything.

Hotel safes were a necessity in the Somerset family world. Along with their bootstrap view of life came the viewpoint that everyone was trying to screw each other over at every turn. Trust no one. Doors must be locked and double-checked before bed. A broom handle inserted at the base of the sliding glass door. Cars locked while in the driveway, even if you've only run inside to use the bathroom.

I had tried to remind my in-laws that they lived in one of the safest neighborhoods in Green Bay and that nothing remotely unsafe had ever happened on their street. The biggest scandal to come out of Apache Drive was that Mrs. Lowerston had a Bears T-shirt in her closet (confirmed by Mrs. Johnston next door, who had seen it) and wasn't that upset when Aaron Rodgers left the Packers.

But their belief that everyone was just a millisecond away from being robbed blind persisted. Thus, Nick had put his precious TripTik in the safe.

I had tried to ease it out of Nick, but as with his love for vacation souvenirs and tacky fridge magnets, I was not successful.

Before we left for the Wild West Water Park, he had carefully placed the TripTik in the safe, along with his wallet, putting his credit card in a plastic bag and then into a zippered pocket of his swim trunks.

"Kids? Did any of you go into the safe?" I called out, too loud, making Nick jump. There was a tinge of annoyance in my voice that I couldn't mask.

Denials all around. I faced Nick, hands on my hips. "I don't know. Maybe you moved it when you got back to the room."

He shook his head furiously. "Nope. I haven't touched it." He frowned and bent down and looked through the safe again, feeling around in the back. He stood up, rubbing his forehead. "It must've been—"

"No. No one has been in here to clean the room." I gestured around to the towels all over the floor. Before we'd left to go downstairs, Sophie had pulled out her entire collection of Squishmallows and scattered them all over the bottom bunk, moving aside blankets and pillows to create the perfect nest for them. None of it had been touched.

"And how would someone know the combination you chose? *I* don't even know it. They wouldn't go to all that trouble and take that but not your wallet," I pointed out. "We must have just misplaced it."

The royal we. Like, *Did* we *get milk at the grocery store? Did* we *pay the mortgage? Did* we *register the kids for school?*

There was no *we*. It was almost always me, but saying *we* softened the blow when Nick would ask the question, even though it took half the credit away.

Nick stared at the safe and then shook his head. "Well, I don't know where it went."

I put a hand around his shoulder and pulled myself to him. "Must've been your girlfriend sneaking in again. She's tricky."

He laughed and relaxed as he hugged me. "I told her not to break in anymore, but she can't seem to stop."

"Relentless. You guys are a perfect match, if she loves TripTiks enough to commit robbery," I murmured. A perfunctory knock at the door. I squeezed him one more time and then released him, turning to the kids. "Pizza's here!"

I patted Nick on his lower back as I went to answer it. "It'll turn up." The glorious smells of take-out pizza wafted through the door.

I just hoped I was right. The TripTik was Nick's bastion of sanity, his trophy that symbolized his organization and planning. Dumbo's feather that allowed him to fly.

If the ghosts had to take something and if they wanted to rattle Nick, they'd certainly picked the perfect target.

Chapter 18

When I was a child, we spent a lot of time during the summers at my dad's family's lake house in Lake Geneva, Wisconsin. Equidistant from Chicago and Milwaukee, Lake Geneva was a summer playground for wealthy families, sporting multimillion-dollar mansions along its lakeshore. The local supper club always had a motley collection of scions of business and tech, fishermen, and locals sitting around the bar drinking cold beers. It would be hard to tell who owned the boat worth more than half a million dollars and who was behind on their utility bills. After all, wealth whispers.

And my ancestral family home was nearly silent.

At the end of the school year, my mother would take me to the Lake Geneva estate—unassumingly called "the lake house," as though it were a modest log cabin in the woods somewhere—while my father would stay back in our suburb of Chicago and work during the week, coming up on the weekends when he could. I would spend the summers diving off the pier that jutted out from the expansive green lawn until our shoulders were pink and freckled. I would run back to the house, passing the gardeners who worked silently like honeybees to tend to the terraced gardens, and up the stone steps.

It was a very 1980s existence of free-range summering, metaphorically drinking from the hose, coming in when the streetlights came on, and playing Wiffle ball in the neighborhood. Not that I did any of those things, but in spirit. There were always so many people at the house, turning the cogs and pressing the levers to keep such a large property not only functioning but ready to host fabulous parties. But none of them paid attention to me, or if they did, it was momentary.

In some ways, I raised myself during the summers. And they would represent the last few years of simpler times, when my future seemed wide open and anything seemed possible.

That all ended with the divorce. Before I graduated high school, my parents would be divorced, and after that, my father would be a guest of the federal prison system. My mother would be a guest of her own denial, lunching at the country club and pretending that we hadn't lost everything.

My father's trial and sentencing for stealing client settlement monies was headline news for years, until everyone moved on, salivating for another fall from grace. They got it, many times, at least in nearby Chicago, with politicians going to jail more frequent than highway construction. But my family's last name remained in people's consciousness, buried somewhere between their grocery list and the name of their first-grade teacher, and when I would introduce myself in college, I would watch as the person first looked confused, and then the realization would happen.

Oh. Isn't that . . .

I think her dad is in jail . . .

My father screwed his clients out of millions of dollars, and in turn screwed us out of our futures. I didn't have a road map to any kind of functional adulthood—my mother usually buried her feelings in gin and gossip—so I had to pretend. Fake it until I made it.

And then I met Nick, who was content with everything. Me, a smaller house, an afternoon spent with a lawn sprinkler and a bathing suit, a weeklong camping trip in the blazing-hot weather of August, restaurants only twice a year. A truly simple life, but a content one.

And in order to have that, I had to do everything the opposite of how I had been raised.

Which is how I ended up at an indoor water park resort in the middle of Tennessee, wide awake as I listened to the sounds of drunk parents and hyperactive kids stomping through the hallways well after midnight.

Since I wasn't sleeping, I was the first to hear the strange noises. It sounded at first like rustling, and I thought one of the kids was getting out of bed to use the bathroom. But it continued far longer than it would take to whip the covers off and get out of bed, even if they were tangled around kid limbs.

I sat up in bed, head cocked to the side to listen. After a long pause, I almost lay back down, certain I had dreamed it.

But then I heard it again. A rustling, someone rummaging around in something soft, like clothes or sheets.

I sighed and threw the covers off my legs.

One of them better not be going through the bags.

As quietly as I could, I opened the door to our bedroom and tiptoed out of the room. Nick was still blissfully unaware and rolled over in his sleep, pulling the covers up to his chin.

In the darkness of the rest of the suite, I could only make out shapes. The couch, the table, a jumble of bags, the white of the sheets wrapped around Piper's body.

I heard it again, from the opposite direction, toward the bunk beds.

I turned to my left and tiptoed toward the rustling, my hands in front of me, feeling around to make sure I wouldn't bump into anything.

I reached the bunk beds.

And then I saw it.

The bunk beds were a dark shape against the wall, two slats on top of one another, white sheets on top with comforters strewn to the ends. Sophie had wound up sleeping on top, after a long negotiation between her and Leo.

The sound was coming from the edge of Leo's bed. He was in the middle of the bed, scrunched up like a caterpillar. On top of him were the sheets I'd tucked around him before I went to bed.

But they were slowly disappearing.

The sheets on Leo's bed were slowly being pulled off, more of his legs appearing as they were pulled toward the end of the bed into a pile. My body stiffened and I couldn't breathe, pressure building in my lungs.

Frozen in my spot near the hallway, I watched as Leo's body appeared, free of the sheets. An unseen hand balled up the sheets toward the bottom of the bed.

I rubbed my eyes and took a step forward, trying to make out a shape or an object. Anything that would explain what I was seeing. I thought about darting back to my room and grabbing my glasses off the end table so I could investigate further, but I couldn't imagine leaving him.

Check on him.

I took another step forward to see if Leo was okay, find a rational explanation for what I had seen. Maybe the sheets were really just falling off the bed and I couldn't see clearly because it was too dark and I was too nearsighted.

But I froze again, like someone had hit Pause on a remote control and stopped me.

Because the sheets were being lifted off the bed by something—or someone—even though I could clearly see the wall behind them.

I started breathing quicker, senses sharpening to a point, fight or flight.

The sheets slowly moved up through the air and then draped around a shape next to the bed. The shape was about my height and rounded at the top.

It was the shape of something human. Like a ghost.

The shape, covered in the sheets, stood facing me.

Nick. The strangled cry for my husband died in my throat and all that came out was a soft whimper.

The white shape and I remained in place, squaring off, even as my brain tried to tell me I was still dreaming, that it was all a hallucination.

Then the shape slowly turned so it was facing my sleeping son on the bed.

The screams were dead no more.

"Nick! Nick! Come out here now!" I continued to shout, hearing Piper wake up and ask what was wrong from behind me.

Nick came barreling out of the bedroom, stumbling and looking around as he tried to put on his glasses. As he did, the shape disappeared and the sheets crumpled to the ground.

"Mommy?" Sophie called from the top bunk, her voice tight with fear.

Leo slowly sat up on the bottom bunk, rubbing his eyes and then his upper arms from the chill in the room.

Nick reached my side and grabbed my shoulders. "What's wrong?" he shouted.

I pointed to Leo's bed and tried to explain what I had seen.

"Leigh, calm down," Nick said, his voice back into the human register again.

"Dad?" Piper called from her bed. She had her arms wrapped around her knees. I could hear the fear in her voice.

"It's fine," he said quickly over his shoulder, and then squeezed my shoulders again, trying to bring me back to the present. "Leigh. What happened?"

I stepped back, shrugging off his hands. I knew what I had seen. With a trembling hand, I pointed toward the sheets next to Leo's bed.

"The sheets moved. The sheets moved off of Leo's bed. And there was someone there," I said shakily. I pointed to the side of the bed where I'd seen the figure, but all that was left was a pile of white sheets on the floor.

Whoever or whatever had been here was gone.

"Someone was in here?" Leo said, his voice in an unnatural register.

"I—I don't—" I walked over to the pile and kicked them. They flopped over, empty inside.

"No," I said, and ran my hands through my hair. "There was something here."

Nick walked over and picked up the pile as I choked out a protest. He looked through them and then put them in a pile on Leo's bed.

"There's nothing in them, Leigh." His voice was calm, placating, with a tinge of irritation behind his words.

"Mommy?" Sophie said, peering out over the railing of the top bunk.

There was a long pause as I stayed in place, my head swiveling from my kids, to the pile on the bed, to Nick. My family no longer looked afraid; they looked upset—upset at me.

"I'm not lying. I saw something standing . . ." The words died as I saw Nick's warning expression. What would be the point in continuing to convince them of what I saw? I didn't even know what it was, and insisting I was right would only scare the shit out of my kids.

I sighed and shook my head. "Never mind. Sorry. I must have been dreaming."

"You don't have your glasses," Piper called from the pull-out couch. "You probably just thought you saw something."

No. Not having my glasses meant things were blurry, not that I would completely hallucinate white sheets on top of a humanoid figure.

But it wasn't the time to have that conversation, and it was likely not one to have in front of the kids at all.

I walked over and grabbed the ball of sheets on the end of

Leo's bed, carefully opening them up to see if anything was inside. They were empty.

"Sorry I scared you, guys. I must have been sleepwalking. Just go back to sleep," I said as cheerfully as I could manage, shaking out the sheets and laying them on top of Leo's body. I bent down and gave Leo a kiss on the forehead. "Go back to sleep," I said again, my voice a whisper.

I heard Piper turn over on the pull-out couch, and Sophie made a noise in agreement as she rolled over, too. I slowly walked back to the doorway to the bedroom, Nick still standing there.

"Are you okay?" he said as I shut the door behind us after he scooted inside.

I lay back down in bed, pulling the sheets over my legs. "No, Nick. I'm not." My voice came out angry at first but then broke, and my tone grew higher and higher. "I'm not. I'm freaking out."

He sat down on the bed across from me and put a hand over mine, our fingers intertwined on my knee. I didn't know where to begin or what to say anymore, so I started with the most simple.

"I saw a vision—or a weird dream, maybe—of you dying recently," I said in a whisper. "It really freaked me out."

His fingers tightened on mine and he scooted closer to me on the bed, leaning forward and resting his forehead on mine.

"I'm here," he whispered.

I nodded, closing my eyes. I wanted to say so much more, to go through each strange event that had happened and lay it all out for him, build one aberrant moment on top of another, until he understood what I was going through.

But I didn't think I had the strength for that, at least not in the middle of the night.

"I'm going to try and sleep," I said to Nick, and he leaned back, watching as I scooted down on the bed and pulled the comforter up around my shoulders.

He bent down and kissed my head. I felt the weight of his body lie down next to mine, the snores coming before my body had even relaxed down into the bed.

Whatever was happening to my family, I couldn't deny it any longer.

Chapter 19

"Did you get a chance to see the magic show? No?" the demonic time-share salesman called out to us as we walked through the lobby, dragging our suitcases behind.

Nick, ever the friendly one, waved to him. "Maybe next time," he said.

I refused to look at the salesman. I had had enough of the Mountain View Resort—on every level. We had hastily packed that morning, shoving clothes back into the roll-aboards and sticking the still-wet bathing suits into a gallon-sized ziplock bag. It had once held a giant bag of Pirate's Booty, so I had to shake out the crumbs, but it was all I had in my backpack. Survive a nuclear winter, I would not. M.J. would have had an entire bag full of water park supplies—a baggie for each wet swimsuit, a box of Band-Aids, special leave-in conditioner for overchlorinated hair, containers to separate the recycling from the regular trash. A backpack cooler. A wagon.

But I was not M.J. in the slightest. And Kerry would never attempt to take her kids to an indoor water park.

So our wet swimsuits were probably being tossed in a light coating of white cheddar dust. I'd wash them eventually.

While I busied myself with throwing everyone's shit into whatever suitcase it would fit into (so much for staying organized), Nick searched the room for his missing TripTik.

"I know I put it in the safe," he muttered to himself while peering into it again. He tapped his phone to turn on the flashlight and looked inside, feeling around in the dark corners.

After a few moments, I said—more harshly than I intended—"We should get going. Aren't we on a tight schedule? Just forget about the TripTik."

He ignored me, and my tone, and continued searching, looking under the beds and through our luggage. He still came up empty and I told him the TripTik was a donation to the resort, like a tithe for allowing us to leave.

After we wedged our suitcases back into the car and Nick checked the straps on the turtle top carrier one last time, we piled into the car, collectively exhausted. The road trip was finally starting to wear at our edges, slowly unraveling everyone's emotional state.

I took a deep breath and turned around, mustering up the brightest smile that I could despite only having had a few sips of coffee from the room's ancient single-serve machine, and said, "Ready? We're getting close now! Florida, here we come!"

All three kids nodded, their excitement buried somewhere in between the cooler of bottled water and the car games. At least everyone was quiet.

As we pulled out of the Mountain Lodge Resort's parking lot, Sophie said, "Can we come back here again? It was so fun!"

Nick and I exchanged a glance, and I watched with satisfaction as the resort grew smaller as we turned down the highway to continue our journey south. "We'll see, honey."

"Did you sleep at all?" Nick said as the hills of Appalachia rolled past my window. After the TripTik fiasco, I'd offered to drive and put the directions in my phone. If Nick had taken the first leg, he would have spent the time behind the wheel adrift, mourning his beloved route manager.

I might have been more irritated about the fact that he was so focused on finding the TripTik, but thinking about what had happened to Patty Vickery—the knowledge that she was on her own when the fire happened—certainly put everything into perspective. Nick's obsession with route management was nothing in comparison. So I tried to resolve to be more patient, understanding, empathetic—things that didn't always come naturally to me.

As we put a few miles between the water park and us, I relaxed slightly, knowing we were headed to our next destination. I shook my head. "I couldn't sleep after . . . all that." I had lain awake while Nick had run through a few REM cycles, replaying what had happened with the bedsheets over and over, trying to make sense of it.

I couldn't.

I knew what I'd seen. But I didn't know how to process it. The law was black and white, a set of guidelines, a literal rule book. That was why I first got into law. Things made sense, even if reading legal briefs wasn't the most stimulating or creative of enterprises. But there was comfort in knowing, for the most part, what to expect. After the turmoil that I'd been through as a kid, I'd learned all surprises were bad surprises, so I opted for no surprises.

Yet there I was. Captain of the Cruise Ship to the Strange and Unusual. And I just wanted off.

"Do you think it was a reaction to those frozen drinks?" Nick said with a half smile.

I laughed and shook my head. "Nope. I didn't even drink the one you bought me." Nick, meanwhile, had woken up that morning with a headache.

"Well, I think it's just maybe all the hiccups in the trip. You must have been half-dreaming when you saw whatever it was you thought you saw." He reached over for his Yeti full of coffee that he had filled in the lobby, feeling around for it. I reached over and lifted it out of the cupholder and handed it to him.

"Maybe. But I don't know. Part of me really believes I saw something otherworldly, even though I know it's impossible," I said. I was tired of pretending what I was seeing, what was happening, was all in my head. I wasn't losing it.

There was a long pause as he took a sip and then slowly put the thermal cup back into the cupholder.

"Whatever it was, it's behind us. The evil spirits can stay at the Mountain Lodge Resort and haunt another family," he said with a laugh.

"Nick, but what if they don't stay there?" I said in a low whisper, making sure none of the backseat passengers could hear me.

"I don't think there's any more room in this car for them." He lifted an eyebrow, his eyes twinkling. "They'll have to hitch a ride out of there with someone else."

"Funny," I said, rolling my eyes. I pressed my mouth into a tight line and looked out the window. It was pointless to continue the conversation. It would just end in an argument, me annoyed that he wasn't understanding what I was saying, him thinking I really had lost it. Not to mention it would terrify the kids.

But the question still rattled around in my brain: what if they don't stay there because we're the ones who brought them?

What if it's us they're after?

Chapter 20

24/7 HOT DOGS, BEER, AND LOTTO

"What more could a person want? I mean, really," I said as I pulled into a gas station, navigating the crowd of other minivans with turtle top carriers sporting license plates from New York, Pennsylvania, Illinois, and Indiana.

"A bathroom. A person wants a bathroom. Two people, actually," Piper said from the third row. She pointed to Sophie, who nodded furiously and unbuckled her seat belt.

"Go ahead," I told them.

Piper grabbed her sister's hand and walked toward the gas station, quickly stepping over what looked like the remnants of one of those 24/7 hot dogs.

I unbuckled as Nick got out to pump the gas and put my foot on the seat, ready to turn toward Leo. Yet the time on Tammy's clock made me stop: 11:14.

I sharply inhaled and stared at the white numbers, waiting to see what happened. I checked the time against my phone, and it was correct. I didn't want to blink as I waited for the time to change, my breaths growing shallow as my stomach clenched.

Then . . . 11:15.

Normal. Perfectly normal.

I slowly exhaled and looked around, waiting for something terrible to happen. Yet, the gas station looked the same. Nick stared at the car commercial playing on the gas station pump, Piper and Sophie were inside and I didn't see any commotion or screaming, and Leo was still behind me.

Safe.

My shoulders slumped in relief and I slowly turned around, fixing my face into a relaxed expression before Leo saw.

"How are you, buddy? Okay?" I gave him a soft smile, exhaling deeply as I stretched my neck from side to side.

He smiled and nodded. "Where are we stopping next?"

"Conyers, Georgia," I said, trying to stifle the dread in my tone. "Should take about four hours."

His smile brightened. "And we're staying with Uncle Ethan at his house?"

I cocked a finger gun at him. "That's the one," I said in a singsong voice, glad I was wearing sunglasses so he couldn't see my expression.

When Nick had pitched the trip to me, he had plotted out all of the proposed stops along the way. After Indiana and the water park resort, he quickly ran through the stop in Georgia. He knew it wasn't a selling point.

At the time, I went along with it, pushing the thought of staying with my brother-in-law out of my brain. It was something I would think about later, when necessary.

Now it was later and necessary.

Nick's younger brother Ethan wasn't a bad guy. He was just . . . a lot. He had moved from the wilds of Green Bay to the wilds of Georgia, swapping ice fishing for boar hunting on the acreage that he owned. We had never visited, since we usually saw Ethan at the holidays when he would come back to visit, so this would be our first time. Our trip's Cousin Eddie. I just hoped it wouldn't end with a family member strapped to the roof of the car. There wasn't much room up there with the turtle top anyway.

"You've been so quiet since we left the water park. Are you sure everything is okay?" I said after I made sure that my family was still inside the gas station. The image of the figure clad in sheets next to his bed was something I couldn't shake, even though everyone else told me that it wasn't real. It stirred a mom instinct to protect, to throw myself in front of my kids. Maybe it would have been better if I had convinced myself I really was half-dreaming. Because then I wouldn't have felt like I should've had Leo Velcroed to my side the way I did.

He shrugged, his shoulders moving up toward his Brewers baseball cap. He looked down, and I couldn't see his expression over the brim of the hat.

"Just tired?" I said, realizing I had used that excuse for everything on the trip. About why I wasn't drinking, about why I felt so unsettled, about why I had a niggling urge to grab the wheel from Nick and turn around to drive home, road trip abandoned. At least I knew Leo wasn't worried because *his* period was late.

"Um, I guess," he said, and shrugged again. "I just want to get there. I'm getting tired of the car."

I nodded. "Same, buddy. Same." I considered whether to end the back-and-forth there. My unanswered questions nudged forward. "Can I ask you something? I promise I won't get mad." He nodded. "Why did you take that necklace?" My voice rose, the desperation behind it clear, even though I was trying to sound casual so he would open up.

He narrowed his eyes at me, and my heart beat faster for a moment; I was afraid of what he might say. "I'm sorry," he finally said.

My shoulders relaxed and I exhaled. He thought he was still in trouble for that. "No, no. You don't need to say you're sorry. I don't care anymore that you took it."

What I didn't say was the truth: *Yes, yes, I care very much that you took it. It doesn't feel right to have it with us.*

"You're not in trouble, buddy, I promise," I added, leaning forward and giving him a tap on the knee with my forefinger. I glanced at the gas station again, making sure the coast was clear. I knew he wouldn't open up at all once his sisters got back into the car. "I'm just curious why you wanted to keep it."

He looked down, eyebrows lowering and cheeks drooping. "I just liked it and thought it was cool. And I thought I could give it back to that boy we almost hit if we saw him again."

"We stopped—" I sat back, his words forming a realization, a question, in my mind. I swallowed hard. "If we saw him again?"

He shrugged. "When we were at the house, I just felt like we were going to see him again, so I wanted to give him the necklace to give back to his mom."

"How did you know it was his mom's?" I whispered. I leaned forward, putting a shaking hand on the driver's seat.

He looked at me, a silent conversation passing between us. He knew so much more than he would say, than he would probably ever tell me.

"He told me," he said.

I slowly closed my eyes and took a deep breath, hearing the sounds of the gas station all around. The car engines revving, the patrons shouting to each other. The dings of the pumps.

A voice scrolled through my mind: *His name is Joey.* From the vision I had seen at the Vickery house, with the child's family portrait drawn, the boy was named Joey.

Could Joey have been the figure by his bed at the water park? No, it was much taller. But that meant that the boy was communicating telepathically with Leo somehow.

I felt sweat beads begin to form on my hairline as I considered this.

His name was on my tongue, waiting to be said. But I pressed my lips together before it could escape. I couldn't give him—it—a name. It would make it real.

None of this is true. I should listen to Nick. I'm exaggerating and jumping to ridiculous conclusions.

Most of all, I didn't want to scare Leo.

I slowly opened my eyes and gave him a smile. "Oh, that's neat." My tone sounded like a ghost's, dubbed over my real voice.

Leo smiled, encouraged that I believed him. "He told me he misses their house and his Big Wheel," he added.

I swallowed and nodded, thinking of the burned house, the trash strewn around the property. If I allowed myself to believe that he was real, that he had come back as a ghost, I couldn't imagine the pain and loss that Joey, just a little boy, felt when he saw what had happened to his home, to his toys, to everything he loved.

My chest felt tight as I saw Piper and Sophie emerge from the gas station. Sophie had her fists balled up and she was saying something to Piper that made her face darken even more. Piper walked a step ahead of her, clearly done with her sister. I heard the gas pump stop with a click, and Nick began to remove the nozzle from the car.

My window alone with Leo was about to close.

I turned around and shot an arm out, putting my hand on his knee and giving it a gentle squeeze as his eyes widened in surprise.

"Just promise me you'll tell me if anything happens. If something weird *is* happening to you. I believe you, so please trust me."

He nodded furiously, moving his gaze from my hand to my face. "Yeah. I will." He moved his knee away. "Ow." He rubbed his knee, where I could see red marks from my fingers.

"Good. I love you, buddy," I said as my fingers tingled where I had grabbed him. "I'm sorry if I grabbed you too tight."

"It's okay," he said, still rubbing his knee.

I hadn't meant to latch on to him so tightly. I needed to know the truth. It felt like something was hatching inside of me, trying to twist out, grab Leo through my fingers.

Sophie and Piper climbed into the car, arguing over who'd used the last paper towel in the bathroom.

"I texted Ethan and he's ready for us," Nick said as he opened the passenger door. "Do you want me to take over? So you can do more of the state prizes?"

"Sure," I said, and opened the door. Walking around the back of Tammy, an idea came to me, sparked by something Leo had said: *He misses his house.*

What of the house? Who owned the land and the property after the fire? Based on the way it looked, no one local had been taking care of it or keeping an eye on the place. The Vickerys had died there, and then everything else around it had been allowed to die, too.

But someone must still have owned it. I figured if it had been turned over to the county, they would have bulldozed the house to deter any revelers and reduce risk.

I'm going to find out more about the Vickerys, and also find out who owns that land. Even though it doesn't make any logical sense, maybe it will explain why this is all happening.

And maybe I can figure out some way to get the hauntings to stop.

I sat back as Tammy ventured onto the highway, taking us to Conyers, Georgia. The state prizes were at my feet, ready to be dispensed. I was about to start researching property records when I was stopped by a burning, a twisting, in my stomach. I placed an arm over my midsection to try to alleviate the pain. It felt like something was trying to claw its way out, rip open my gut and spill into the car.

Maybe Rosemary's baby, I quipped silently.

But then I thought about everything we had seen and been through, and the fact that I still hadn't gotten my period, and suddenly, it wasn't so funny. It wasn't something to even joke about.

It was something to fear.

Chapter 21

"Did you hear me? Leigh?"

Nick's disembodied voice wafted across the console to me. I shook my head mutely, eyes fixed on my phone screen. I scanned the web page I had found, pulse quickening and vision sharpening.

"Leigh?" he said again.

I snapped my head up. "What?" I said more harshly than I intended, and his eyebrows lifted in surprise. "Sorry. I didn't mean to react like that." I forced my body to relax and my hand to drop to my lap. "What did you say?"

"We're about an hour away," Nick said. "What were you reading so intensely?"

I hesitated. I didn't want Nick to talk me out of researching the Vickery family and what had happened to them. Googling them felt like an obsession, like scratching an itch. It was uncomfortable but satisfying.

Yet I hadn't found anything that I could actually latch on to. As Piper had told me before, there wasn't much information about the family. The first few searches I tried linked me to a professor in Indiana who had gotten a local award for his gardening—congrats to Dr. Vickery Szymnsky. And an article on a Vickery who was arrested a couple of years ago for stealing a tank of gas from the local 7-Eleven. Condolences to Martina Vickery.

On the second page of search results, I finally saw something relevant. It was an article titled "The Unexplained Mysteries of Marion County." It was a simple web page that looked like it had been created in the days of dial-up. The web page had a fuzzy graphic of a creepy-looking house, straight out of clip art, and a black background with white lettering. I had to squint at my phone to read the paragraphs on the Vickery family.

> **Another, less well-known mystery surrounds a family in central Indiana, near the town of Locksmith. The Vickery family—recent widow Patty and her three children, sixteen-year-old Lyssa, eleven-year-old Joey, and seven-year-old Annie—moved into a farmhouse off Route 28 sometime in the late 1970s. The exact year is unknown. What is known, however, is that on the night of June 21, 1982, the Vickery family household caught fire and burned to the ground. The family perished inside, the fire department not alerted to the fire until the next morning, when a neighbor saw the smoke and rang the police. According to reports, the firefighters arrived to only a smoking rubble. Only a small section of the foundation remained. The family's car was outside, half-burned, and it was assumed the family had died inside, although no bodies were ever found.**
>
> **The cause of the fire was never determined, and the event was shrouded in suspicion and gossip and became a local urban**

> **legend. Visitors to the house's remains reported smelling smoke and seeing sparks years later. Some even claimed to have seen a ghostly woman calling out for her children. Still others described seeing the children playing in the rubble, especially the boy riding a Big Wheel tricycle.**

I stopped and a cold front moved through my body.

The Big Wheel. The one that Leo mentioned Joey said he missed.

> **Throughout the years, the charred remains became more of a magnet for local teens and young adults looking for a place to party, the police often breaking up gatherings.**

> **Sightings of paranormal activity have never been validated or documented, yet the local chatter remains strong, nearly every person in town having a theory as to what happened, yet reluctant to speak about those theories. No one I spoke to would go on record. The mysteries of the family, and how they died, seem to have perished in the fire. Their story is, unfortunately, lost to time.**

It wasn't anything I didn't know, or hadn't suspected, but it still made the hair on the back of my neck stand up. Reading it felt like validation. I bookmarked the web page, which went on to talk about phantom cars and trains in nearby Clermont, Indiana, and then went back to the search.

Nothing. That was it. Not even old newspaper articles on the fire.

I chewed on my lip and stared at my phone screen, quickly swiping up to scroll through the results, certain I had missed something. *How does a whole family die in a fire and no one even writes it up in the local newspaper?*

Or maybe the newspaper in Locksmith was so small that it wouldn't have any archives.

So, in that case, they were as good as burned up in that fire, too.

I clicked over to social media and searched for a few hashtags. #vickeryfamily #vickeryghosts #vickeryfire yielded only a few results from a family reunion in Montana a few years ago. Nothing on the mystery in Indiana.

Next, I went to Facebook and tried to search for any Vickery family members in Indiana. It was after my eyes had nearly crossed from staring at names that I stopped myself.

Even if I had found a relative, I didn't know what my plan would be. It was far from appropriate to send one of these distant cousins a Facebook message and tell them their tragically deceased family members might be haunting my family.

I looked over at Nick and gave him a shrug. "Nothing. I don't know what I'm doing anymore. Just messing around and doing some research on the Vickerys," I said in a low tone, hoping the kids wouldn't hear. "But I didn't really find anything."

"Sorry you didn't find anything. But we're not too far now," he muttered as he looked at his phone screen for directions to his brother's house.

I glanced down at the phone in my lap and saw that the screen had gone dark. For the best. I'd need the next sixty minutes to mentally prepare myself for arrival at Ethan's homestead.

"Keep your eyes open for Old Possum Road," Nick said, his head on a swivel as we looked around the neighborhood. The Maps app on everyone's phone had gone wonky, so we were left to find the house the old-fashioned way: by looking for it.

Nick, to his credit, didn't mention that he wished we had the TripTik, although I was sure he wanted to shout it many, many times. Even I missed the damned thing.

There wasn't much of anything off the highway exit, minus signs proudly pointing the way to Conyers. Tall pines with red needles underneath bracketed the roadway, the sight lines occasionally broken by a rotting shed or fallen tree.

"This town is so weird," Piper said from the backseat. I heard the clicking of her phone as she took pictures to document it for Instagram. "This is a good place to play I Spy."

"My turn. I spy . . . ," Leo said. He looked around the car's interior and then outside. "I spy something orange."

"Hmmm, orange," I said. I turned my head to scan the backseat. I caught a glimpse of Sophie's face, which wasn't orange but a shade of green. Carsick green.

"Soph? You okay?" I said, and poked Nick on the shoulder.

"Can I put my window down?" Sophie said, and before I could answer her, she hit the button. A mass of humid, thick air filled the car, the windows instantly fogging up.

Despite the putrid air, her face lost the greenish tint and went back to something resembling normal.

"Mom? Something orange?" Leo said impatiently.

"Oh, right. Sorry. Hmmm." I started to look around the car, but Piper blurted out the answer.

"It's a clementine, Mom. Right there." She pointed to the small orange that had halfway rolled under Sophie's captain's chair. I had given it to Piper in her present at the Georgia state line. Though, apparently, she wasn't "into clementines anymore this summer." Of course.

"Piper! You ruined it!" Leo said as he whipped around. "You always ruin everything!"

She chuckled and raised her eyebrows. "I thought we were all playing. Calm down."

I held up a hand as I saw Leo lean over to grab the clementine.

"No! No one is throwing anything at each other, okay? Piper, you should have let us play. And, Leo, you—what?" I saw he was staring at the window, face transformed from anger to confusion.

"Mom, why is our car so dirty?" he said as he stared at the smudges on his window. The humid air rushing in had really revealed how dingy Tammy had gotten on the road.

"Well, I can give you three reasons," I said. I smiled and pointed to each of my kids. "I'm not the one who—" I stopped as my vision sharpened on the window behind Piper. There were more smudges and fingerprints than on the rest of the windows, almost like someone had been running their hands down the back windshield, palms against the glass.

I cocked my head to the side as I studied a shape in the corner, near the top of the window. It was round and had two black holes toward the top, and a wide gaping stretch of black toward the bottom.

It looked like a face.

I leaned back a little, blinking a few times. As I did, instead of the shapes all forming together and mixing like a group of clouds, the scene became more clear. It was a head, and the smudges on either side were fingerprints and palm impressions.

It looked like someone had pressed their face against the window and run their hands down the glass. Like someone had been trying to get inside.

My head snapped back as I felt a pain inside my body again—right in my stomach. I quickly turned around and faced forward, my heart thudding. Nick didn't notice, leaning forward to study the road signs buried in the pines.

I wanted to turn around and point out the shapes to my family, to try to have them either tell me I was seeing things or tell me that they saw them, too. But I couldn't scare the kids like that. And I didn't want Nick to think I had really lost it.

I ran my thumb over the dark screen of my phone, and I remembered that I wanted to find out who owned the Vickerys' land. I pecked out a quick email to Dawn O'Callaghan, a paralegal I worked with at my office. She was in her midtwenties, wore serious tortoiseshell glasses, and twisted her hair into a topknot every morning for work. Yet I had seen enough social media pictures of her to know that as soon as billable hours were over, that topknot came undone and the glasses came off. It made me happy to know that she was at least attempting to have a social life, something I'd forgone at that age to focus on my career.

I sent the email with an approximation of the location, giving the last known owner: the Vickerys. I was vague on the *why* of the request, just asking her to send me anything she found.

"Old Possum Road!" Nick said triumphantly as he pointed to

a brown and white lettered street sign that looked like it had all but given up.

I inhaled sharply as I looked around at the scene down Old Possum Road. It was mostly open land dotted with scruffy pine trees and piles of needles. On the right, the remains of what looked to be an old outhouse surrounded by boulders. On the left, a rusted-out car parked just off the road, as though it had died and someone pushed it into the woods.

At the end of the road was a small white ranch-style manufactured home. In the front yard was an aboveground PVC swimming pool that looked like it had seen better days. The left side sagged down, the water level dangerously close to breaching it. A fire pit with dusty lawn chairs was next to it, and on the other side was a camper parked under a carport.

We had arrived at the Southern Somerset Camp.

I picked up my phone and sent a text to my friends.

Prayer circle: Have arrived at my brother-in-law's house and it's everything you're picturing.

Chapter 22

"Where's your broth—" The words died in my throat as I saw my brother-in-law, Ethan, come around the side of his house in his bathing suit. He was shirtless and held his arms out as we parked the car.

He didn't wait for Nick to open the driver's-side door, wrenching it open with a smile.

"You made it!" he said, leaning into the car and wrestling Nick out. "Magic Land or bust, eh?"

I slowly opened my door and got out, watching as Ethan put Nick in a headlock, his face against his brother's bare chest.

And so it begins, I thought.

"Kids, come on out," I announced as I opened my door. I walked around the front of the car and stood near the brothers, my hands on my hips.

Ethan looked up from where he was bent at the waist, my husband's head in his armpit. He dropped his vise grip on Nick and stood up. Nick pitched forward and stumbled around, trying to regain his footing. At least he was laughing.

Ethan's face relaxed from mischievous younger brother into

accommodating brother-in-law. He might have moved from the Midwest, but the overly polite Wisconsinite in him couldn't be broken. He held his arms out, walking forward for a hug.

"Oh. Um, hi," I said as he pressed his bare, sweaty chest against me. "Good to see you."

"Sorry. Where are my manners? I should have put a shirt on but I thought you guys were coming tomorrow." Ethan smiled and looked over at Nick, punching him lightly in the upper arm.

I gave my husband a questioning look. "No, it was always today," Nick said. He looked over at the kids, who were warily standing beside Tammy. "C'mon, guys. Say hello to your uncle."

Ethan clapped his hands together and then walked over, giving each of them a bear hug. I saw Piper's look of horror as he went in for her last. She half-patted him back, unsure of how to reciprocate.

"Where's Donna?" I asked as I put a hand up to shield my eyes from the sun. It was hotter than hell on the driveway, and even though the pool looked like it was one ripple away from bursting, I had half a mind to walk over and jump in.

Ethan shook his head and gritted his teeth in a grimace.

"Really? I'm sorry," I said. I had only met Ethan's girlfriend Donna once, at Christmas last year when they'd come to town. She was in her midforties and tattooed, tanned, and looked like she had Seen Things. But I liked her. She was down-to-earth, and kind, and the variety of tough lady that you would want on your side.

"That's awful, man. When?" Nick asked as he put an arm around Leo. Leo's gaze was fixed in the distance, on the pond at the edge of the property. It was covered in a thick green moss, and I shivered picturing the enormous mosquitoes that were probably guarding the water.

"Last week," Ethan said. He waved a hand around nonchalantly. "You know how it is." He smiled, but I saw his chin quiver and his eyes water. Poor guy.

I made a sympathetic noise, and there was a long, awkward silence as Ethan stared at the ground, thinking of Donna, and Nick and I exchanged a glance. I gave him a slight shrug.

Now what?

"Listen, man, we can stay at a hotel tonight. With the mix-up on when we were coming . . ."

I surprised myself with the self-restraint to not react when he said that. There wasn't a mix-up. I had overheard their conversation over speaker the day before we left, and Nick said at least three times, "Wednesday. We will see you Wednesday." And that was in addition to the reminder text message.

"We can hang out today," Nick continued, "and then stay somewhere else tonight. We don't want to put you out."

I saw Piper's face brighten at this suggestion, at the thought of staying at a motel somewhere as opposed to Ethan's house, especially since he was going through a breakup and I doubted cleaning his house was high on the priority list.

A loophole.

"Yes, yes," I said, trying to keep the hope out of my tone. "I'm sure there are plenty of places to stay nearby."

Ethan laughed. "You all are funny." He shook his head, still laughing. "No way would I let my brother"—he paused to punch

Nick in the arm again—"stay in a hotel when he's visiting. Especially when he's headed to the most magical place on the planet!"

Leo and Sophie gave half-hearted cheers, still wary, while Nick laughed nervously and rubbed his arm where he'd been hit.

"Red Woods Inn," Piper said, staring at her screen. "They have two rooms available tonight."

"Why wouldn't you want to stay here?" Ethan said, his tone quiet. "I have the room."

Nick and I exchanged a quick glance. "Of course, we'd love to stay here," I said, a too-bright smile on my face.

"We just don't want to put you out, is all," Nick said, putting a hand on Ethan's shoulder.

Ethan waved his hand around. "Bullshit. You're family."

And so it was done. Piper's eyes went wide, and her head snapped to me. I pretended I didn't see.

"Can we swim in your pool?" Sophie said, pointing.

Ethan clapped. "Hell yes. Oops—I mean heck yes." He smiled at us.

His language wasn't what I was worried about.

"If anyone gets hurt, don't sue me, okay?" he said with a laugh, flinging a heavy arm around my shoulders.

"You got it." I gave him a thin smile and extracted myself. No matter how many times I had told my brother-in-law that I wasn't that kind of lawyer, it didn't matter. In his mind, lawyers were for monetary settlements and getting the district attorney to drop a few charges.

"Well, c'mon, c'mon. Let me show you guys around the ol' camp," Ethan said. He put an arm around Nick's shoulders and led him toward the front door. The kids and I followed, my face frozen into a smile.

The trilling of emails from my phone distracted me as we walked into Ethan's house. I pulled it out of my back pocket and opened up my mail. Dawn O'Callaghan—my unexpected savior—had already gotten an answer for me on the property records. The land where the Vickery house stood was, in fact, owned by someone: a Jillian Samson in Tucson, Arizona.

"Tucson?" I whispered. "No wonder the land looks like . . . that." I wondered if she was a relative or someone close to the family, and if she would be the one to finally give me some concrete answers. I was about to open up social media and search for her when I heard my name.

"Leigh?"

I looked up and tucked my phone back into the pocket of my cut-off shorts. Nick and Ethan stood in the center of the common space, staring at me.

"Sorry! Work texts," I said with an apologetic smile.

"No problem. Welcome to my palace, guys." Ethan spread his arms out wide, beaming a large smile at us.

I glanced around the space. From my vantage point, I could see cooking gadgets dotting the kitchen countertops, mirroring my mother-in-law's house. She had never watched an infomercial she didn't love, so her kitchen was crammed with food dehydrators, pasta machines, and an automatic vegetable chopper. I had never seen her use any of them.

Dark wood paneling was dotted with a few nondescript

paintings of nature and forest scenes, a family photo from a reunion over ten years ago, a few framed beer advertisements, and a skyline picture of downtown Green Bay.

Speaking of Green Bay, in one corner there was a near collage of Packers pennants and posters, a recliner tucked into the space with a green and yellow blanket thrown over the arm. Next to the chair was a scuffed wooden end table holding a lamp with a Packers-logo shade.

No question here who the occupants were rooting for come the fall.

"Ethan, I didn't know you were a Packers fan," I said wryly, smiling at my brother-in-law.

He laughed and walked quickly toward the refrigerator, pointing to all the magnets, which were also all from the Packers. "What gave it away?" he said. He gestured toward the recliner and couch. "Have a seat. Take a load off."

I looked around the room and peered into the brown-carpeted hallway that presumably led toward the bathroom and bedrooms. "Where are the kids?"

"Walking around outside," Nick said. I opened my mouth, and he held up a hand. "I told them not to go in the pool."

Ever, I added silently.

Ethan walked back with three cold bottles of beer in his hands and passed them out. I was about to take a long sip when a wave of panic ripped through my chest. I still hadn't taken a test. Or gotten my period.

"I have other kinds of beer if you don't like High Life," Ethan said, his brow creased with concern.

I realized I was sitting straight up, arm stiffly holding the beer bottle nearly touching my mouth. Nick stared at me, too.

I stuttered, then decided to take the path of least resistance. I held the bottle up to my lips and tilted it back slightly, pretending to take a sip.

"Mmm. Refreshing," I said. A wave of nausea passed over me like a warm ocean current. Suddenly the room felt stifling, claustrophobic. "Can I use your bathroom, Ethan?"

After splashing water on my face and drying it with the cream and gold hand towel that my mother-in-law had gifted all of us for Christmas a few years ago, I took a few slow, deep breaths staring into the mirror. The color returned to my face, the sweat drying. I had managed to stave off any puking, thankfully. I didn't think I would have been able to hide the sound.

And then there would have been a whole lot of questions to answer. Questions I couldn't answer.

I reached over to grab a piece of toilet paper to dry my mouth (no tissues in the bathroom; deemed unnecessary, I supposed) and saw the roll was empty.

Luckily, I was no stranger to this problem. I don't think my children could put a new roll of toilet paper on the holder if their lives depended on it.

I opened the cabinet underneath the sink and rooted around for another roll of toilet paper. As I grabbed one off the top of the stack, I saw something behind it.

A pregnancy test.

It must have been left over from Donna. It had probably been in there for years.

My hand shaking, I slowly picked it up and stared at it.

Quick results! 99.98% accurate.

I turned it over, searching for an expiration date. I found it, in red lettering on the side. It hadn't expired yet.

If this isn't a sign from the universe, I don't know what is.

Take it.

Get it over with.

I had just lifted a finger to slide under the flap of the box when I heard the front door open and close.

"Dad, where are our bathing suits?" Leo said.

Nope.

I tossed the pregnancy test back under the sink and quickly stood up, leaving the new toilet paper roll on the sink.

"No swimming," I called out as I opened the bathroom door.

"This water feels great!" Sophie splashed around in the quasi pool, lifting her arms up.

I eyed the collection of leaves that she brushed aside to swim to the other edge.

I obviously had lost the battle of the swimming pool. Leo and Sophie had jumped in, with Nick on the edge, his feet invisible under the cloudy water. Piper had opted out, propping herself on two lawn chairs and leaning her head back. She fell asleep within minutes.

Ethan was next to Nick. He had decided that it was easier to just bring the beer cooler outside rather than go to the fridge every four minutes for more drinks. The "cooler" was a laundry basket on wheels lined with a garbage bag, with beers and ice dumped inside. I had to give him points for ingenuity.

Just past the swimming pool, I saw a round black grill on the side of the house. Smoke was drifting out of it.

"What's that? Something seems like it's on fire," I said, pointing across the lawn.

Ethan followed my gaze and nodded. "Those are the ribs. I just put them on. They should be ready in a few hours, just in time for the barbecue."

Warning bells flipped on in my head, and my eyes flicked toward Nick. "Barbecue?" he asked before I could. He took a sip of his beer.

"Surprise! I knew you would want to see everyone, so I invited everyone to come over tonight. I told everybody it was tomorrow, but I just sent a message that we're changing it to tonight." He held out a hand and began to count on his fingers the friends he invited, which seemed to be everyone within a fifty-mile radius.

After he had moved on to the third set, I said, "That seems like a lot of people. You really don't have to go to all that trouble."

I hoped the panic in my voice wasn't as obvious as I suspected.

Nick put a hand on my knee, silently letting me know that I hadn't done a very good job of covering it.

Ethan drained his beer and set the can down under his chair, adding it to the growing collection. "Horseshit. We're going to have a party tonight!" He clapped his hands and let out a whoop as Nick and I exchanged a defeated look. "Buckle up, big brother. It's going to be a long night," Ethan added with a wink.

Fantastic.

Chapter 23

Over the past couple of years, I had distanced myself from social media. In election cycles, the cesspool of Facebook became a car crash, and I was tired of watching people eviscerate each other. Not to mention the constant solicitation from old high school and grade school classmates, asking me to join their "accountability" group or "wellness team" to peddle wax candle melts, spice blends, vitamins, jewelry, skin care.

I usually just deleted the message, which often led to an increase in the solicitation—something behavior analysts, I had learned from working with one on a client case, call "uptick." Negative behavior first increases but then will extinguish.

It had always worked.

But that was online. I was in real life now.

"So this pattern has been discontinued, which makes it ultra rare. Look, feel how soft it is." LuAnne, Ethan's coworker, held out a garishly patterned pair of leggings.

We were seated around the makeshift campfire that Ethan had created from dried branches and lighter fluid. It looked small but had the smoke of a large fire.

I quickly ran my finger over the red, white, and blue striped pants. "Soft," I said with a smile.

LuAnne still held them out. "Well, go on. Take it. Really get a feel for it."

Her blond hair was piled on top of her head in a messy bun, but her face was a burlesque-show level of made up—contouring and glittery eyeshadow, hot-pink lips, black liquid eyeliner. She thrust the pants forward another inch.

I murmured and took them from her. I set them in my lap and lightly ran my hand over them.

"Mom, are you petting a dog or something?" Piper said as she came up behind me. She peered around my shoulder and started laughing. "Are those Suvi leggings? They're so—" She stopped as she realized what was happening.

"Soft. They're so soft," I finished for her, giving her a glare over my shoulder. I turned back to LuAnne. "Really nice."

Not sure what to do next, I bent down and picked up the water bottle at my feet and took a long, slow sip, hoping that someone else would jump into the conversation and I would be set free.

Nick was over at the cornhole area playing with Ethan, Leo, and a few close friends whose names I had immediately forgotten. In my defense, they were "old friends" of Ethan's, or "next-door neighbors" of the actual old friends. The barbecue seemed to be more about gathering around the campfire, drinking, and playing games. We were just the excuse.

An hour before, partygoers had started to arrive in a near crush of people, parking their cars all over Ethan's front yard. I guess it helped that most of them were driving either pickups or SUVs outfitted with what looked like tractor tires. I didn't have to ask if these folks were hunting enthusiasts. I received that information from prominently displayed bumper stickers, such as **HONK IF MY DEER FALLS OUT**.

LuAnne leaned forward and patted my knee. I noticed her fingernails were each decorated differently, with elaborately painted designs and a few rhinestones. I couldn't imagine how long that had taken her, but from an article that I'd read online, sales for Suvi leggings were tanking, so I imagined LuAnne unfortunately had some time on her hands as of late.

"You go ahead and keep that pair. Consider it a gift. You start wearing those around town, and I guarantee you will get stopped and asked about them," she said with a firm head nod.

"Thank you," I said as I carefully folded the leggings and placed them on my lap. I might get asked about them, but probably not for the reasons LuAnne was picturing.

She held a pointer finger in the air, which looked almost monstrous, so sharp in the glow of the campfire. "And then you come back to me, and we can get you set up as a partner. We really don't have a lot of partners in Wisconsin."

"Do you have any Packers leggings?" I laughed. "That might help."

LuAnne looked horrified, and her friend next to her—JoAnne—placed a hand on her arm.

JoAnne whispered to LuAnne and then turned to me, her hand still on LuAnne's arm. "Suvi has a whole team of designers. Some from Paris, France. And they spend hours on each design, like high-fashion charcuterie."

Couture, JoAnne, I silently corrected.

I nodded, still not grasping what I had said that was wrong. "My apologies. Of course."

From the limited amount I knew about IP laws and corporate branding, I figured Suvi just didn't want to pay to use the NFL logos. No, they preferred producing designs from Microsoft clip art. But more power to all of them, girlbossing and whatnot.

LuAnne and JoAnne nodded with satisfaction, although they each gave me a wary look. I was a person not to be completely trusted, apparently.

JoAnne bent down and rifled through the enormous black handbag at her feet. She pulled out a hot-pink spray bottle and misted herself with a body splash called Honeysuckle Dreams. The cloying smell blanketed my cheeks and forehead, some of it working its way into my mouth.

I swallowed, and it felt like I had eaten a dusty flower bouquet.

I gagged and bent down to rinse my mouth out, sneezing, eyes burning.

At that moment, I heard a shout from across the expansive lawn.

"Ribs are ready!" Ethan walked around from the side of the house holding an aluminum tray, stacks of animal bones inside.

Still chugging water and already a little queasy from the smell, I stood up and slowly walked over to where the crowd gathered around a white folding table, where Ethan placed the ribs.

I stared at the piles of bones, making out each individual curve. Ethan held one of the racks up, pointing to it.

"It's a beaut," he said, beaming.

With the barbecue sauce dripping off the end, it looked gory.

It looked like he had reached his hand into the pig and pulled out the ribs like a xylophone, the pig's body collapsing, boneless.

I felt the burning of bile as it surged up my throat. I put a hand on my stomach and took a deep breath. My insides clenched and I gagged, vomit held back only barely.

I quickly turned and walked toward the house, still gagging.

"Where are you—" Nick said as I passed the cornhole pit.

I shook my head and kept walking, breaking into a jog as I felt my lunch dangerously close to spilling out on the porch.

I made it to the bathroom, thank God.

When my body had gotten rid of everything I had eaten, I took a few deep breaths and splashed some cold water on my face until I felt semihuman. I rinsed my mouth out with water, but still an acidic taste coated my teeth. I opened the medicine cabinet, searching for mouthwash or even toothpaste to finger-brush my teeth.

Nothing. An old comb crusted with concrete hairspray residue and an empty miniature bottle of Pert Plus shampoo. I bent down and opened the cabinet under the sink.

Success. There was a bottle of bright yellow Listerine in the back left corner. I reached to grab it, and my gaze fell on what I had seen earlier: the pregnancy test.

It wasn't the right time or place—not by a long shot. A terrible idea.

But I was worn down by the trip, weak from my body rejecting the sight of the ribs.

So I gave in to the terrible idea.

Before I could stop myself, I grabbed the box, ripped it open, and peed on the stick. I didn't read the directions. I figured not many technological advances had been made in the realm of pregnancy tests, although I did sometimes see the fancy digital ones at Walgreens that were kept under lock and key, away from shoplifters looking to get a piece of that sweet black-market pregnancy-test world.

I set it down on the counter next to the sink and checked the time on my watch.

Eight twelve p.m.

The front of the box said "three minutes," so I stood, staring at myself in the mirror—I looked like a woodland monster who'd lurched from the trees to join the party—trying to decide how I felt about all of it.

While I couldn't comprehend the idea of having another baby at forty-two, one thing I did know was that I'd never pictured I would find out life-altering information in my brother-in-law's bathroom while a kegger raged outside.

I nearly fell over at a loud rap on the bathroom door.

"Someone's in here!" I said, my voice high and squeaky. I looked at my watch and saw I still had two minutes left. "I'm busy," I said weakly.

Undeterred, the waiting party guest banged again. "We've gotta go."

It was a deep voice, so I retorted, "Go outside. In the woods."

More raps and bangs. "No, ma'am! I gotta go. Ribs are going right through me."

Great.

Then more banging.

I didn't think I could hold whoever it was off for another two minutes. Panicked, I looked around the bathroom, thinking I could stick the test in the medicine cabinet, hidden, and then return to check it after whoever was outside finished.

But what if they take forever? And do I really want to go back into this bathroom after whatever's about to happen happens?

I grabbed the pregnancy test and held it horizontal, carefully wrapping the end of my shirt around it to conceal it.

Still holding it under my shirt, I wrenched open the door with my other hand, and came face-to-face with a very stocky, very drunk man wearing a black T-shirt.

"All yours," I said to him. He nearly knocked me over as he surged toward the bathroom and slammed the door shut. I definitely made the right choice in sneaking the pregnancy test out of the bathroom. I couldn't go back in there, maybe forever. I would pee in the woods the rest of the night.

I slid into the guest bedroom, where Nick and I were staying for the night. I sat down on the pull-out bed across from Ethan's old desktop computer, a Compaq that looked like it had seen Gore lose the election.

The metal springs dug into my bottom as I slowly unwrapped the shirt until my hand was free.

I didn't want to look, couldn't look.

But of course, I did. And of course, there it was.

Two lines, both pink.

I was pregnant.

Just as I had feared.

I carefully set the test down on the scratched wooden desk, next to the keyboard. I blinked a few times, making sure it wasn't a trick of the light. I watched as the second line grew darker, as though it were mocking me: *You're pregnant, stupid. Need more proof? Here ya go.*

Jostling the desk to put the pregnancy test down had made the desktop computer come to life. Ethan's screen saver was him holding some kind of large fish by the mouth, smiling proudly.

I stared at it, unable to move or breathe.

The fish was huge. I wondered where it was caught. The background told me it was somewhere around here. I wondered if he'd won a trophy for it.

A whoop and a cheer broke me out of my trance. I listened and realized it was people applauding during some kind of drinking game.

The air in the bedroom felt heavy, musty. A lone window-unit air conditioner lamely hissed out lukewarm air, making the room feel like it was slowly filling with water and my head was sinking underneath the surface.

I had to find Nick. No way could I pretend everything was fine, not after that second pink line appeared.

He will calm me down, tell me everything will be okay. He always does and always will. He'll be so excited that it will quell my fears and anxiety. Right?

Chapter 24

"Hey, asshole, beer me!"

"Yeah, get me one too, asshole!"

"Me too!"

"Gimme a minute," I heard Nick say as I walked around outside toward the cornhole pit.

The group playing cornhole had moved over to one of the folding tables just off to the side. They were seated with cards in their hands, beer cans on the table. Nick stood and walked over to the cooler filled with beer next to the cornhole boards.

"Two clears!"

I realized what was happening. It had been, oh, twenty years since I played the card game Asshole, but the dark recess of my brain where I stored that information lit up like a firecracker.

As I walked over, I saw Nick try to juggle the beers in his arms as the other players jeered at him.

Right. So he's the "asshole." The one who lost the last round and now has to be a servant to everyone else during this round.

My pace slowed as I took in the scene. As Nick passed out the beers, I could tell that he was buzzed. When I arrived at the card table, it was confirmed.

He smiled too brightly at me and held out his arms. "Leigh! There you are! I was looking for you."

"I was inside," I said, putting my hands in my back pockets. My lips were quivering with nerves, and I gave him a shaky smile. More than anything, I just wanted him to hug me, tell me everything would be fine. That I wasn't too old, too tired, too much of a disaster to have another child.

"Here, take my seat. I'm vice asshole," said a skinny guy with a goatee and a Braves baseball cap. He stood, gesturing toward the empty seat.

I held a hand up. "Oh, no thanks. I'm good."

Amid the mild protests from the rest of the group, I bent down to whisper to Nick. I planned on telling him I needed to talk. Immediately. But as I got closer, I got a whiff of the beer and my stomach turned again.

No, this isn't a good time. You can't tell him like this.

Not that I'd listened to that voice earlier when I decided to take a pregnancy test in the middle of a drunken barbecue, but still. I needed to listen this time.

"Where are the kids?" I said instead, keeping my voice low to steady it.

"They just went to bed," he said, and pointed toward the house. "They went in the back way."

I frowned, wondering why I hadn't seen them. He put an arm around my waist and gave me a squeeze. I briefly closed my eyes and swallowed down the pregnancy news, pushing aside any need for comfort and support until I could find a better time.

"I'm going to check on the kids and then go to bed," I said, and bent down to kiss him. He smelled like a campfire. "I'm exhausted."

"I won't be up too much later," he said.

I turned and waved to the rest of the people around the fire, who responded with half-hearted waves back. I slowly made my way to the house, careful not to step on any rocks or tree roots in the darkness.

I hoped he would have his wits about him by the time he came to bed, although I doubted it.

As I shut the door behind me once inside, I heard Ethan shout that Nick was the asshole again.

Perfect. Tomorrow's drive should be extremely pleasant. And no way are we talking about anything tonight.

I walked into the other back bedroom and saw that the kids had collapsed on the queen bed. Piper and Leo flanked Sophie in the middle, who was curled up like a pill bug in a garden bed. All three were dead asleep.

"That was fast," I whispered. I smoothed back the hair on Leo's head for a moment as I felt a pressure cooker of emotion start to boil over in my chest.

Another child.

It was impossible to imagine. Impossible to process.

But I did know this: I had three really great kids in that bed.

I gave Leo a pat and then turned and tiptoed out of the room, gently closing the door behind me.

I brushed my teeth and crawled into bed, pulling the hunter-green comforter up, willing myself not to think about how often bachelor uncles were likely to wash their guest sheets.

I closed my eyes and felt the exhaustion seep through my bones, tethering me to the bed, tentacles outstretching to the ground. I was just about to drift off when a flash moved across my eyelids. Then another.

I sat up and looked around, just before another flash came from the window. I ducked and looked out, to see angry streaks of lightning crisscrossing the sky. It looked like an invisible Michael Myers was slashing his butcher knife through the air, tearing the fabric of the sky in long rips.

I heard car engines starting in the distance, low rumbles as partygoers began to leave with the storm blowing through. I heard the front door open and Nick and Ethan walk in, voices raised.

I lay back down as a low rumble of thunder sounded in the distance. Then, a flash of light.

The thunder and lightning weren't more than two seconds apart. As a kid, I was always told to count the number of seconds in between the lightning and thunder to judge how close the storm was. The smaller the number, the more imminent the threat.

The knowledge was burned into my brain after I watched the movie *Poltergeist*. In the movie, the little boy lies in bed counting down, until finally the tree outside his window comes to life and tries to murder him.

I did not want that to happen to me.

A loud wind rattled through the property, knocking on windows and waving the tree branches. I heard what sounded like trash cans blowing over and the clatter of beer cans set free.

Nick creaked down the hallway to the bedroom, his steps uneven. As the doorknob turned, a loud blare made me jump out of bed.

It was a tornado siren. The sound reverberated through the walls, rattling the wood paneling and nudging the glasses in the kitchen cabinets.

The bedroom door flung open, Nick looking wild-eyed with his hair slightly sticking up.

"Tornado siren!" we both shrieked at the same time.

"Mom!" I heard Sophie call out from the bedroom, her voice high and afraid.

"It's okay," I heard Piper say before I opened their door.

"C'mon. C'mon." Nick waved them out of the bedroom and into the hallway while I opened my phone's weather app and tried to load the radar.

It was completely pixelated and wouldn't come into focus.

"Shit. Turn on the television," I said as I looked toward the family room. "Where is your broth—" I stopped as I saw Ethan, asleep face down on the floor of the family room, a brown shag rug framing his head. I walked over and nudged him with my toe. He responded by rolling over and grumbling.

Nick turned the television on and flipped it to the Weather Channel. A stern-looking scroll was at the bottom of the screen.

"What county are we in?" I said to Nick as I watched the names run across the bottom with messages like **Take Cover Now** and **Extremely Dangerous**.

"No clue." He walked over and bent down to shake Ethan awake, telling him there was a storm coming.

Ethan slowly sat up, rubbing his head, looking like a man who had just time traveled. He shook his head a few times and widened his eyes. He looked up, glanced at the television, and then did a double take, pointing at the screen.

"That's really bad. We have to go to the basement," he slurred.

Next to me, Sophie began to cry.

"Mom, the basement is probably creepy," Leo whispered to me.

I nodded and whispered back, "Most basements are creepy. But we'll be safe down there."

Five minutes later, I tucked an arm around Leo's shoulders and pulled him tighter. We sat on a faded brown corduroy couch in Ethan's basement, me in the middle, with Leo on one side and Sophie on the other; I had one arm around each of them. Piper sat on an armchair across from us, and Nick and Ethan stood off to the side, trying to get an antique weather radio to work. Cell phone service was spotty, Wi-Fi nonexistent.

At first, when Ethan had brought us down to the basement, it was nicer than I had expected. I'd pictured a haunted root cellar or a crawl space that regularly hosted family reunions of the arachnid variety. But it was a 1970s-style wood-paneled basement, with linoleum flooring and a few sad posters of beer advertisements.

All very standard.

Except for the Christmas decorations.

Ethan's ex-girlfriend Donna loved Christmas and collected boxes upon boxes of holiday decorations, usually things she found at Goodwill or garage sales. And she had left every box at Ethan's.

Against one wall were boxes labeled **ORNAMENTS**. Against another wall were four boxed artificial trees. Four! In the utility room stood row upon row of plastic light-up Santas.

And across from us on the couch was a five-foot-tall Santa statue, facing us, his eyes seemingly moving as we did. Or maybe that was just a trick of the light.

"Nick?" I said. "Can you turn that thing around? It's freaking the kids out." I pointed to Satanic Santa and felt Leo and Sophie furiously nod.

He stopped fiddling with the weather radio and obliged, swiveling Santa around and then turning back to his brother. He seemed to have instantly sobered up, but with dark circles around his bloodshot eyes.

We heard the blare of the tornado siren outside and the rattle of the windows upstairs. From the egress windows, I could see rain falling through in the well, soaking the leaves below.

Extricating myself from Leo and Sophie, I stood for a moment, stretching my arms over my head. I walked over to Ethan and Nick, who was still fiddling with the dial on the radio. I could only make out every other word, the static was so thick.

". . . County . . . shelter . . . winds . . . reports . . . basement . . ."

"Well, that's extremely informative and helpful," I muttered as I rolled my eyes.

The smell of beer still wafted off of Ethan and Nick, although my husband definitely was the more alive of the two.

"Damn it. This thing is a piece of shit. What's the point of having a weather radio if it doesn't work when there's any weather?" Ethan said as he slapped his hand on the wooden bench. The radio hopped on the wood, still unwilling to cooperate and give us actual sentences.

"No kidding," Nick said. He stood up and shook his head. "Remember when we were kids and that storm came through when we lived in the house on Red Cardinal Lane? And the tree branch that went through the window downstairs?"

Ethan laughed. "It was the greatest thing that happened to us that summer."

The two carried on, reminiscing about tornado watches and warnings and memories of hunkering down in their basement with flashlights and batteries. Of nights spent camping out on the living room floor when there was no power, candles on the table. Of throwing away everything in their fridge after the power had been out for a couple of days, and of watching a funnel cloud descend from the sky and touch the ground before their parents made them come inside.

Whenever the weather would get bad when I was a kid, my parents would just ignore it and send me to my room to wait it out. There was no family bonding moment, no shared adrenaline rush.

No, we just kept to ourselves until the storm passed, which it always did. Until the day it didn't, and we were forced to change our lives.

I walked over to Santa, who was now facing the wall like a child in time-out. I put an elbow on his shoulder to steady myself. The air in the basement had been cool at first, but since we had been down there, it had quickly turned humid and muggy, our body heat warming the air.

Piper curled herself into a ball on the armchair and closed her eyes, unaffected.

Lucky, I thought.

Even Leo and Sophie looked more calm, bored almost, as we waited for the thunder and lightning to stop. We heard the wind whipping against the siding and the sounds of tree branches cracking and falling as the sirens blared on.

My children were better than me in a crisis, it seemed.

I internally rolled my eyes at my own reaction and went to sit back down and wait for the storm to pass. My ears pricked, though, at a few words that came clearly through the weather radio.

Interspersed between the crackly bursts of static and low buzzing, a voice was saying "eleven fifteen."

I froze, certain I'd heard the radio wrong. It was back to total static.

No one else in the room seemed to have heard it. Then, in between the hums on the radio, a different kind of humming. A song.

Recognition moved through my body before I understood what was happening, my brain singing along before I identified the song.

It was "You Are My Sunshine." The same song that I'd heard Patty Vickery humming in my vision, the same song I used to sing to my own kids when they were little.

I shook my head, squeezing my eyes shut, trying to silently will it to stop.

No, this isn't happening. Not now. Not here.

The pleas seemed to work, and the humming stopped. The radio was back to jumbled buzzing. I relaxed my shoulders, blinking very slowly. I tried to focus on something in the room to calm my nerves. I chose a dark corner of the basement, in the direction of where Santa stared, almost a straight line from his gaze.

A few boxes were stacked, and I focused on the cardboard, the angles of the corners, and tried to remain in the basement, tried to remind myself what was real. The three boxes I had chosen to stare at were marked "Suvi," the legging company's name written in a fancy pink cursive.

From Donna also, I assumed. Or maybe LuAnne had left them there after she pitched Donna.

The more I stared at them, the more I realized something was very wrong. One of the boxes was slowly opening. From the inside.

I stood, frozen—pulse skyrocketing, insides seizing—as I watched the flaps of the box begin to unfurl outward, like a flower blossoming. One at a time, they opened, gently, unseen hands peeling them away. A strangled cry rose and died in my throat as my vision tunneled, and all I could do was watch and stare.

Like a disjointed child with broken limbs climbing out of a crawl space, a pair of leggings with Fourth of July fireworks and "Happy Birthday America" written down the legs slowly pulled itself out of the box. One limb first moved out of the cardboard, sniffing around like wounded wildlife checking for danger. It lifted the end, the black space devoid of a leg, and looked at each of us. It looked like a worm surveying the landscape.

Sensing no danger, it placed the end of the leg on the ground, and from behind, the other leg followed, similarly looking around and checking out the basement to be sure it was safe.

I remained frozen. My body shook slightly, and I held my breath as I watched it place the other leg on the ground. There was a pause before the rest of the leggings slowly stood up, steadying itself on the two openings on the ground.

Then they unfurled upward, straightening out and smoothing out the wrinkles as the leggings filled out with an unseen body.

The clothing was opposite me, in a view that was blocked by the support beams in the basement.

It stood, twitching slightly.

A real-life MLM advertisement, sans human.

I lifted a shaking finger, pointing at it. "Nick—" I started to say as I felt Leo jump next to me. He reached forward and wrapped his arms around my waist and buried his head into my mid-section.

"Mom, who is that?" he whispered into my stomach.

So he had seen it, too.

I wrapped an arm tightly around his shoulders and put a hand on his head.

"Nick—" I said again, my voice trembling.

He didn't hear, as he was still next to Ethan fiddling with the weather radio.

I jolted as Piper screamed from across the room. She flung herself up out of the armchair and began to run around the basement, arms flailing.

"Ew. Ew. Ew. Ew. Ew. Ew. Did you see that? Kill it!" she said, her voice high and squeaky. She pointed down to a baseboard near the armchair.

"What?" Nick said as he rushed over.

"A roach! A gross crawly roach almost touched my hand!" She hopped up and down and pointed toward the empty ground.

Sophie screamed and jumped into my lap, nearly crushing her brother, who was still processing the trauma of seeing the leggings.

Ethan's booming laugh echoed across the basement. "That's just a palmetto bug. Regional mascot of the South."

"It's a roach. Kill it!" she shrieked, flailing her arms in the air as she scooted around Nick and came over toward me. Now I had all three kids nearly in my lap.

Nick bent down and examined the floor around the chair, finding nothing except a couple of old beer bottle caps. He looked at me and shrugged.

I carefully, slowly, slid my vision over to the corner, where the leggings had animated. They still stood there.

It was then that I realized they weren't just regular Suvi leggings. No, they were maternity leggings. As the pants had inflated and stood, so had the front panel of the waistband, stretching and expanding outward until the ghostly leggings looked like they were hugging a pregnant woman.

"How?" I tried to speak but it died in my throat. *How would they—how would anyone or anything—know?*

I understood the message, though: They knew. They knew I was pregnant.

As though the leggings had heard my thoughts and knew the message had been received, I saw them slowly beginning to deflate. A few wrinkles appeared across the front, horizontal lines. Then deeper creases appeared as they slowly melted into the ground, an empty pile of cotton and polyester.

I blinked a few times and leaned forward a little to make sure I had truly seen it. I had. The mail-order leggings were in a pile on the ground, next to the box.

I shut my eyes tightly and wrapped my arms around my kids.

Did I imagine it?

No, I couldn't have. Leo saw it, too.

Didn't he?

"Piper, you're just going to have to deal with it," Nick said as he ran a hand through his hair. "The bug is gone and won't come back to bother us."

"No, he's just telling his friends to come and hang out with us," she muttered under her breath. She turned to me, eyes wide. "Mom, I'm not having fun."

Girl, same.

I gave her a sympathetic look and put a hand on her head, smoothing back her long hair, which was tangled around her shoulders.

"I'm sorry," I whispered.

Then I silently added: *I don't know what we got ourselves into, but I would give anything to get out of it.*

Chapter 25

"Nick, I have to tell you something."

We stood outside Ethan's house the morning after the storm, packing Tammy and securing the turtle top. It was the first time we'd been alone since I took the pregnancy test.

"What's up?" he said as he stood on the running board, tightening the straps of the carrier.

"Nick?" I said, and he turned toward me, his expression one of slight confusion.

He stepped down from the running board and I deeply inhaled, ready to tell him.

"I took a—" I started to say before I was interrupted by a low whistle from Ethan. He emerged from the front door, surveying the storm damage in the yard.

"Well, hot damn," he called out, and he looked out over the fallen tree branches and party debris.

Annoyance and anger flooded my veins. It felt like we would never get a free moment alone for me to tell him. I was about to ask him to go inside so we could have some privacy when Piper appeared behind him.

Not the right time, I quickly realized. Because while I could probably stave off Ethan, Piper was too smart not to know something was going on.

"Nothing. We'll talk later," I said. I saw Nick hesitate, but his attention was diverted as his brother walked up to Tammy.

"Helluva night last night," Ethan said.

"You sure you don't want help with any of this before we leave?" Nick asked him. He gave the straps one final tug and muttered, "That's not going anywhere," before he turned back to his brother, eyebrows raised.

Ethan's front yard was littered with tree branches, debris from the party, and leaves from nearby trees. The storms had swept through the night before, and while there were no tornadoes reported, the damage appeared to be widespread.

Red Solo cups were everywhere, as were beer cans. A flag with a political message about stopping the steal was torn in half and covered part of our car. I was the lucky one who had gotten to remove that in the morning when we came out to survey the damage. Ethan had snatched it out of my hand and insisted he could fix it.

I didn't want to tell him that maybe the universe had sent him a message by tearing it in half, but I had learned early and often that it was best to pretend I didn't either hear or understand half of the things my in-laws said.

"Nah," Ethan said. He looked rough. He had a sheen coming off his face, and dark circles were parked under his red eyes. A faint odor of stale beer came from his pores, soaking his white tank top. "Some of my buddies are going to come over later and help."

Good enough for me.

I saw Nick hesitate, to insist we help him clean up, but I quickly opened the driver's-side door. I figured I should drive since Nick was in such rough shape. I had hoped to do some research on Jillian Samson from Tucson, Arizona, who owned the Vickery property, while Nick drove, but safety first and all that.

"Sounds good. We should get on the road."

I wanted to leave everything at Ethan's house behind us. All of it—from the drunken shenanigans, to the pregnancy test, to the self-animated leggings.

I didn't ask Leo what he had seen in the basement, ask him if he had seen what I had. I didn't want to further traumatize him if he had, or try to explain what it was I had seen if he hadn't.

Instead, after the storm had ended and our phones told us the coast was clear, I'd walked over to the leggings on the floor. My heart was pounding and my hands shaking, but before I could stop myself, I reached down and grabbed them off of the floor.

Part of my brain whispered the possibility that I might feel something solid inside of them.

But they were empty, just cheap fabric for pregnant women.

I did have a moment of hesitation before I quickly stuffed the leggings back into the box and closed it. I could actually use some pregnancy clothes. I had given away all of my maternity pants after I had Sophie, confident our infant years were behind us. Famous last thoughts.

I then grabbed another box, marked **NEWSPAPERS**, off the floor and placed it on top.

There. Try and get out of that one next time, asshole.

"It was great to see you all. You should come down every

summer," Ethan said as we hugged him goodbye. The kids were lined up along the car, waiting to say farewell, itching to plug in their devices. Perfect storm for a vacation meltdown.

I accepted a very sweaty and beer-soaked hug from Ethan, silently promising myself that we would never come back to stay with him—the Red Woods Inn seemed like the way to go—and then we were all journeying down the gravel driveway in Tammy. I watched as Ethan's figure grew smaller and smaller in the side mirror, until he was just a white blob waving.

I felt a slight pang of guilt at not telling him what I'd seen in the basement. What if the leggings reanimated and tried to attack him? Or worse?

But, really, whatever haunted the leggings wasn't a danger to Ethan. It was only a danger to me.

Something—or, terrifyingly, someone—was inside of me, attached to me, and was making these things happen. It wasn't situational or coincidental.

Something was trying to send me a message.

"Are you sure you're all right?" Nick said, his gaze moving from the windshield to me as I drove. "Did you want to talk about something?" he said in a lowered tone.

"Of course! No, nothing," I said brightly. My voice was too high. I sat in the driver's seat with my back ramrod straight. I looked like I was an enraptured attendee at a weekend Bible revival, and the lead speaker had finally taken the stage to save my soul and lead me into the promised land (for the low, low price of several hundred dollars).

"Leigh?" Nick said, suspicion in his voice. "What's going on?"

I stared straight ahead, chills running down my arms. I wanted more than anything to body swap, to replace the fear and anxiety pumping through my blood with normal worries like reservation confirmation numbers, possible room upgrades, and making sure the Magic Land tickets were loaded into the app on my phone.

To swap with someone who hadn't taken a pregnancy test and now had to wait to tell her husband until they were alone.

But, no. I was entirely in a different world and life.

"A lot," I finally said, my voice low. "We'll talk later."

I didn't know which "talk" I should start with. The strange visions? The leggings?

The pregnancy test? The fact that our lives had spectacularly changed in an instant, and I was terrified?

Or maybe just the fact that I never even wanted to go on this vacation and was only going along with it for the kids and for Nick, yet it seemed I was the one to pay the price.

"Leigh, are—" Nick had started to say when my phone began to chirp with an incoming FaceTime.

It was M.J.

"Who is it?" Leo said from the second row.

I didn't answer him and hit Accept for the FaceTime, setting my phone in the cupholder, angled toward me as I drove. There was a whoosh and M.J. and Kerry's faces filled the screen. They looked like they were in a restaurant. Behind them was a large floral arbor and a grass wall with a neon sign that said **ROSÉ ALL DAY**.

"I see you guys are at Moveable Feast," I said with a smile.

"Leigh! We caught you," M.J. said. From the bottom of the

screen, both of my friends lifted their wineglasses, pink liquid inside, and clinked the glasses together.

My eyes slid over to Nick, and I said, "I'm in the car right now. We just left my brother-in-law's place. We are all in the car," I repeated the last sentence so they would know not to launch into twenty questions, asking if Ethan was still Ethan and if my kids had driven me bonkers yet.

"Hey, Somersets!" Kerry said as she smiled. Her eyes twinkled as we made eye contact, and I tried to silently convey all that I felt in that look. "How's the trip? When do you arrive? Leigh, you look pretty bad. Are you getting any sleep?"

From a quick glance, I watched as a waiter appeared behind them and a white-shirted arm placed what looked to be a charcuterie board in front of my friends.

A pang of homesickness ran through me. In an alternate world, I would be sitting across from Kerry and M.J. at Moveable Feast, sipping a crisp rosé, and digging into that charcuterie platter. Instead, I had a half-eaten bag of gas station Cheetos in my lap, a positive pregnancy test wrapped in an old T-shirt in my suitcase, and a possible haunting.

"Thanks a lot! We get to Florida later today."

I hadn't even told my friends about our final stop. I had been in denial when it was planned, only half-listening to Nick's arrangements. I think I was also making dinner as he was talking to me, and I remember nodding and grunting as I pulled the garlic bread out of the oven, not really comprehending what I had agreed to until this very moment, two hours away from the stop.

"Did you guys get a nice hotel for your last night on the road?" M.J. asked as she popped a dried fig into her mouth. She squinted and leaned closer, until the screen was just the top of her face and the bottom of Kerry's.

I pressed my mouth into a tight line and nodded, raising my eyebrows. They knew what that meant.

"Oh no," Kerry said. "Dare I ask?"

"Nope," I said. I rolled my eyes. "I'll fill you in later, assuming I survive. How's everything at home?"

"Good! I got those soccer forms from the parent meeting like you asked," M.J. said as she tucked a strand of hair behind her ear. "They're looking for a new team mom since Candice Bloodgood is pregnant again. I gave them your name."

I snorted and shook my head. "You did not. Very funny."

M.J. laughed and Kerry groaned.

"Can you imagine having another baby now? Candice is—what—like forty-three?" Kerry said with a frown.

Yes, suddenly I can imagine that.

M.J. raised her eyebrows and a faraway look appeared on her face.

"No," Kerry said to her. "You can't have any more kids. You already can't fit your family into a normal car. Plus, your next kid would be an indoor theater kid, and Leigh and I would have to raise it while you guys were going to travel soccer tournaments."

M.J. laughed. "You're probably right. Never mind. But you never know!"

Indeed.

"I'll call you guys in the next couple of days and fill you in on everything," I said.

"Can't wait to hear where you guys are staying tonight!" M.J. said before I clicked off.

I put my phone back in my lap and there was silence in the car. The kids and Nick knew why. It was because we were doing something I had said I would never do, something that, while I had agreed to it, I couldn't believe was actually happening.

We were going camping for the night.

In Florida.

In the summer.

If the trip hadn't killed me yet, this definitely would.

Chapter 26

It was two hours to the Citrus Grove Campground and Family Fun Park, and I knew I needed to mentally and physically prepare for the overnight. I vaguely recalled that Nick had told me he had booked a cabin with a loft and a private bathroom, so it wasn't going to be tent camping. But close enough.

After ninety minutes on the road, Nick looked more like a human, so he offered to drive. I gladly switched since I was itching to find a certain Jillian Samson. With Nick in the driver's seat, I was finally able to scratch.

Google wasn't much help, and it took me through several wrong turns—congrats to Jill Samson in Phoenix for winning that 5K—until I finally located a Facebook page for a Jillian Samson in Tucson. I clicked on her profile, which had an American flag as the cover photo and a Bible quote as her profile picture. Neither looked like it had been updated in a long, long time. Under "About" she had typed out: **I don't give Facebook permission to use my photos.**

So I was less than optimistic that Jill regularly checked her page or even knew how to read Messenger notes. But I was desperate.

When my family was in the bathrooms at the next rest stop, I typed out a short message to Jillian, telling her that I was on a road trip with my family to Magic Land and we had passed through a town in Indiana, seen the farmhouse and land, and wanted to know more about them.

I realized before I hit Send that it all sounded creepy and like we were nefarious real estate investors, but I was too tired and too anxious to think of anything better.

After I sent the message, I placed my phone in my lap, trying to send good energy behind the request, praying Jillian Samson woke up that morning and decided to check her social media. And that she knew something that could help me. Maybe she would even want the locket back.

I reached forward for the backpack and unzipped the front pocket. I shoved my hand inside and pulled out the locket, holding the chain with two fingers so the charm spun wildly.

I eyed the V on the front as it circled in front of my face, then dropped the whole thing into my hand. I squeezed it, hard, and then slowly opened my palm, studying it. The metal left indentations in my palm when I squeezed it but didn't burn me, and I watched as the lines slowly plumped and faded.

The locket in my other hand, I opened the car door. I speed-walked toward the garbage can, making sure my family was still in the bathrooms, and stopped in front. McDonald's and Burger King brown bags were piled high in the can, precariously balancing in the rest area wind.

I held my fist, closed over the locket, over the trash and finagled a drop spot better than a *Price Is Right* contestant playing Plinko.

I started to open my hand but stopped. I wanted one last look at the locket before all of this was over.

Before I dropped it in the trash, my gaze landed on the hinges on the side. It had been empty when I opened it the first time, but for some reason, I felt compelled to check again.

I pressed the latch's release button quickly, and the locket swung open.

But it wasn't empty at all.

My hand began to shake with the locket in the center, making it bounce around on my skin.

Because in the center of the locket was a tooth. A baby tooth.

Sophie's lost tooth.

Chapter 27

I screeched as I looked down at the tooth and then quickly turned my hand to let the locket fall. It slipped down into the dirty blue trash can and quickly disappeared beneath the towering fast-food trash pile.

I saw my family coming out of the rest area's bathroom, grimaces on their faces that told me exactly how clean and sanitary the bathrooms were.

Still standing in front of the trash can, quaking, I took a step toward the bathrooms. I speed-walked past them, saying I really did have to go.

Once inside, I was afraid to touch anything. Everything was wet—the floors, the walls, the toilets, the trash cans.

I stood, ramrod straight, and stared in the mirror, trying to understand. Logic told me there was obviously no way Sophie's tooth could have gotten inside the locket.

Unless . . .

Unless one of the kids stole it as a prank and put it in there. But who? I couldn't imagine any of my kids taking a prank that far. Or being creepy enough to come up with something like that.

And Nick certainly wouldn't. He was having enough trouble keeping the dream of his perfect family vacation alive; he wouldn't risk pushing me over the edge and jeopardizing that.

I washed my hands, letting the cold water soothe the tingle in my palms. After I rinsed them off, I flicked my palms a few times, realizing they no longer hurt.

I slowly lifted my gaze to look in the dirty and cracked mirror. I froze as I saw the image in the mirror wasn't what I'd expected. No, not frazzled, tired Leigh.

Instead, I saw someone who was half me, half Patty Vickery.

My own eyes. The cheeks were longer, thinner than mine. The hair was auburn instead of my brown messy bun.

Patty.

I took a startled step backward, my heel sliding on the wet floor and never getting traction. My foot slipped out from under me, and I tried to put my hands down to cushion my fall, but I didn't get them down in time.

I crashed down on the concrete floor with a loud bang. My teeth chattered together as they absorbed the impact.

"Oh God. Gross," I said as I placed my palms down on the disgusting floor to hoist myself up.

I tried to push myself up with my palms, but I couldn't get enough traction, so I had to roll over and get onto all fours first, the bathroom floor sludge soaking my knees. My hip ached where I'd fallen on it. I shoved myself upward as quickly as possible, wiping my hands on my jean shorts. I held my arms out from my body in a ballet dancer's position and slowly walked out of the rest area, wet and moaning like a yeti.

I could hear my family's laughter from inside the car.

As I hobbled over to them, I couldn't help but smile and laugh, too. I realized how ridiculous I looked, and with the way that everything had gone so far, I was thrilled to hear their laughter, even if it was at my expense.

As I reached for Tammy's door handle, I started to laugh, too. And I decided not to say anything to any of them about the locket or tooth or what I'd seen in the mirror. I had thrown the locket away, so hopefully our troubles with the Vickerys would be over. And I wouldn't say a word about it to my family. Jillian Samson in Tucson, Arizona, probably wouldn't respond to my message, and I bet it wouldn't matter anyway.

I would keep quiet for their benefit, like a good mom.

"'Florida Man Arrested for Stealing Shoes from Walmart.'

"'Florida Man in Jail After Running Naked Through Church.'

"'Florida Man Picked Up After Threats to Eat Corn Flakes to Death.'

"Should I keep going?" Piper sat in the third row, proudly announcing every Florida Man headline she could find on Google. While Nick and I had laughed along at the first fifty headlines, as she continued, the humor dwindled and reality set in. While none of us were going to steal shoes from Walmart, I didn't doubt that we could find a way to be featured in a "Florida Family" headline.

"Okay, okay. Let's give Florida Man a rest. We're not too far away," Nick said. He adjusted himself in the driver's seat and sat up straight to stretch his back. He looked less tired than he had before, but worry and stress still creased his face.

I had kept up a steady stream of conversation and questions to

Nick and the kids, until Piper finally interrupted me with her Florida Man information. I wondered if she really had wanted to tell us about those or if she just wanted a topic that would shut me up.

"Why can't we just keep going all the way to Magic Land?" Leo said with a frown.

I turned around in the passenger seat. "Because . . ." I trailed off as I tried to remember why. Truth was, I was asking myself the same question. I'd rather have slept in the car for the night than have another cup of bad motel—well, the office at the campground—coffee.

"Because it's fun." Nick's voice was tight, and I could tell he was straining to keep positive.

"Magic Land is fun. Not camping," Leo said as he rolled his eyes. "I want to go on the Mystic Twister."

"Yeah! And I want to go on the unicorn carousel!" Sophie added, her face brightening. "Why can't we go there now?"

"They're right," Piper said. "This is stupid."

With their collective voices, the kids had managed to fully extinguish any wind Nick still had left in his sails. I saw his hands clutch the steering wheel as he blinked slowly, eyes on the road.

I waited for him to say something optimistic, something positive, as he always did to bring our family out of a funk. He'd once managed to turn things around after a storm wiped out our power, causing our sump pump to fail and our basement to flood. Somehow, some way, he made us laugh.

But, nothing. He simply continued staring straight ahead, blinking slowly.

"Because it's fun!" I said as brightly as I could muster. "It's going to be great!" My voice cracked in the middle of the sentence. "And hey, I just realized I never passed out the Florida prizes." I raised my eyebrows in exaggerated surprise.

None of the kids so much as looked at me.

"Guys? The state prizes?" I said in an even tone.

"I don't even want any more prizes," Leo said, and Piper nodded.

"Soph?" I said, hopeful that my last state bribe would be successful. It was the one thing I'd contributed to the planning of this trip while Nick and I brainstormed. My one good idea.

She shrugged and then looked out the window.

I had successfully managed to push what had happened at the rest stop out of my brain. But seeing the kids slowly losing their cheer and excitement throughout the trip threatened to break me.

"Well, we can wait for the state prizes until later, I guess," I said. I glanced at Nick, who still stared blankly. I gently touched his arm. "You okay, honey?"

He didn't look at me, just slowly nodded. I turned my head forward and folded my hands in my lap.

We were all breaking. Even Nick.

"Look! Isn't that where we're going?" Leo pointed to a billboard in the distance.

"Citrus Grove Campground and Family Fun Park," Nick said. "Yup, that's our next stop."

The car was silent as we passed the billboard for Citrus Grove. It looked like it hadn't been updated since Nixon was in office. It was a picture of a lake surrounded by tall pine trees, with a cabin in the background. All peeling and faded.

At the bottom, a slogan: **GET LOST IN NATURE**.

"I do not wish to get lost in nature, Nick. For the record," I said with a laugh. The grim reality of what we were doing was starting to set in.

I had never been camping before.

I had never wanted to go camping before.

Yet here I was, at the tail end of what was the most stressful and bizarre vacation of my life, about to go camping.

In Florida.

In June.

"'Citrus Grove: two miles this way,'" Nick muttered to himself as he turned off the highway onto a dusty white gravel road.

Tammy bumped and lurched along the country road, slowing down for water-filled potholes and branches randomly scattered along the ground.

Thick forest lined the gravel driveway. The trees formed a canopy over the car, and it grew dark enough that I could only make out the kids' shapes in the back but not their features.

I opened my phone and saw that I had, thankfully, three bars, so at least we weren't starring in a horror movie where phones don't work. I typed out a quick text to M.J. and Kerry.

> **About to arrive at a Florida campground. Will report back. Keep that prayer circle up.**

I had decided not to tell my friends about the locket, either. I had other horrors to share with them.

When I was twelve, we took a weekend family vacation to St. Joseph's, Michigan. It was back during the years when my parents were still trying to give their marriage a go, back before the times when we were in the newspaper.

My mother had gotten the glowing idea that we should go away for Labor Day weekend together. And she picked the Lake View Motel, a small establishment on the shores of Lake Michigan just past town in St. Joseph's. She chose it because my father had spent a few weekends there as a child and she was hoping the nostalgia would score some points. Or at least put him in a good mood for the weekend.

As we pulled into the parking lot of the motel my father had visited thirty years before, we all realized at the same time that it hadn't been touched in thirty years.

Thirty years of the same bedsheets, comforters, remote controls, carpeting, and shower tile. There was a small pool that seemed to be the big draw, and a hot tub. The hot tub was located in a glorified gardening shed that locked from the outside, and to use it, one had to pay by the minute.

On one unfortunate afternoon, we accidentally got locked in and were only discovered after the front desk clerk realized we had paid for fifteen minutes and it had been twenty-five without any sign of us emerging.

Ten extra-long minutes of banging on the door to the hot tub shed and calling out for someone to help us.

We left after the front desk clerk freed us, and that was our last trip to St. Joe's. Actually, to the entire state of Michigan. We had never gone back. And after a year, there was no more "we" anyway.

I always thought that would be the worst vacation I had ever taken, that the crown jewel of disastrous vacations had already happened. Nothing to fear from future vacations.

Except the Citrus Grove Campground and Family Fun Park in Victory, Florida.

Tammy made it through the long winding road toward the check-in area of the motor resort. It was really a small clearing with a few metal lawn chairs placed in a circle, facing each other, with a smoldering pit of coal in the center, metal skewers that had long disposed of their s'mores propped up next to it.

An old, cream and brown trailer had a dry-erase board on the exterior with *Check In* written on it with a flourish.

A bicycle with the front tire missing rested against the steps leading up to the trailer.

Nick put the car into Park in front of it and we all sat silently for a minute, absorbing the surroundings.

"Look, a doggie!" Sophie said, and pointed out of her window. A thin, not-friendly-at-all black dog was sniffing around the perimeter, looking ready for the Junkyard Dog Show.

"Lassie better go pull Timmy from the well," I muttered as I unbuckled my seat belt. "I'll go check us in."

I hopped out of the car before Nick could stop me, closing the door quickly, his mouth still open.

I gingerly climbed up the rickety wooden steps to the trailer, certain my foot was about to go clean through, wooden splinters shoving themselves into the skin around my ankle.

"Hello? Checking in the Somerset family," I called through the door, giving the metal storm door a couple of quick raps. When no one appeared, I repeated the knocking.

I turned back to the car and shrugged, lifting my palms in the air. I tried the door to the trailer. Locked.

A metal scratching sound, and I looked down and saw the mail slot toward the bottom of the door was slowly opening. I took a quick step back, stumbling a little, and watched as a key attached to a plastic placard dropped out of the mail slot, hand unseen.

I bent down and saw it was a gold key, with *Cabin 7* on the placard dangling from the metal. I picked it up and walked back to the car, holding it between my two fingers.

"Customer service is top-notch," I said to Nick as I climbed back into Tammy. "Cabin seven, here we come."

I waved goodbye to the junkyard dog, who was warily watching us drive back down, following the signs for **CABINS/OUTHOUSES**.

"Outhouses? Do we have to go to the bathroom outside?" Piper said, her voice squeaky.

"Only if you misbehave," I said. I looked over at Sophie, whose eyes were wide as she took in the forest surrounding the car. "You okay, Soph?"

She slowly lowered her chin and pressed her lips together. After a moment, she whispered, "They're here with us." Then she smiled, wide enough so I could see where she was missing her tooth.

Chapter 28

"Yes. I will get the conditioner out of the red bag in a second. Just let me go to the bathroom," I called out as I quickly shut the bathroom door in our cabin.

When Citrus Grove had advertised "rustic cabins," they weren't fucking around. Our humble abode for the night was a twenty-foot-tall structure with a great room, a small dorm room fridge, a bathroom with a sink and shower, and a microwave. It was like sleeping in a much larger, slightly tricked-out Tammy.

There was a ladder that led to a loft area, for which we had brought a blow-up mattress for Piper and another for Nick and me, and the small kitchen table folded down into a bed that would sleep Sophie and Leo.

As we put our bags down on the floor, a feeling of suffocation began to build in my chest. It was too much. Too much togetherness, too many stressors. The bathroom was the only place where I could escape.

I splashed some cold water on my face, refusing to look in the mirror. Out of the corner of my eye, I didn't see the reflection of the woman that I had last time, but I wasn't going to give her the satisfaction of searching for her.

I leaned forward and closed my eyes and took a few long, slow, deep breaths. It felt like the walls were closing in on me, and I couldn't keep track of everything I needed to hide, everything I needed to figure out.

I wanted more than anything to tell Nick about the pregnancy test, but the more hours ticked by without my telling him, the harder it felt to bring it up.

Never mind finding Sophie's tooth, the locket, and my increasing visions of the Vickerys.

Get a grip. Get your shit together. You're a mom of three kids and a successful lawyer. You like gardening. You pulled up flower beds full of English ivy ground cover last year while listening to a murder podcast that Kerry had recommended. You're married to Nick. You love him. You'll be able to handle another baby.

Yet none of it felt familiar anymore.

None of it felt safe.

"Mom, the conditioner?" Piper's voice came out like an accusation.

"Coming!"

"This has to be one of Florida's greatest landmarks." Nick chuckled as he looked up at the neon sign in the parking lot of the restaurant the kids had chosen for dinner.

We had passed by the gray clapboard shack before we turned down Misty Pines Drive to the campground. The color of the building was unassuming-dark, drab, looking like it would blend in during hurricane cleanup, but the outside was dotted with various brightly colored signs. They detailed things like **KIDS EAT FREE ON MONDAYS** and **MUD WRESTLING COMPETITION ON WEDNESDAY**.

For some reason, that piqued my kids' interest.

So that's how we wound up eating at Fudlicker's for dinner.

The inside of the restaurant was set up like a beach shack, with fake netting on the walls and plastic dead fish that were supposed to look like trophies. The server who greeted us and brought us to our table wore a fishing hat and fishing shirt with multiple pockets.

"Welcome to Fudlicker's. I'm Jake and I'll be your server tonight. I'll give you guys a minute to look over the menu." Jake deposited sticky plastic menus on the table and turned away, walking in a manner that made it clear he wanted to run far, far from us but propriety (and his financial status) dictated that he walk politely.

"Well, what fried abomination am I going to treat myself to tonight?" I said as I reached for a menu. I rolled my eyes and smiled at Nick. The kids were surprisingly quiet, worn out by all of the driving. Not to mention the ghosts, tornadoes, and uncomfortable beds. Tonight two of them would get the treat of sleeping on a table converted to a bed. Lucky ducks.

"Do I dare order the crab legs?" Nick muttered as he scanned the menu.

"You do not. They're fifty-four dollars, according to the sign out front. Fudlicker's isn't a place where you order anything that could be listed as 'market price,'" I said without looking up. I was trying to decide between the chicken fingers, mozzarella sticks, and popcorn shrimp. I figured any of those played to Fudlicker's strengths.

"Fettuccine Alfredo," Sophie said proudly as she slid the kids menu across the table, knocking over the plastic cup of crayons.

"Soph, I would order something different," Piper said, her nose wrinkling as she scanned the regular menu. "Like mac and cheese. It even says it's Kraft brand here."

Sophie's face darkened, and her brows lowered. "No. Fettuccine."

Piper gave me a look and then shook her head. I waited to see if Nick would jump in and weigh in, but he seemed absorbed in choosing between the full boil with corn and potatoes and the half boil with only corn.

"There's only one bathroom in our cabin so everyone should choose accordingly," I announced. Popcorn shrimp it was. Although food poisoning would be particularly appropriate at that juncture, given all that we had experienced. At least I had gotten rid of the awful locket and hopefully all of its eerie juju.

A young couple with a little girl walked past our table, toward the exit. The little girl had a Little Mermaid costume on, and I smiled. She looked about four years old, and Sophie wouldn't leave the house without wearing some ridiculous ensemble at that age. Halloween costumes, bathing suits, princess dress-up outfits, all of it. The fact that I might get to experience something like that again made me smile. One bright side.

"What's up?" Nick said as he looked up from his menu. "What are you smiling at?"

"Oh." I adjusted my posture and sat up straighter. I realized it would be a perfect opportunity to tell him I was pregnant.

I glanced at the kids, and Piper looked over. "What?" she said.

No, it wasn't the right time. Too many ears.

"That little girl is so cute. She—" I stopped and shrank back as she started screaming after the tiara fell off her head. She turned bright red and closed her eyes, balling up her fists, as her parents tried to frantically shove the tiara back on, to no avail. Finally, the dad picked her up and carried her out of the restaurant over his shoulder like a sack of potatoes.

Never mind. I had forgotten about that part of small childhood.

"Ew," Piper muttered as she watched the display.

I pressed my lips together and looked down at the menu again.

"I really thought I had it," Nick said dejectedly, looking at his dinner plate, a crab legs graveyard. Random pieces of shell were scattered around the plate and a few rested on the table, having been pushed off by his aggressive cracking and finagling.

Yet one cluster remained, still attached to the joint. Its pristine appearance mocked Nick, who had been certain he could finish the whole plate—ten pounds—and thus earn himself a free dinner. According to the wall of fame that our waiter, Jake, had pointed out when we ordered, only three other individuals had accomplished the feat. I didn't ask if they were all dead from coronary artery disease.

I patted his shoulder sympathetically. "I know. But I think you're a close runner-up."

He stared forlornly at the crab cluster on his plate. He reached for the claw cracker, hesitating, before sighing and putting it back down on the table, admitting defeat.

After the bill came, and we got the extreme pleasure of paying in full for Nick's crab legs, we moved over to the attached gift shop. None of us were ready to go back to the cabin and sit in silence or individually watch random content on our electronics.

"Mom, look! Gators!" Leo pointed to a corner of the gift shop, hopping up and down a little from the excitement.

Of course there were alligators. This was Florida.

I followed Leo through the gift shop, twisting in between the circular racks of T-shirts that said things like **I GOT LICKED AT FUDLICKER'S**. Charming. In the back of the gift shop, next to a man who looked like he had a concealed carry permit, was a small plastic child's pool with two baby alligators inside, unmoving. Probably contemplating how the trajectory of their lives had led them here, to a gift shop inside Fudlicker's.

I honestly was wondering the same thing.

"Ten dollars to pet them. Twenty bucks to hold one for a picture." The alligator wrangler didn't even look up from his phone.

A hand from behind me moved across my shoulder, clutching a twenty-dollar bill.

"Nick . . . ," I'd started to say when Piper and Sophie appeared behind him. They shouldered past him and me and stood next to Leo, ready for the photo.

Alligator Man finally stood up and pocketed his phone, reaching out to accept the twenty dollars. Then he bent down with a flourish and picked up one of the gators, who didn't even move his eyeballs before he was handed to Piper. She stood, holding the alligator out perpendicular to her body like it was a bomb.

Leo and Sophie gathered on either side of Piper, frozen smiles on their faces.

I laughed and reached into my pocket to pull out my phone for a picture, but Nick already had his out. He snapped the picture and then showed me. I nearly doubled over from laughing. It was a perfect hostage photo, one that encapsulated the entire trip in one quick click: everyone looked terrified, but with huge smiles because it was supposed to be fun.

"Thanks, man. The pictures are great," Nick said as he shook his head.

The handler grabbed the alligator from Piper and deposited it back into the plastic pool. Then he stood and stared at us, waiting.

"C'mon, kids. Wasn't that fun?" I said brightly, watching him out of the corner of my eye. He continued to stare at us, and I had visions of kidnapping and tearful appearances on *Dateline* cloud my vision.

Then I realized what he wanted: a tip.

I looked over at Nick and jerked my head slightly toward the alligator guy. I didn't have any cash.

Nick quickly caught on and reached back into his pocket and pulled out his wallet. There was one one-hundred-dollar bill inside. Not exactly proportional to the need.

I bent down to pick up a Woodman's Food Market receipt that had fluttered to the ground, near the handler's boots. As I reached for it, I heard Nick say, "Goddamn it." Followed by several not-kid-friendly words as he rifled through the various compartments of his wallet.

I snatched the receipt and stood up, the kids all groaning at hearing their father use profanity.

Nick shook his head and patted at his pockets again. Now Alligator Man was really getting agitated. We had to get out of there.

"Dad, let's go," Leo said.

"Here," Nick finally said, shoving forward the one-hundred-dollar bill. "It's all I have," he said with resignation.

"Hey, thanks, man."

Nick just nodded, as graciously as he could.

As we turned to walk out of the restaurant, Piper said, "Dad, why did you give that guy a hundred bucks? That was way too much."

"All I had," he repeated, his tone flat. Gone was the childlike excitement for the trip, the ability to laugh off whatever sticks were thrown into our spokes. No, he was right in the shit with the rest of us.

I kept walking behind the kids, sidestepping a family pushing a double stroller and wearing looks of grim resignation as they walked past a waitress selling Shit in the Grass shots off a tray by the entrance.

Nick reached the car first, opening the driver's-side door. He paused as he watched the kids approach and then glanced inside the open door. He did a double take and then slowly turned to face the seat, his back to us.

Something was wrong. I could tell by the way his shoulders stiffened and his arms were frozen down by his sides.

Oh no. What now?

I jogged up behind him and tapped him on the shoulder. He slowly turned, his face stricken and eyes wide. He turned his head and gestured toward the seat. I peered around him and saw it: his TripTik, sitting on the driver's seat. Where we definitely had not left it.

"Kids?" he said as he pointed to the booklet. "Did one of you do this?"

I shook my head. "The kids? No way. They've been with us the whole time. We all left the car together, remember?"

Piper elbowed me out of the way and looked at the TripTik. "Oh, cool. You found it. Now you can be happy, Dad." Then she turned and climbed into Tammy.

"Where did it come from? I wasn't sitting on it the whole time," Nick said. He looked rattled, afraid, confused. He looked the way I felt.

"Nick, I really can't explain anything that's happened on this trip," I said quietly. "I'm glad you have the TripTik back, though." I lifted my hand to rub his arm but lowered it without touching him. I didn't know what I was supposed to say or how I could help him process what had happened.

"Me too," he finally said before he carefully lifted the TripTik off of the seat and slowly tapped the sticker on the front that read **SOMERSET**. "Well, it's definitely ours." He put the booklet on the console and got into the van.

"At least we got it back," I said grimly as I settled into the passenger seat.

"I don't feel good," Leo moaned, and closed his eyes. Before I could react, he threw up, all over the back of the car.

"Mom. Mom, wake up. Mom!" Piper's disembodied voice floated through my dream. I was standing in the middle of a grocery store, trying to decide what ice cream flavor to buy. Dream Leigh really wanted rocky road, but they only had cookies and cream and cookie dough. A true conundrum.

I felt a hand on my shoulder and my body move around.

Piper was shaking me. But I really needed to decide on the ice cream.

"Mom!" she shout-whispered in my ear.

That did it. I opened my eyes and slowly sat up, my vision adjusting to the dark shape of her next to the bed. Nick was still fast asleep.

"What are you doing? What time is it?" I glanced over at the end table next to me and saw the time: 4:18 a.m.

"Mom, my phone charger doesn't work. Can I take yours?" she said. She didn't wait for me to answer before she unplugged it, making me wonder why she had woken me up at all.

I rubbed my forehead as I hissed an agreement. I tried to close my eyes and return to sleep after she left, but I kept picturing the Vickerys' ghostly hands carefully replacing the TripTik.

I sighed and reached for my (now unplugged) phone. I swiped through my apps, not really sure what I was looking for, until I saw the Messenger app had a notification. My heart beat faster as I tapped on it.

I had a message from Jillian Samson, sent while we were battling alligators at Fudlicker's.

> Hello,
>
> Thank you for your message. I do have information on that property and would be willing to share. It is easier to explain over the phone. You are welcome to call me anytime.

I stared at her phone number, the digits displayed with a blue line under them. All I had to do was click on the line and it would call Jillian, maybe, possibly, someone who could give me some real answers.

Yet if my calculations on the time zones were correct, it was almost one thirty in Arizona. And Jillian did not seem like someone who would be partying all night. The phone call would have to wait.

Besides, I needed to rest since we were finally reaching Magic Land the next day. It required all of my energy and mental faculties to present the appropriate amount of excitement—at least at having our road trip come to an end for seven days. Honestly, I never wanted to see the inside of Tammy ever, ever again.

Chapter 29

"We aren't going to make the admission adventure today, but we will tomorrow," Nick said, his voice apologetic, as we left Citrus Grove for our first day at Magic Land.

"Admission adventure?" I said.

He nodded and eased Tammy onto the highway. "Admission adventure. I told you about this, remember? The admission adventure is when the park opens and everyone lines up to be the first to run into the park and get on the best rides. I really wanted us to make it today, but—" He shook his head.

"I must have forgotten. I'm sorry," I said. I didn't remember him ever telling me about an admission adventure, but there was probably an ocean of Magic Land trivia and vernacular that he had tried to teach me, only for it to disappear into the ether of my brain.

I looked out the window, wishing I had told Nick about the test. But it was for me, really. Whether he was happy at the news or not, it would cast a shadow on the trip and change the focus. This was supposed to be Nick's dream trip and core memories for the kids. The Vickerys had already changed that, and even though it was nearly impossible to keep the secret for much longer, I decided as I watched the tall pines on either side of the highway whoosh past that I would wait.

I would wait until we got home, after the trip, to tell Nick. Or at least until after we had visited Magic Land.

Three hours later, the air was thick with theme park anticipation as Nick turned Tammy down Magic Land Way, the long, winding entrance road. We had started to see signs for the park as we grew closer to Orlando. At first, it was things like **MAGIC LAND: 30 MILES**, which wasn't quite as exciting, but the fever pitch in the car began to climb as we watched the mileage to our destination decrease.

Even Nick, who somehow had managed to keep his cool for most of the morning, began talking in staccato, like he had suddenly ingested a whole suitcase full of cocaine and was now going to tell us every piece of Magic Land history he had ever heard.

"The park officially opened on June 1, 1987, at eight a.m., with a red-ribbon cutting ceremony even though there was a tornado warning . . ." He continued on, his words melting together into white noise.

I glanced back and all of the kids were silent, sitting in stunned excitement, at hearing their father officially lose his mind.

Finally, Sophie squealed and put her hands over her mouth. Leo rolled his eyes but couldn't hide the glee on his face. Even Piper's teenage ennui paused for a moment and she threw her hands in the air.

I put a hand on Nick's shoulder. "You okay?" I said with a laugh.

He smiled. "I'm just so happy we're finally here." What he left unsaid was his presumption that all of the trouble was behind us, now that we had reached Magic Land's heavenly gates.

I murmured in agreement and nodded. At least our road trip was over.

"One mile!" Sophie screamed from behind me, and I jumped, spilling the to-go cup of coffee I had in my hand all over my lap.

"It's okay, it's okay," I laughed as I reached down for some napkins to soak it up. I was just happy, after everything we had endured, that we had this moment. We would always have this moment: the few minutes where everything was worth it.

Nick threaded the car through the crowded parking lot. Families were setting up full tailgates from the back of their cars: card tables, charcuterie platters, Magic Land flags, and someone even had a small charcoal grill.

It looked like we had missed a very important Magic Land vacationer memo.

"They must eat out here to avoid the food prices inside," Nick said, echoing my thoughts.

"That seems like a lot of work," I said as I watched someone setting up an elaborate fruit display. "But they don't look like they're messing around."

Those people must have been the Facebook group moderator types, who knew everything and anything about visiting a Magic Land park and had the whole thing down to a science, including logging on to the website when they opened dinner reservations thirty days in advance at midnight.

I had thought about doing that but had fallen asleep doing a client motion, and by the time I woke up, every reservation was booked. Probably by the people currently tailgating in the parking lot.

Nick finally pulled into an empty spot (for the low cost of eighty-seven dollars for the day), which looked like it was two miles from the park's entrance.

"Well, let's get to it," I said. We were lined up outside of Tammy, taking a few deep breaths, just having had a few sips of Gatorade and water to hydrate us for our parking lot trek.

"You guys heard your mom," Nick said. He clapped and motioned for us to follow him across the parking lot. "This is going to be the best day of our lives."

"Mr. Mystero!" Leo and Sophie shouted as we approached the park's entrance gate. We were covered in sweat, panting a little, overwhelmed a lot. It had taken almost a half hour to walk to the gates. And then as we approached the entrance, I pulled out my phone and started double-checking that the tickets were in my Apple Wallet. Unfortunately, my phone kept freezing, so I walked slower, and soon I was several paces behind.

But I did hear the excited outbursts as Leo and Sophie spotted the first character walking around.

The mascot was a classic Mr. Mystero character, with the black and white tuxedo top, black pants, and top hat. He stood next to the entrance gate, waving slowly at everyone, his eponymous smile pasted on his face courtesy of the costume's head.

"Whoever is in there has to be melting," I said. I glanced upward, squinting in the sunlight. The actual temperature was close to ninety. With the humidity and all of the concrete and asphalt, it felt somewhere north of a hundred degrees. I couldn't imagine being encased in stuffing, waving to toddlers who were about to have the most epic, expensive meltdown of their parents' lives.

I paused as I walked through three arches of water misting, enjoying the beauty and break from the heat as I entered the park's gates.

I turned and waved too enthusiastically at the Mr. Mystero character, trying to get hyped for the theme park. The kids began to lose their minds as we approached the ticketing gate. It reached a near fever pitch, with Nick included, as I pulled out my phone to let the attendant scan my tickets.

"So, Mystic Twister first, right, guys?" Nick said from behind me.

"Yes!" they all replied in unison.

I had heard their plans for the order of the rides for weeks at that point. At first, it was the carousel as the first ride, but that slowly changed based on what Nick learned from the message boards and Facebook groups that he joined. At least I knew that if I died any time soon, Nick could easily have a boatload of Magic Land–loving women to choose from as his next wife. The catch of the Magic Land Facebook groups.

"Why is Mr. Mystero doing that?" I heard Sophie say from behind me. I swiped at my phone, bringing up another ticket, and looked over to where she was pointing.

Off to the side of the entrance gates, about twenty feet from us, Mr. Mystero stood under an arch that displayed a sign: **Welcome to Magic Land, folks! Mr. Mystero invites you to explore his home. Experience the thrills of the rides and the wonders of his magic! But first, take a picture with him to start your journey!**

When we'd seen him from afar, Mr. Mystero had been enthusiastically waving at people and stopping to take a picture with families, arms around their shoulders.

But now his arms were down at his sides, and he was staring straight at us.

I watched as a family approached him with big smiles, waving frantically and motioning for Mr. Mystero to join in on the picture with their twin girls in matching dresses.

Yet it was like he didn't hear them. He continued to stare straight at us, arms by his sides, even as the family asked again.

"Next ticket?" the gate attendant said impatiently.

"Oh, sorry. Right," I said as I swiped through the last two tickets.

I looked over at Mr. Mystero. He was still staring at us, still ignoring the increasingly desperate family, before they finally gave up and walked away.

"I think Mr. Mystero is having an off day," Nick whispered to me with a laugh.

"Let's get a picture, Mom!" Leo said as he pointed toward Mr. Mystero and then broke out into a slow jog toward him.

A strangled protest died in my throat as he ran off. I shrugged at Nick and followed my son over to Mr. Mystero, who still hadn't changed his stance.

"Hey, Mr. Mystero! Can we get a picture with the family?" Nick said. He immediately began to scan the crowd to ask someone to take our picture with his phone.

"Mom? This feels weird," Piper whispered in my ear. "He looks like an NPC."

I racked my brain for the acronym before it hit me: non-player character. A character in a video game coded to give predetermined answers and actions, without any self-awareness.

I turned to her and nodded slowly, stealing glances out of the corner of my eye.

"Spooky," was all I said back.

Nick finally located an older couple wearing matching T-shirts and pristine white shoes and handed over his phone to the woman. It was a smart move—we had too many wonky pictures of us taken by male strangers.

"Ready?" he said with a smile as he jogged over.

"Kids?" I said too brightly, still eyeing Mr. Mystero. He hadn't moved.

"C'mon, c'mon," Nick said, motioning for us to group around the character.

Nick stood in the back, next to Mr. Mystero, and I was on the other side of him, so he was in the middle. Piper stood next to me, and Leo and Sophie lined up in the front.

"Say, 'Magic Land,'" Nick said as the woman holding his phone stepped forward and aimed it at us. After she was finished, Nick jogged over to thank her and swiped through the pictures. "They look great," he said. He glanced up from his phone and looked at Mr. Mystero. "Tired today?"

Mr. Mystero still hadn't moved. It was like he had turned to stone.

"Well, okay, then," Nick said with a slight eye roll. "Mystic Twister, up next."

I glanced back at Mr. Mystero as I followed my family in the direction of the ride. He was still staring at me, unmoving. Like he was afraid.

Behind him was the marquee for the Sorcerer's Showplace,

advertising the daily shows. Today was *The Magician's Secret*, showing at two forty-five p.m.

I stood and waited for what I already knew was coming.

I watched as the start time for the show blinked and then the numbers melted together, pooling and then birthing a new time: eleven fifteen.

I raised my eyebrows at it. *I see you*. Then I slowly blinked until the numbers switched back to two forty-five p.m. At the same time, a smiling father wearing a Magic Land top hat walked by, humming "You Are My Sunshine."

The Vickerys were at the park with us; there would be no reprieve.

➡

No one with a heart condition, missing limbs, or who is pregnant may ride Mystic Twister.

I eyed the warning sign as we waited in the switchbacks for Mystic Twister. I had passed the sign five times as we snaked through the metal labyrinth.

I can't ride Mystic Twister. But how can I get out of it? I have to fake some kind of illness or injury. Why didn't I think of that before? Why didn't I just tell Nick that the test was positive? I could have even gone straight to the hotel and sat by the pool—alone.

"Nick? My stomach is hurting a little," I tried to say casually, to start planting the seed of why I wouldn't be getting on Mystic Twister.

"Oh really? Do you think a funnel cake would help?" Nick said earnestly.

"No, Nick. I'm just going to take some deep breaths and hopefully I will feel better," I said. I gave him an encouraging smile, knowing that my "upset stomach" wasn't going away any time soon and I would quickly be relegated to the snack bar for all of the thrill rides.

I turned toward Leo, hoping Nick wouldn't ask any more questions.

"Excited?" I patted Leo on the shoulder.

He turned and gave me a grin that softened my insides. "Yes!" he said. "I can't believe we're really here! I'm going to dominate on Mystic Twister."

I nodded, a serious look on my face. "Of course you are. I'm sure the employees here were warned about you. No one can stop Leo Somerset."

He raised his eyebrows and nodded. "I'm going to crush it," he whispered, mostly to himself.

My irritation and annoyance and fear over everything that had happened on our trip melted away—at least for a few seconds—because no matter what nightmares I would have for years afterward, my kids were happy.

"Still don't feel very well. Go ahead. I'll be waiting for you at the bottom of the exit ramp." I said it all very quickly and very much as I was stepping through the ride to the other side, before my family could protest or try to stop me.

I stood off to the side and watched my family secure their safety harnesses on the ride. I waved to them as the train left the station and then slowly walked down the exit ramp, watching them twist through the first corkscrew.

I found an empty park bench that was only partially covered in melted ice cream and collapsed down onto it.

We had made it to the park, the entire reason for the road trip. But instead of arriving at the theme park with renewed bonds and shared family memories, I was exhausted, terrified, and in shock.

The Vickerys, the locket, Sophie's tooth, the positive test. All of it. I felt like I was keeping so much inside, so many emotions, that my chest would explode. No one fully understood what I was feeling, and I realized that was entirely my fault for keeping things secret.

It was exactly what my mom had done.

Screw that, I thought.

I picked up my phone to call my friends but then set it back down. I needed to talk to Nick first, not M.J. or Kerry. I needed to lay everything out for him, let him try to help, and I was quickly becoming aware of how little I had let him in. It was time to fully open the door—just as soon as we were out of this cursed park.

I opened the Messenger app and clicked on the note from Jillian Samson.

Call me anytime.

I tapped the numbers and the phone began to ring.

Chapter 30

"Oh, that is so wonderful that you are on a trip with your family. What a blessing," Jillian Samson from Tucson, Arizona, said after I had sputtered out an explanation as to who I was.

"It's been a lot. But we are grateful to have the time together," I said, a wide smile pasted on my face even though she couldn't see me. "We're at the park right now, actually."

"I was told Patty just loved trips. They all did," she said with a soft laugh that morphed into sadness.

I cleared my throat. "I'd love to know more about her. What would you feel comfortable telling me?"

Another soft, sad chuckle. "Well, it was such a tragedy. The fire and all that. You know"—her voice lowered another octave—"the police and fire department were never able to find their remains. That was the hardest part, honestly."

"Yes, I believe I read that. I'm so sorry." My breath hitched as I paused, trying to figure out how to ask what she thought had happened.

"'Course everything I know about what happened is secondhand. I've never even been to Indiana. Born and raised here in the desert," she said. "So I never met Patty or Greg, or any of the kids. I only heard about them from relatives."

I've met them, I wanted to say. *In fact, they won't leave me alone.*

"What a tragedy," she mused. "A whole family, just gone. You know, everyone always said that all Patty wanted her whole life was to be a mom. Three, four, five kids." Jillian made a muted noise that dissolved into reverence. "Everyone said she would have had more kids if . . ."

I sat up straight on the bench. The air was suddenly thicker and warmer, making it hard to inhale. Thick clumps of oxygen sat in my lungs, invisible tendrils grabbing on and refusing to move.

Patty's dreams had died in the fire: her three kids.

I thought of Greg's funeral card. So many lives lost in one family. So much pain. And for what? Why?

"Just a tragedy," Jillian said again, her voice even.

"When I saw—" I stopped, unwilling to finish. Jillian, whom I had found out was a second cousin to Patty, didn't need to know I had been inside the Vickery house, seen the family, felt them swirl around me.

"Anywho, do you have a price in mind?" Her voice had changed to all-business.

"A price?" I said, rubbing my forehead. *Does she want money for information?*

"You'd have to clear it out, I'd imagine, but as I said, I've never been to the property." Jillian sounded impatient, and I realized she thought I was calling to buy the Vickery land. That we had stumbled upon the house and seen a business opportunity.

"Oh. I'm sorry if there was a miscommunication, but we aren't looking to purchase the plot," I said evenly.

Jillian Samson did not appreciate that, and the conversation ended abruptly, with me still sitting on a park bench in the middle of Magic Land, sorting through what she had said.

Patty wanted to be a mom. It was so cruel, what had happened to her. First her husband, then everything else: her home, her children, her life. Everything she had ever wanted was taken from her until there was nothing left but an abandoned plot of land.

Forgotten.

Until now.

"All right, now put on your top hats for the picture," Nick said. He passed out the five Mr. Mystero hats he had purchased at a gift shop—I didn't want to know what the going rate for one was, let alone five.

Piper perched hers on her wavy hair and popped her hip out. This was her moment—the Instagram picture that was supposed to be worth all of this. The quintessential social media shot that appeared on my feed approximately once a month. The perfect picture: the five of us looking happy, wearing Mr. Mystero hats, with the magic castle in the background.

It was blazing hot—at least a hundred degrees, with a humidity index somewhere in the realm of the Amazonian jungle. We were surrounded by strangers who were also presumably broke from paying twenty-two dollars for a hot dog.

There was no way hell wasn't some version of Magic Land.

We gathered together for the picture, which had to be retaken four times because people kept walking in between our group and the camera. Usually the parents of toddlers, who were in their own special kind of hell—spending money on the vacation, being miserable, all for something their kid wouldn't even remember.

The crowd finally cooperated for a few seconds, and we got the picture. We moved off to the side by a bench and gathered around Nick's phone as he swiped through the pictures. They were perfect. No one would ever be able to guess at the things we had gone through to get that dumb picture.

Sophie took her Mr. Mystero hat off her head and started swinging it around, windmilling it through the air in the fidgety way kids have while they're waiting for adults to finish with adult tasks.

"Dad, can you take one of just me in front of the castle?" Piper said as she adjusted her hair over the front of her shoulders.

Nick obliged and followed Piper back out into the promenade, waiting for her to adjust her hair once again and get in the proper pose: flashing a peace sign, one leg popped in the air, and making a kissy face at the camera. He paused before he took the picture.

"Okay. Next I get to take one with that pose," he said.

"Mom, I want to go on another ride," Sophie said. Her Mr. Mystero hat was still in her right hand, swinging around. Leo was sitting on the bench next to us, looking bored.

"Just be a minute, Soph," I said. I laughed as I watched Nick and Piper change places, with Nick popping his leg for the camera as Piper laughed but took the picture.

"But, Mom, I—" Sophie started to say, holding her Mr. Mystero hat, arm pumping wildly, when she lost her grip and the hat went flying across the pavement, bouncing on the ground and landing upturned in a pool of congealed nacho cheese from one of the taco kiosks.

"Mom! My hat!" she screamed. "Get it! Get it!"

"That thing is a goner," Leo said as he put his head in his hands.

Sophie started to scream, pointing at her hat just as someone stepped on the side of it, kicking it across the pavement. A few more guests kicked it and it volleyed around like a beach ball at a sports game.

Her screams caught the attention of Nick and Piper, who started to jog over wearing looks of concern.

I bent down on my knee and put my hands on Sophie's upper arms. "It's okay. Take a deep breath. We can find another one."

She nodded and gave me a small smile, and I stood up.

"Let's go back to the gift shop," I said to Nick, and pressed my mouth into a line, grimly determined to save this day.

After we bought Sophie another Mr. Mystero hat, we went on a few other rides, but it was mostly in silence and weak attempts to cheer each other up. We had finally reached our destination, but it didn't feel like a prize at all.

Even Leo asked after three more rides when we could go back to the hotel and rest. The trip had taken it all out of us, and we had no enthusiasm left to enjoy the park.

As we waited in line for Flight of the Dragon, I looked over at Nick. The disappointment was written all over his expression. He knew the road trip had been a failure, since before we even left our driveway.

We are never doing this again, I thought.

"Mom, I'm still tired," Sophie said after we got off the roller coaster. "Can we go swim at the hotel?"

I saw Nick's shoulders sag further. I looked from Nick to Leo's overheated, flushed cheeks, to Piper scrolling on her phone, to Sophie, young enough to be honest. "Okay, kiddo."

As we trekked back through the exit gates, another half hour of walking ahead of us, I saw the same Mr. Mystero character standing off to the side, waiting to take pictures with kids as they entered. He was waving this time, with none of the robotic catatonia from before.

I hoped that maybe he was just having an off day.

Heatstroke. Bad news from home. A bout of stomach flu coming on.

I smiled at Mr. Mystero and waved. His arm dropped back down to his side, and he stared at me stiffly, like a marionette with the strings cut.

"What the hell?" I said, and stopped. A man eating a waffle cone nearly collided into my back.

I waved tauntingly at Mr. Mystero, daring him to respond in kind.

Nothing.

I felt the rage and anger and disappointment and frustrations of the entire trip pressing against my rib cage. The muscles in my arms tightened and I held my breath, allowing the pressure in my chest to continue. All of it needed an outlet, and it looked like Mr. Mystero was the valve to turn it on.

Unbeknownst to me, Nick had watched the interaction. And that was what finally broke him.

"Guys, hold up," he said. He balled his fists and marched over to Mr. Mystero, moving crossways against the flow of foot traffic. I heard a few curse words as he tried to sidestep everyone.

Mr. Mystero remained motionless as my husband worked his way over.

"Stay," I said to the kids, and jogged behind Nick. Warning bells were going off. I had never seen Nick this angry, not even when Piper sideswiped the mailbox at the end of the driveway with my car and didn't tell us until the next day, hoping we wouldn't notice our mailbox was in two pieces.

"Man, what's your problem?" Nick said just as I reached them. His voice was sharp enough to cut through metal.

But Mr. Mystero wasn't affected. His black plastic eyes gleamed with nothing behind them.

Nick leaned forward. "I said, what's your problem?" His voice was louder now, catching the attention of a few people who were walking by.

I put my hand on Nick's arm. "C'mon. Let's just go. You're causing a scene," I whispered.

"Mom, what are you guys doing?" Piper called from across the crowd. "We want to go."

I held up a finger in their direction and tilted my head toward Nick. "Nick, let's just go," I said, and tugged his arm again. Everything around us felt too loud, too difficult, too dangerous. We had to leave before the situation got even worse.

Nick leaned forward again, and my grip on his upper arm tightened.

"I said: What. Is. Your. Problem."

The character didn't move, didn't twitch. Didn't breathe.

I noticed the frozen cartoon grin was actually made of black netting, so the person inside could see out from the costume. I saw Nick hesitate for a moment before leaning forward, trying to make eye contact with whoever was inside.

But it was just black inside. A hollow space.

Nick relaxed under my grip, and I loosened my fingers. He was finally coming back to reality.

Then he lifted an arm, finger outstretched, as though preparing to poke or shove Mr. Mystero.

He'd started to move forward when the air around us crackled and I scrambled forward, putting myself between him and the character.

"Stop," I said, eyes wide. "Nick, stop. Please." I moved his hand down, back to his side.

He looked like a deflated balloon as he began to come back to himself. Sweat was beading on his forehead, and his cheeks were flushed.

"He—I—" He tried to sputter out an explanation.

"I know. It's okay. C'mon. Let's go to the car," I said. I turned him around and nudged him back toward the kids. He shuffled forward through the foot traffic while I waited for a beat.

I glanced back at Mr. Mystero one final time. We locked eyes, and he slowly lifted a hand and gave me a wave. His mouth seemed to draw upward into an evil grin and his eyes shone with delight. He was *enjoying* Nick's meltdown.

I narrowed my eyes at him and widened my stance, crossing my arms over my chest, in the hopes of taking up more space to intimidate him like a hooded cobra. I had done it more than a few times in meetings with opposing counsel.

You wanna go, asshole? I suddenly have no problem being a "Florida Mom" headline.

As though he had heard my thoughts, Mr. Mystero mockingly put his palms up in a surrender gesture and then shook his head. He was laughing at me. Then he turned his hands toward the sky and his fingers made a beckoning motion. An invitation to truly lose my shit.

I leaned toward him, finger raised. He didn't get to scare my kids, push my husband to the brink of a breakdown. Put the final nail in the coffin that had become our trip.

But my last shred of level-headedness told me I probably shouldn't punch him.

"Fuck you," I growled at him.

Then I whipped back around and followed my family out of the park, my confusion and terror only slightly more annoying than the heat and the walk.

Chapter 31

I don't know what came over me. I really don't," Nick said from the next pool lounger over. "I'm so sorry. That wasn't me." His face crumpled and he looked down.

Nick was supposed to be the steady one, not the parent who threatened a beloved children's character with possible violence. Not the parent who publicly had a meltdown and freaked everyone out.

The trip had eroded the essence of who he was—it had taken him from himself. From me. From all of us.

"I know. It's been one awful thing after another with this trip. And I'm sorry—really, I am—I know how much you were looking forward to this trip and family bonding time and all that, but it's doing the opposite of that. We're all exhausted and scared by what's happened." I leaned back in my pool lounger, grateful I was wearing sunglasses so he couldn't see my red eyes. When I got back to the hotel after we left Magic Land, I had planned on taking a shower to give myself space to cry. Instead, Nick had gotten there first, I'm assuming with the same intention.

I didn't want to spend another minute in Florida. Another

second on the trip. I wanted to go back home to where it was safe and I could worry about my clients and my garden and if I had paid the travel soccer summer fee. I wanted normal, however boring or mundane my normal was.

The kids were playing in the outdoor pool at the Magic Land Wilderness Resort, having scampered off the second we found lounge chairs. Piper was in the lazy river on an inner tube, floating around into oblivion, and Sophie and Leo were playing in the water, waiting for the bucket to overflow and splash everyone down below. Apparently water buckets were the hottest attraction at any water park.

Nick reached over and put his hand on top of mine. "I know. You're right—it's been one thing after another. And I can't believe I lost it today. I promise it won't happen again. It all just . . . got to me. But I think we've had some good times, too?"

The look on his face was so hopeful, so innocent, that I couldn't completely break his heart. So, I nodded. "Yes, of course. But I can't do this anymore. I want to go home."

If we had flown, we could have hopped on a flight that evening. But of course, we had to bring our car back with us. In a moment of insanity, I had tried to google services where someone would drive our car back to Wisconsin for us while we flew home, but after I saw some of the estimated costs, I figured we could survive a quick road trip home. We would have to figure out how to break it to the kids, of course.

Nick squeezed my hand. "I know, I know. But please, it's only for six days. We can enjoy the park as much as possible and then head home. I need to redeem myself, if only for the kids. We'll have a great time tomorrow, and then we'll laugh about all of this in a couple of years, I bet."

I felt frustration bubbling in my chest. He wasn't understanding. He wasn't getting it.

Then I remembered. There was so much that I hadn't told him.

I would start with the Vickerys. The locket.

I leaned forward and put my forearms on my thighs. "Nick, you might feel differently after I tell you this."

To his credit, Nick didn't jump up and start screaming the way I would have. As I told him about the locket and Sophie's tooth, his eyes grew wider and wider and his mouth dropped open slightly. But never enough so that if the kids had seen him, they would know he had heard something terrible and shocking. Once again, why he was a principal. Nearly unflappable, or at least, he covered it better than most. Of course, I knew that could change after I told him about the baby. But I still didn't know how to tell him.

"Now do you understand?" I said softly. A downcast satisfaction bloomed across my chest as I saw his expression. He was fighting to keep his face neutral, fighting to find some loophole to exploit, fighting for the words that would make me change my mind.

"I do. But I still think we should ride it out," he finally said. "Make good memories to offset all the bad ones."

I felt my satisfaction turn to white-hot anger. I folded my arms across my chest like a tantruming toddler and refused to look at him. There was nothing else to say. It wasn't like I wanted to fly back on my own, and I'd never leave my husband and kids on a family vacation.

I was on my own.

"Do you want something from the snack bar?" Nick said after several quiet moments.

I shook my head and didn't answer. Giving him the silent treatment was beneath my maturity level, but I couldn't help it. I needed to act out.

I grabbed my phone and swiped at it, checking my work emails. I had one from Chester, the lawyer representing Lenny Black. Apparently the Instagram model Lenny was dating had moved into the house, with Michelle and the kids still living there. The mistress was sleeping in the pool house but sunning herself nude each day. The kids saw her before they went to school in the mornings.

Not surprisingly, Michelle was not happy about this. So she told Lenny she was going to get a cease-and-desist letter sent to the girlfriend, making her wear clothes outside when the kids were at home.

I had my work cut out for me when we got back home. But I was still on vacation—at least, technically—so I put my phone down and vowed to ignore Michelle's emails until we were back in Germantown. Assuming we ever made it back.

Nick returned from his snack bar excursion with a plate of nachos and two beers. He silently placed one next to me as a peace offering and nudged the nacho plate closer to me on the table in between us.

I then realized I needed to tell Nick, right at that moment, about the pregnancy. I needed him to fully understand all of the conflicted emotions I was feeling. It wasn't that I wanted to use the information for my benefit—that felt wrong and deceitful—but more so to help Nick process why I felt so unsettled and anxious.

It was time to tell him.

I took a deep breath and kept my face forward, watching the kids jump around in the splash pad area.

"Thank you, but I can't drink that," I said quietly, still looking forward.

Out of the corner of my eye, I saw Nick reach over and pick up one of the beers and take a sip. He winced and then wiped his mouth with his hand.

"It's not the best but it will get the job done," he said with another grimace.

There was a pause, and I knew I could just claim I didn't want to try the unpleasant beer. But I was sick of keeping things inside. Weren't we supposed to be bonding, getting closer, on this trip?

"You're not hearing me. I can't drink that," I said again, this time my voice a bit louder.

Nick turned his head and slowly sat up, swiveling his body to face me. He put his palms on the lounge chair. "What do you mean?"

I slowly turned my head to him and whispered, "I took a test at your brother's house." I didn't finish the rest of the sentence, just raised my eyebrows. I still couldn't bring myself to say it.

"A test?" he said, looking confused for a moment. Then I could practically see the light bulb go off over his head. "A test." This time, not as much of a question.

"A test," I echoed. I turned to look at him, shoulders sagging.

This was not how it was supposed to go. People don't announce their pregnancy to their spouse while at a water park in Orlando, and certainly not after a day that involved nearly beating up a Magic Land character.

Nick looked down and clasped his hands together tightly. I saw him blink a few times rapidly and take a few long deep breaths. Then he looked up at me. And smiled.

"Really?" It was in the same hopeful, excited tone that he had used when I told him I was pregnant with our other three kids. Anxious excitement.

I nodded. "Yes." My face made it clear I did not share in his pure joy. I pressed my mouth together to keep from saying anything else. It wasn't fair to Nick.

He reached over and gave me an awkward hug, with me still sitting in the lounge chair. He whispered in my ear, "This is amazing." He squeezed me closer, and I could feel his hands were shaking. "I can't believe it." His voice broke. "Holy shit."

The fragile chains that had held back all of my emotions since before we even left our driveway broke. My eyes filled with tears and my chin began to tremble. I shut my eyes tightly but the tears still escaped. My breath became ragged.

"I'm scared," I managed to whisper back through exhales. "I don't know if I can do it all over again."

He nodded against my shoulder and then sat down on the end of my lounge chair as I tucked my feet underneath me and sat crisscross. He took my hands in his.

"I know. It's a little scary. But it's also a gift. We didn't expect this, but I know we're going to be great. Look at our kids." He pointed across the water park to where Piper, Leo, and Sophie all waited in line for a twisty slide. Piper held Sophie's hand and tousled Leo's hair with the other in a teasing gesture. Then I saw them all laugh.

They were great kids. Nick was right. I never doubted that for a second. And we would be lucky to have fifty more just like them.

But it still scared the shit out of me to go back to buying diapers.

"People are going to think I'm the kid's grandmother," I said with a morbid half smile.

Nick laughed and squeezed my hand. "A hot grandmother, at least." He pointed to his graying temples. "At least to grandpa over here."

"Do you know how old we will be when the kid graduates high school?" Before he could answer, I said, "I've done the math every day. We will be like sixty. Sixty—just let that sink it. We will almost be old enough to join AARP."

He pursed his lips together and thought for a moment. "Before the kid is even in high school, we can get the senior discount at McDonald's."

I rolled my eyes. "Oh good. I can get a cup of coffee for fifty cents off as I go to my office each day until I'm dead because we have another college tuition to pay."

"We can buy baby food pouches along with our denture cream. All in one trip. We'll be going to the pharmacy anyway," Nick said.

"Well, I'm glad it's convenient, at least."

We sat in silence for a few minutes. Then he slowly reached his hand over and I put mine in his. Tentative, afraid. He gave me a quick squeeze and then held my hand.

"Why didn't you tell me this sooner?" he said quietly.

I gripped his hand and pulled it toward me and leaned forward. "I should have. I'm so sorry. I was too afraid and anxious to say anything until I had processed it. And with all of the creepy stuff happening it just wasn't the right time. I was going to wait until we were back home, after the trip."

He pulled my hand toward him and put his arms around me again. "It's okay. I just wish you would have said something. I don't want you to feel like you're on your own."

I nodded against his shoulder, closing my eyes. "I know. You're right."

I was still afraid, still anxious, but I felt lighter after telling him. The secret was finally out. I didn't have to carry it alone.

I had spent my entire life ignoring truths and uncomfortable realities, disassociating from pain. When now I knew that I didn't have to. I finally understood that, in real time.

We settled back, close together, and watched our kids wait in line.

One more child.

An exclamation point in our family, as though we didn't have enough excitement already.

Chapter 32

I dreamed of the house again that night. Of flames licking at the walls, of the Vickery children screaming because they were trapped, of windows exploding and Joey's Big Wheel melting in the heat. I reached out to save the bike, but my hand just went through it.

I woke as the fire danced around me, consuming everything in its path.

When I opened my eyes, I hunched my shoulders and looked down at my hands. Even though it was just a dream, I couldn't save them. I was a mom. I was supposed to be able to protect kids and have an instinct to keep them away from danger. I couldn't even do that in my dreams.

I slowly stood up to get a glass of water, careful not to disturb Nick. He had collapsed into bed after we got back to the room and fallen asleep immediately. He'd had quite the day.

I tiptoed toward the bathroom and began to fill up a rocks glass that I'd found next to the ice bucket. While I waited, my eyes flicked to the TripTik carefully placed against a corner of the vanity. I stared at it until the water began to overflow and spill on my hand.

I set the glass down and turned off the faucet, wiping my hand on my pajama pants and slowly lifting the TripTik. I ran a hand over the cover, breathing slowly. Then I slowly flipped through the pages, looking at the yellow highlighted route we were supposed to take in each state.

No, the trip had not gone according to plan. And the TripTik was the perfect symbol of that. We had barely stayed on the yellow highlighted route, despite Nick's months of planning. He had put so much importance on the trip. There was no way to live up to his expectations.

I paged through the TripTik and then stopped in Indiana. I ran a finger down the highlighted route, then veered away where we took our first detour and wound up at the Vickery house. It was just greenery and open land on the map. Not even AAA showed the road they had lived on.

As I looked down at the green swath on the map, it began to change. I lifted it closer to my face and I saw words swirl from nothing.

Come. Please come.

My heart thudded as I stared at the message, blood whooshing through my ears. My hands began to tremble, making the words bounce around in front of me.

"Ni—" I started to sputter before the words dissolved, the plain green page back to normal.

I slowly closed the TripTik, placing it flush against the corner of the wall. I remained in place for a moment before I took the glass of water back to bed and carefully lay down next to Nick.

I didn't have to wonder what the message meant—that was clear. And I didn't have to muse about who had sent it.

Patty.

Patty Vickery had something to tell me. That much was obvious. But what?

Their souls were in unrest, chained to the earth.

Maybe they had been locked away in a purgatory of the spiritual realm without anyone to help release them. Maybe whatever had actually happened had been traumatic enough to keep them tethered to earth, to their house in Indiana. Maybe they had chosen me, for whatever reason, to tell their story.

What really did happen there? Maybe if I found out what had happened to them, their souls could finally be at peace. They could move on. And people would remember them, one of the most simple of human wants. To be remembered, cared for, thought of.

If I couldn't save them from the fire—in my dreams or in reality—then I would find out what they wanted now.

Maybe I could still save them.

Come. Please come.

Chapter 33

"Mom, Orlando is on the Weather Channel."

I turned over in bed and shut my eyes tighter, throwing the white hotel comforter over my head. It felt like the middle of the night, even though I had fallen asleep just an hour before.

"Mom?"

I heard Leo's voice again and felt Nick shift and groan getting up.

I opened my eyes under my white comforter fort. I could see through the material that it was morning. And when I listened, I could hear the murmur of Sophie talking in the other room.

I exhaled and threw the comforter off my head. I closed my eyes again as the sunlight assaulted me. Slowly, I walked into the kids' room to find out what was going on.

"Look," Leo said.

I rubbed my eyes and plopped down on Piper's bed. She was just a shape on the bed covered in sheets. She groaned and rolled over as I jostled her.

On the television, the Weather Channel had a map of Florida with green, red, and orange blobs moving across it. It looked like someone had spilled cans of angry paint across the state. A huge storm system.

And Orlando seemed to be the epicenter.

". . . strong to severe thunderstorms are certainly possible in the central portion of the state, especially the Orlando area . . ." The meteorologist seemed a bit too perky, slightly too excited, to be reporting on a weather event that would be so destructive.

"What time is it supposed to hit?" I asked the television.

"She said this afternoon," Leo said from the doorway. His eyes were wide and filled with anxiety.

Sophie came out of the bathroom holding her Magic Land toothbrush. "Is there going to be another bad thunderstorm? Like at Uncle Ethan's house?"

I didn't answer her and stared at the screen. "Nick? Come in here." I walked over to the sliding glass door to the balcony and thrust the curtains back with a flourish.

The sun was shining brightly, reflecting off all the cars in the parking lot below. Nearly every car had a Magic Land decal.

Yet the sky held a scarlet hue in the distance, a warning of the storms approaching.

Red sky at night, sailors' delight. Red sky in the morning, sailors take warning.

"It's not raining." Piper's voice came from underneath the comforter, a disembodied voice from the teenage lump on the bed.

"Thanks. I can see that," I said dryly.

Nick appeared at my side. "What's wrong?"

I silently pointed to the television, then to the sunshine outside, and then shrugged.

He put his hands on his hips and looked from the radar to the sky. "Well, we should get moving if there is a chance of rain today." I sensed the defeat in his voice, the cracking at the seams.

"No. I'm not getting out of bed. That park was horrible," Piper mumbled from under her comforter.

"Is Dad going to get mad at Mr. Mystero again?" Leo said, eyes darting from me to his father.

"Yeah, Dad, you can't defeat Mr. Mystero. He has magic powers," Sophie added.

I held up my hand. "Your dad wasn't mad at him. He was just . . . talking about something. Mr. Mystero wasn't feeling well and he was trying to help." The words sounded ridiculous even as I heard myself say them—with conviction.

Nick looked stunned, finally realizing the full impact of his confrontation with one of the most beloved children's characters in history.

"I'll apologize to him if we see him again," he finally said.

"Give it back! Leo, give it back!" Sophie started to shriek as Leo jumped off the bed, his sister's narwhal Squishmallow in his hands. He scampered toward the bathroom, Sophie chasing after him. He slammed the bathroom door shut, and Sophie started to pound on it, screaming.

"I hate you!" she yelled through the closed door.

I sighed and walked over, threatening Leo until he opened the door. By then, Sophie was hysterically crying and red-faced. She reached forward and shoved him, causing him to fall back into the bathroom and slam against the bathtub.

Then more screaming as Leo fought back.

Nick and I finally extricated them, pulling them apart, both crying and spitting insults at each other. We put them on separate beds, Piper still a lump under the comforter, hiding.

"Don't move," I said to them, and gave Nick a nudge to talk privately.

Back in our room, I turned to him. "Nick, we just can't keep pretending everything is fine," I said, tears sliding down my face. He reached an arm out to hug me, but I moved away and shook my head. I didn't want him to comfort me. I needed to feel this; I needed him to see how I was coming apart. That he was coming apart, whether or not he realized it. "The kids are ready to kill each other. It's been nothing but disaster after disaster, and I can't do this. *We* can't do this."

He knew I was asking to head home, to skip the next five days at the park. To go back to the site of the Vickery house and make the unexplainable stop. To make it so that we could return home and forget all about it.

"We've come this far, Leigh. Magic Land is the whole reason for the trip." He stared at me, an incredulous look on his face. "We can't just give up now."

I took a deep breath before I responded. "Nick, you said the reason for the trip was family bonding. The theme park was just the icing on the cake, so to speak. I just can't go back to that park and pretend things are fine." I looked down, waiting for him to agree with me. When he didn't say anything, I looked up. "I can't even go on any of the rides anyway."

He looked down, staring at the carpet, and I got the sense that he was sorting through the possible reactions to what I'd said, trying to select the right one.

Finally, he looked up. "If we don't go to the park, the whole trip will be pointless."

I realized what he was saying. This was his emotional line in the sand. He wanted us to go, to have one decent day there, to make the whole trip worth it. But I knew having one decent day was out of our grasp.

"There's a tropical storm coming, ghosts are haunting us, I feel like I'm losing it, and who knows what terrible things will await us at the park. It's not worth it, Nick," I said, my voice rising.

He shook his head. "It's worth it. I promise. Let's just do one more day. We can just spend the morning and head home tomorrow." Even as he was offering the compromise, I could see the disappointment on his face. This was his worst moment: admitting defeat.

I didn't want to spend another second inside that park, but I would do it for Nick, and for the kids.

One more day. I could do one more day.

I exhaled and nodded. "If that's the compromise, then fine. I just can't pretend anymore."

He reached forward and pulled me to him. I rested my head on his shoulder and closed my eyes.

"I never want us to pretend," he whispered.

"I know. That's why I married you," I said with a laugh into his T-shirt.

"Then I should tell you the truth: the kids are going to kill each other today."

Chapter 34

If I thought the Vickerys or sibling-cide was my biggest worry that morning, I definitely did not check the Facebook group for updates on the park. It seemed that everyone in a four-state radius had heard the weather forecast and had decided the exact same thing as we had—to get to the park right as it opened and ride it out for as long as the weather held.

We saw the line of cars before we even saw the sign for the park.

"Well, that's not good," Nick muttered as he put the car into Park approximately half a mile from the park entrance. "Everyone must be here for the admission adventure."

Forty-five minutes later we were walking to the entrance gates with hordes of other people, everyone speed-walking to get inside and start having fun—goddamn it—before the weather ruined everything.

We made it inside and the kids decided the first ride they wanted to go on was the Sorcerer's Carousel. So we crossed the park and headed straight there, not stopping for a funnel cake or passing Go. At least I could actually ride on this one.

"Three hours?" Piper screeched as we arrived at the carousel, which had unicorns and dragons instead of horses. "The sign says the line is three hours long. No way."

"Um," I said as I saw the crowds of people inside, going through the metal turnstiles looking defeated and discouraged. I looked at Nick and the kids.

"I want to wait," Sophie said, and Leo nodded.

I gave Piper a sympathetic look. "Sorry. Hopefully it's wrong."

Nick put an arm around her shoulders. "C'mon, you can show me some TikTok reels or whatever they're called while we wait."

"Well, Mom, you were right," Piper said as we walked down the exit ramp after riding the carousel. "It wasn't three hours."

I grimaced. "Sorry. That wasn't what I meant." The wait had taken three and a half hours and we all looked like we had been through boot camp by the time we reached the front of the line. Piper's phone was on low battery, Sophie was whining that she was hungry, and Leo said he was hot and tired. Even Nick had had the pep in his step obliterated.

At the end of the exit ramp, I turned to face everyone. I looked up at the sky and saw a few clouds beginning to gather, but they were fluffy and white, so we weren't in immediate need of shelter. Evil dark clouds would be our sign to hightail it back to the car.

"Nick, how about we get the kids some food?" I said, and they nodded. Meanwhile, my stomach flipped in protest.

We quickly walked over to the food court and surveyed the menus. The best options appeared to be a cheeseburger and a hot dog, and not the Korean corn dogs that seemed to be all the rage:

a deep-fried corn dog rolled in Flamin' Hot Cheeto dust and drizzled with sriracha. Even if I weren't nauseated, I didn't think I could handle that.

After a quick lunch of hockey-puck cheeseburgers—for the low cost of thirty-four dollars each—we were ready to head to another ride.

Lucky for me, the kids chose another ride I figured was safe: Enchanted Carpet Ride, a leisurely boat ride through tunnels hosting animatronic characters. Mr. Mystero was thankfully not one of them.

As our boat returned to the station, we heard the distant rumble of thunder. The sun was still shining, but it wouldn't be for long. I unbuckled my harness and helped Sophie do the same, then caught Nick's eye. He gave me a slight nod that meant it was time to round up.

When we walked out of the station, we saw that half of the sky was now covered in the puffy, cute white clouds but on the fringes, the storm clouds were beginning to arrive.

"Mom, we should go," Leo said nervously as he looked up.

At least he said it first.

We began to walk to the exit gates leisurely, figuring we had time. Yet, such is the Florida weather way: one moment it was sunny and hot, and a second later the sky opened up and released sheets of rain down on everyone, with booming thunder and jagged lightning streaking the sky.

We broke into a run in the parking lot, Nick lifting Sophie up and putting her on his back, piggyback style, and me keeping a death grip on Leo's hand while Piper jogged next to me. The rain was nearly sideways, pounding down on the asphalt in the parking lot, steam rising, giving the eerie effect that we were trapped in a fire.

"Mom!" he said.

I felt a tug as Leo tripped over a crack. My arm tightened, and I was able to lift him up enough to avoid any major damage, but his hand was scraped up. One more injury from this trip.

We reached the car and threw ourselves inside, soaking wet and panting. We closed the doors just as a particularly nasty form of lightning lit up the sky.

Red sky in the morning, Somersets should have taken warning.

Chapter 35

Are you guys sure?" I kept my voice neutral, soft. The last thing I wanted to do was to intimidate them into agreeing.

"Hell yes," Piper said as she flung herself down on the hotel room's bed. She splayed her arms out, crucifixion style, like a true martyr.

I looked at Sophie and Leo, who were sitting on the opposite queen bed.

"What about you guys?" I said. Nick shifted from his vantage point in the doorway between the two rooms, one arm on the doorframe.

Sophie nodded and clutched the narwhal Squishmallow in her lap, giving it a squeeze. Leo looked down for a moment and then back up to me.

"I want to go home, too," he said.

I looked at Nick and he gave me a slight shrug. It had started on the very wet car ride home from the park after the storm began.

Piper was the first to say it.

"We should just go home tomorrow." She muttered it, so none of us reacted, and I thought it was just another teenage throwaway comment. Like the time that Piper said she was never eating fast food again and walked through the door three days later with a grocery bag full of Taco Bell, mocking us for believing her.

But then Leo joined in. "Yeah, I want to go home."

Sophie added her two cents: "I miss my bed."

"I think that's what we'll do," Nick said quietly. We rode mostly in silence back to the hotel.

Once we were in the room, the kids started fighting again.

Oh, Nick, I'm so sorry, I thought as I saw him hang his head and put his hands in his pockets after listening to them argue.

"Your mom and I will start packing," he finally said.

"Please don't kill each other," I said before I left the room. I gently closed the connecting room door behind me, leaving it slightly cracked so one of them could come in if there was an emergency.

Nick stood near the sliding glass door, and I sat on the bed, scooting closer to him and tucking my legs underneath me.

My stomach clenched and a wave of sadness settled across my shoulders. In an effort to keep things moving for the kids, and in the pursuit of the perfect family vacation, we had done the opposite of what we intended. We had traumatized them, even though very little of the horrible things that had happened were our fault.

I heard the kids begin to argue in the other room, and the sound of their tired, sad, and overwhelmed voices made me hang my head. I felt like a failure.

"Nick, I'm so sorry. I know how much you wanted this to be a great memory," I said quietly, checking to make sure I didn't see any eavesdropping eyes peering through the door's crack. Luckily, they were all too busy arguing.

He looked outside and watched the raindrops angrily smash against the sliding glass door. The storm was so intense that we couldn't see more than five feet out from the balcony.

"I failed us. I wanted this to be their best memory ever, and I failed," he whispered.

I shook my head. "No. You didn't fail. I let you take all of this on, because you always do, and that's not fair. You always put us first. And hey, we did have some fun, right?" I said in a thin voice.

He smirked. "No need to lie."

I stood up, extricating my legs from the bed. "No, really. There were a lot of good times. And we definitely have family stories for, oh, forever." I wrapped my arms around his waist and hugged him.

He nodded and rested his chin on my head. He didn't say anything for a long few seconds.

Finally, he gave me a squeeze and then stepped back. "I'll tell the kids to start pulling stuff together," he said before he walked into the other room. He closed the adjoining door behind him so I could change out of my wet clothes.

Dry and clothed, I stretched my arms over my head and looked around the room with a sigh. Even though we had only been at the hotel for a day and a half, it looked like we'd been there for a year. Clothes thrown all over the floor (mine), nightstand full of empty water bottles (his), and a plethora of sunscreen bottles all over the dresser (the fair-skinned Somerset crew in totality).

I should pack something. Anything.

I walked over to the bottles of sunscreen and began to collect them. Once I had my arms full, I walked over to my backpack, unzipping the main pocket and shoving as many of the sticks and sprays into there as I could, but the different, awkward sizes made it so that only a few fit inside, and I still had three left.

I zipped the main pocket closed and opened the smaller front pocket. I dropped one of the spray bottles into the pocket, but it stopped halfway, caught on something.

I made a harrumph noise and reached my hand into the front pocket.

My fingers stopped as they felt something cold, hard, and metallic. Small interlocking circles of metal with a pendant at the end.

My entire body turned to ice, a quick deep freeze that turned me into a statue. A prickling began on my scalp and it felt like tiny bugs were moving through my hair. My peripheral vision went dark, and the hotel wall in front of me blurred.

Without consciously doing so, I hooked my fingers under the chain and pulled it out.

Holding it in front of my face, I stared at the swinging circle spinning around in front of my eyes. It slowed, the circles becoming smaller and smaller, until it stopped. Swaying slightly, the V engraved in the center of the locket stared at me. Taunting me. Smiling at me.

"I thought you said you threw that out."

Nick's voice made me jump. I lost my balance on my haunches and tipped backward, hitting the ground hard.

"Ow," I said as I struggled to sit up.

"Are you okay?" Nick knelt down next to me and held out his hand.

I nodded and allowed him to pull me to a standing position. After lifting my hand to rub the ache in my back, I realized I was still holding the locket. I slowly opened my palm and looked at it, coiled innocuously in my hand.

"Didn't you get rid of that?" Nick said, looking confused.

My hand began to tremble under the locket, making it flinch and wave. "I did. I swear to you, I did." I looked up at Nick, tears forming, and I felt my face drain of all color. "I did."

He didn't say anything, staring down at the locket. I saw several conflicting emotions pass over his face: disbelief, fear, anger, annoyance, confusion.

Then he looked up, and I saw that he believed me.

"They want us to come back. Patty does—she sent me that exact message. She wrote it in the TripTik, Nick. We have to go back to the house on our way home," I said, my determination strengthening with every word.

"What? No. We can't go back to that house. What if something even worse happens?" Nick asked.

It was a fair question, and one I hadn't really considered. I was so worried about getting everything to stop, about finding out what the Vickerys wanted to tell me, that I hadn't paused to consider that it might not all work out. What if it hurt us even more?

I stared at the carpet as I responded. "This family lost everything. Their house, their father, their names, what happened to them. My biggest fear is something happening to you guys, and it actually happened to them. Patty lost her husband, and she had to do it alone." I looked up at Nick, my voice cracking. "And then she couldn't keep the children safe. For whatever reason, they chose us. She chose me. I'm the only one who knows and wants to help. Please—I have to go back to the house." Tears spilled onto my cheeks as I realized I knew it was the right thing to do.

There was no guidebook for supernatural encounters during a road trip—no TripTik for this situation—but I knew I had to go back.

"Keep packing," was all Nick said.

We packed for what felt like hours until the exhaustion finally kicked in and we slowed down, preparing to leave at sunrise. I sent a quick text to Kerry and M.J., letting them know we were coming home early. Then I put their texts on mute. I didn't want to have to lie and come up with a reason why, and I didn't want to tell them the full truth. Mostly because I didn't want them to talk me out of it.

Before she went to bed, Piper asked if she could drive on the way home. She caught me when I was in the middle of trying to shove a pile of joggers into my suitcase, lying on top of it to get it to close.

In other words, she caught me at a weak moment.

"Please?" she added, clasping her hands together.

I slumped down over the top of the suitcase, limbs full of rubber.

"Fine," I whispered into the suitcase.

"Really?" she said carefully, like she was afraid I would change my mind.

I picked my head up. "Fine. Sure. But not through the mountains." It felt like a small way I could brighten her vacation.

After Piper stopped cheering, we told the kids to go to bed, and then Nick and I got ready ourselves. As I was about to flip off the light, I stopped and stared at the black object near my feet. It was my backpack, resting where I'd left it since I'd slid the locket back into the front pocket.

I slowly crouched down and opened the pocket again, feeling for the locket. I wanted to make sure it was still there, that it hadn't hopped into some other, more terrifying location. My index finger quickly located the jewelry, so I zipped the pocket back up and stood.

"What's wrong?" Nick said, already lying down in bed, covers pulled up. His eyes were half closed.

I frowned and pointed to the bag. "Feels weird to sleep with it two feet away."

Nick didn't respond, so I looked up. He had fallen asleep.

Well, if he could sleep, I guess I could try.

Chapter 36

The sun was just beginning to rise over the green bracketed landscape outside the Magic Land Wilderness Resort. Brilliant oranges and pinks streaked the sky—no red hues in sight—promising a beautiful day and none of the flooding rains the meteorologists had predicted. I wasn't surprised.

Piper took the first leg, buoyantly climbing into the driver's seat with Nick in the passenger seat. I stretched out in the third row with one of the Squishmallows in my lap, and Sophie and Leo were in the middle row, electronics on their laps and a bag of snacks tucked on the floor in between their seats.

"Ready?" Piper said as she reached for Tammy's gearshift.

"No," Leo shouted. "She's going to kill us."

I tossed the Squishmallow in his direction. "Yes, Piper. Just listen to your dad."

She shifted the car out of Park and Tammy lurched forward, the turtle top holding tight on the roof.

"Now, just ease her out of the spot. Here . . . pull forward . . . now stop . . . now gently brake," Nick said.

I had started to put my AirPods in, unable to listen to the constant stream of Nick's instructions—although I was certainly glad he had taken up that mantle so I didn't have to—when I heard the brakes squeal and was pitched forward in my seat belt.

"Dad! Stop! I didn't hit it!" Piper sputtered.

"I didn't say to fully brake there!" Nick said at the same time.

"Well, you confused me and made me nervous!" she said.

We were stopped barely an inch from one of the light poles that bracketed the welcome sign in the front of the resort.

WELCOME TO THE MAGIC LAND WILDERNESS RESORT

Indeed. Welcome, motherfuckers, I thought, and then burst out laughing. My family turned to look at me in unison as I cackled, tears streaming down my face.

"Leigh?" Nick said.

"Sorry. I think that broke me," I said, wiping my eyes. "Let's keep going."

And so Piper continued without any more near accidents. The three of us drove for twelve hours, switching off, Nick riding shotgun while Piper was driving.

When I wasn't at the wheel, I periodically stuck my hand into my backpack, making sure the locket was still there. I would reach in, feel the cool metal chain and rub my thumb over the charm, and then zip the pocket back up.

I hadn't told the kids that I had thrown the locket out or it had been returned to me. (How would I have explained that?) But they did know we were stopping at the Vickerys' house before we went home.

I planned to return the locket. I figured that was what Patty really wanted. After all, it was the locket that had started everything, the genesis of the attachment, the bond, between our families.

I hoped if I returned it, buried it back near the house, everything would stop. And I was going to ask Patty myself when I got there.

"We're going back there?" Leo had asked somewhere in Alabama when we told the kids.

"Just to return what we took." I looked back at him and gave him a reassuring smile. "It should be back with them, not with us."

I held my breath, hoping Leo would take that as sufficient explanation.

"Boring," Sophie said in a singsong voice.

Leo didn't say anything else, but Piper did.

"Can I put it on Instagram that we're going back there?" she asked, excitement dripping from her voice.

"No," Nick and I said in unison.

Indiana State Line

"We made it to the Midwest, at least," I muttered as I drove on I-65 North twelve hours later. We had just put Kentucky behind us, the last of the Southern states. Indiana was the last state line before I completed my mission and we could go home.

Nothing spectral had happened since we left Florida, so I took it as a sign we were on the right track. Maybe Patty had listened to our plan to return the locket and was satisfied.

Or maybe she's just waiting for you to get to the house to show you what she really wants.

I shook the thought off, refocusing on my gut feeling that it was something we needed to do. Something we were supposed to do.

And then hopefully they could rest, and so could we.

I continued on I-65 for another two hours, everyone asleep behind me. As I would round each curve, their bodies would shift slightly and I would expect one of them to wake up, but nothing. The exhaustion had set in for everyone.

I felt my eyes growing heavy and my shoulders wanted more than anything to relax down, to allow my body to drift off. I reached over and took another swig of coffee. I figured the stress of getting rid of the poltergeist problem outweighed whatever effect a few cups of coffee would have on the baby.

The baby.

It was still almost unfathomable to me that we would have another child, another little one. And what a story we would have to tell about the way this child's existence began.

As we grew closer to the Vickery house, I put cross streets into my phone. Since the highway had been blocked and we had the detour to urgent care, I knew there was a quicker, more direct way to get there.

Forty-two minutes later, my phone's navigation announced, "You are on the fastest route."

Fast, yes. Safe? I had no idea. My anxiety and fear had begun to build in the silent car, every worry and worst-case scenario playing out in my head. Flashes of every horror movie I had ever watched danced across my thoughts. While I had faith that going to the house would make things better, there was also an excellent chance they could get worse. We could all be traumatized by this, haunted forever, destroyed, possessed. Every possibility suddenly seemed very real.

But I didn't know what else to do. I didn't speak ghost, so I had to rely on instinct. And I felt I needed to do this to make things better.

I thought of the screams at the house as the fire burned, of Patty's voice asking me to come. They wanted me. They had something to show us.

No more running, no more ignoring. No more pretending.

I had to face it with my family. We had to fight it together.

➡

"Turn left up ahead."

I slowed Tammy down and realized the tree line looked familiar. It was the strangest sense of déjà vu. I had seen the area, dreamed about it, had visions of it, but it hadn't felt real. It seemed like something out of a false memory or fever dream. Until I came back.

The car was eerily silent. Everyone was awake, rousing at various times as we got closer to the exit. I expected more questions, more heightened emotions, but no one said a word. I figured that was for the best. There were so many questions I didn't have the answer to. Didn't *want* the answer to.

"Right there," Nick said, and pointed to a clearing. The gravel driveway seemed to wave to me, and the trees bordering it looked like they were opening up for our return, swaying in the early evening summer sunshine.

Welcome back, they seemed to say.

I turned Tammy left and started down the long driveway, the

car's undercarriage bumping along on the uneven gravel. We continued for a few seconds, sitting up straighter in anticipation of seeing the rubble and debris.

But instead, we gasped when we saw something else.

Where there used to be a burned-out structure with beer cans and fast-food wrappers littering the property stood a house. A two-story, foursquare white farmhouse with a front porch and a swaying porch swing.

I slammed on the brakes about thirty feet from the house.

"What is that?" I said as I gripped the steering wheel. I looked at Nick.

His eyes were wide and his mouth gaped. Fear moved across his face, and he whipped around to look at the kids but said nothing.

All three of them were poker straight in the seats.

"That's not the house," Sophie said as she craned her neck to get a better look through the windshield. "The other one was burned down."

"I don't understand," I whispered. I leaned forward and studied the house. It was the same house I'd seen in my dream, in my visions. The same front porch, the same swing, the same trees around the property. It was the Vickery house, but from the past.

"You guys can see this too, right? We should get out of here," I said, and moved to put Tammy in reverse. I figured I could throw the locket out of the window, toward the house, in the hopes that would be enough. It was too much, too terrifying.

"No way," Piper said as she began to unbuckle her seat belt.

"Piper!" Nick finally broke out of his shock and whipped around to face the backseat.

But Piper was already reaching for Tammy's handle, half-smushing Sophie, who tucked her feet up on her captain's chair to let her sister through.

My hand shot out to hit the child lock button on the door and prevent her from opening it, but she was too quick. She slid the door open just as I pressed the button and jumped out of the van.

I unbuckled my seat belt and wrenched my door open as Nick did the same. "Stay here," I said to Sophie and Leo before I stepped down. Piper had gotten only a few paces toward the house before she stopped, hands on hips. Nick and I came up on either side of her.

"Piper, we need to . . ." I trailed off as the pull of the restored house gained my full attention. No doubt, it was beautiful. I could see why the Vickerys bought it, thinking they would raise their children there, lovingly paint the shutters baby blue, hang the porch swing, and spend long afternoons sipping iced tea or lemonade while lazily moving back and forth on the swing during a balmy Midwest summer afternoon. Yet Mr. Vickery had died, the beginning of their dream unraveling. And then everything that followed.

"Go back to the car, Piper," Nick said.

"Yeah, right," she retorted. She looked at me. "Mom, we need to face this together."

"No, I should be doing this alone," I said, raising my voice. I looked at my husband and daughter. "Go back to the car. I'm the one they want. I'm the one they've been talking to. Go back to the car and don't get out no matter what."

Nick shook his head and grabbed my hand. "No. This started with our family, and it will end with it."

Piper grabbed my other hand and squeezed it. "Nothing will hurt us if we're together."

I realized in that moment that I'd built a family stronger and better than my parents had. I could do difficult things, but only *because* of my family. And I would do everything possible to ensure our challenges brought us closer together.

The house seemed to shimmer and blink. An illusion. Yet, when I took a few more steps toward the front porch and reached a hand out, half expecting it to go through the ghostly steps, they were solid. They felt as real as the steps on my own house beneath my feet as I climbed up.

"Mom, did they rebuild the house while we were in Florida?" Leo asked. He and Sophie had also disregarded my instruction and gotten out of the car through the driver's-side door. Nick and the kids were in a line at the base of the porch.

I didn't answer him and turned toward the house. I felt it pulling me forward, like a string was attached to my midsection and the spool was inside the house somewhere, with a ghostly hand slowly turning the crank, reeling me in like a helpless fish.

At the top, I reached for the front door.

Chapter 37

Life was on pause in the Vickery house. Clearly, a family lived here, but the house was empty. I walked into the dining room, the first room to my right. Plates of food were set around the table. Meatloaf, mashed potatoes, and peas. I could smell the food, as though dinner had just been placed on the table seconds ago.

"What the fuck," Nick said as he pushed an index finger into a pile of mashed potatoes. He held his finger up and sniffed the white fluff on his fingertip. He started to bring his finger to his mouth but stopped as he thought better of it. "It seems real," he said before he wiped his finger on his T-shirt.

I walked through a swinging door that led to the kitchen. Inside was a 1960s kitchen that would have made the midcentury modern enthusiasts in our neighborhood die from ecstasy.

"Look," Nick said, and pointed to the sink. The faucet was dripping water, a slow, methodical sound.

I walked over to the sink and tightened the faucet. I then realized the lights were on.

My wonder began to tinge with fear and uncertainty as I looked around the kitchen. Dirty dishes piled in the sink, and a crumpled dish towel on the floor. I automatically bent down to pick it up and folded it, placing it on the counter.

"Was that important?" Nick said as he looked at the folded dish towel.

I lifted my palms. "Muscle memory, I guess."

"Mom? Dad?" I heard Piper call from, thankfully, outside.

"Just a second," I said. I looked at Nick. "We should go."

"Agreed. Where's the locket?" Nick said as he pushed open the swinging door to the dining room.

I patted my pocket and rolled my eyes. "I forgot it in the car. I'll go get it."

In the foyer, I looked to the left of the front door, to the living room. The television was on, but only static was playing. I remembered my vision, with Patty watching *Days of Our Lives* as the kids played on the coffee table next to her.

It was as though the Vickerys were about to walk back into their house and continue on with their evening. And possibly wonder why two strangers from the future had decided to join them.

"The clocks," Nick said. One hand reached for the front door and the other pointed to the grandfather clock on the wall. It was stopped at eleven fifteen, the same time I had been seeing on our clocks. The same time that had followed us all the way to Florida.

I slowly craned my neck around, catching glimpses of the other clocks in the living and dining rooms. They were all stopped at the same time. A wave of anger and heartbreak moved through the house, making my breath quicken as I *felt* their pain. Whatever it was that Patty wanted me to see, it suddenly didn't seem like a good idea to stay. There was too much pain in this house.

The restraints that held back my panic broke, and my body flooded with fear. My blood turned to ice despite the sweltering temperature, and my hands began to shake.

"Go," I urged Nick, putting my hand on top of his on the door and pressing the latch, his thumb under mine.

"Get the locket," Nick said as I ran down the porch steps.

As I passed the kids, Leo said, "Mom, I think I hear a car coming."

I made a noise and turned back to run to Tammy for the locket. Nick joined the kids at the base of the porch as I ripped open the car door and shoved my hand into the backpack, quickly palming the locket. I held it tightly in my hand as I jogged back to my family.

"So now what? Do I put it on the porch?" I said, suddenly uncertain. I had been so sure that just being here, with the locket, would be enough for Patty to tell me what she wanted. That a message from beyond the veil would appear and I would follow the instructions. But thus far all we had understood was meatloaf and clocks and an increasing sense that all of it had been a mistake.

"Throw it into the house," Piper suggested. Her arms were around her siblings, who flanked her. She was the tentpole that held up the Somerset kids, and I was never more grateful for her rare protective instincts.

Nick nodded, and I squarely faced the house and lifted my right arm. I wound it back, ready to launch the jewelry into the house and be finished with the Vickerys.

But then a strong wind came through the site and nearly knocked us all over. It started in the trees, with branches rustling and leaves swaying, and then picked up momentum, lifting the porch swing from the porch and slamming it back down.

It looked like the house was having a temper tantrum. A toddler being denied an extra yogurt pouch at lunch.

The wind began to organize and solidify, forming a swirling pattern. It kicked up the dust and debris around us and spun like a funnel cloud, with the house and my family in the eye. I looked back and couldn't even see the van anymore through the thick, swirling dust clouds.

I huddled next to my family, putting my arms around Piper as she pulled Leo and Sophie closer, with Nick behind us.

We watched as the vortex continued, and then a small flickering orange spot appeared on the front porch. It grew higher and bigger, dancing around, as smoke began to drift up toward the porch ceiling. It turned the floor of the porch black, singeing the worn wooden boards. It reached for the porch swing, causing it to crash down on the porch in a tumble of wood and metal chains.

Inside the house, the flames moved quickly, engulfing the stairs and melting the clocks. I saw the light fixture in the foyer come crashing down to the floor before disappearing into the fire.

I tightened my grip around my family as we remained frozen, trapped in the otherworldly tornado, unable to leave. Unwilling spectators. The fire was close enough so that we could feel the heat, feel how it wanted to scorch our skin and peel off our hair.

Nick broke free from our huddle and tried to walk through the swirling wind around us, to breach the perimeter and get us back to Tammy, but he was pushed back. Either by unseen hands or the wind, or both. He returned to us, gripping us tighter than before.

I knew it wouldn't work. I knew the Vickerys wouldn't let us go that easily. Not when we were in their territory, in the place of their power.

Is this how it ends?

I closed my eyes and felt tears run down my face. We were helpless. And I was the one who had trapped us.

I felt the heat from the fire grow closer and heard the crackle of it licking at the hydrangeas that bordered the porch. We retreated to the edge of the vortex, our backs to the wind stream.

Through my shut eyelids, I saw a flash of light.

I felt Nick's hand tighten around my shoulder as Leo said, "It's him!" I peeked through my half-closed eyes, squinting.

In front of us was Joey, the child who had started all of this. He faced us, the burning house at his back. His face was serious, the corners of his mouth downturned and his eyes quiet, studying us.

I reached a hand forward to him. For help. For understanding. For escape. Seeing him had started everything, and I just wanted him to end it.

Piper squeaked next to me, and I moved my hand forward. She grabbed my biceps and yanked my arm away, shoving it back to my side.

"Mom, don't," she yelled.

The wind whipped around us, fueling the fire at the Vickery house. We were trapped in the center of the storm that went around the house, us, and now the little boy. There was no escape. Either the wind, the fire, or maybe the Vickery child would take us all out.

"Help," I whispered to Joey. "Let us go. I know you and your mom wanted our help, and we listened. Here is the locket. But please, let this end."

He shook his head, and I felt Piper's knees buckle as she gripped me tighter.

Joey slowly turned and looked at the burning house, and then shook his head again. He looked back to us once and then to the house. He lifted a hand in the direction of the flames and just as quickly as the fire had started, it stopped.

There was the feeling of pressure, of a cosmic vacuum above us, sucking away the image. A new one replaced it in front of us. It wasn't the current state of the house, all broken glass and trash, but the Vickery house as we'd seen it before, just before the fire.

We looked around in wonder, the danger gone. I looked down at my arms and then at Nick and the kids, examining them for any injuries or damage. Everyone was physically unscathed.

Joey was also gone.

I heard a car moving across gravel, headlights shining on the path. It was then that I realized it was nighttime in this vision.

It must have been eleven fifteen p.m. The time when the clocks stood still.

We froze, huddled, as we watched the car that Leo had heard earlier approach the house. I recognized the blue paint on the sedan—it was the same car that I had seen in the *Days of Our Lives* dream.

The driver pulled up to the side of the house and the passenger-side door opened. Out popped a teenager, with long dark hair curled around her shoulders. Lyssa Vickery. She leaned back in the car and gave the driver a peck on the cheek, then climbed out, bounding toward the front steps to enter the house. It was then that I noticed she had a cigarette in her hand. She stopped before she opened the front door and flicked the cigarette over the side of the porch. Then she waved her hand around, trying to clear the smoke.

Lyssa opened the front door and closed it behind her as her boyfriend drove away, the outside silent again.

Silent, but not at peace. From our vantage point, we could see that the cigarette that she had tossed away, expecting it would burn itself out, had landed on a pile of leaves and brush that had been stacked on the side of the house. It caught the edge of one of the dried leaves and started a fire. The other leaves in the bushel also caught fire, and the blaze began to accelerate. The flames licked closer and closer to the house, before igniting the laundry line tied to the house, where sheets were hanging dry. The fire hopped the rope directly to the house's upper half. Just a few feet from the danger, I saw Joey's Big Wheel bike.

"Fire!" I yelled fruitlessly through time. "Get out!"

Of course, no one heard me. We were just watching a movie reel, camcorder footage from the past. We were the spectators.

The roof began to burn, and there was no sign of the family rushing out, nor that they had noticed the house was on fire.

I turned back to the house and everything went quiet again.

There was a crackle in the air and the vision of the house catching fire was gone, and in its place, the reality was back, all half-burned wood and forest trash.

Joey appeared in front of us again, the emcee of this spectacle.

"I'm so sorry for what happened to you. I wish someone could have saved you," I said.

The weight of what had happened to the Vickerys pressed

down on my chest, and I felt my eyes flood with tears. My stomach bottomed out and I sank down onto one knee with Joey—the little boy who never had a chance—in front of me.

His eyes filled with tears and his chin began to tremble. His shoulders shook; he was just a little boy trying to seem brave, but it was too much.

"I'm sorry," I whispered to him, sinking further down into the gravel so I was sitting on my hip in front of him.

I was a mom, even though so often I didn't feel like it was something that came naturally to me. It felt like part of my identity, but not one that fit easily. I was a mom—but was I a good one? Did I deserve to be one?

Yet in that moment, every maternal instinct I had reached toward him.

Joey didn't have his mom anymore, but for a few seconds, I offered myself up to him.

"Your mom loved you very much," I whispered to him. Because I knew it was true. I felt it. The same way that I loved my children despite all of my self-doubt, the way that I worried that I was constantly screwing them up even though I loved them more than my own life.

He gave me a small smile and nodded.

"Thank you for showing me what happened to your family. I know now and will tell the story. You can rest," I said. I reached into my back pocket and pulled out the locket, the charm swinging from the end. The engraved V caught the light and twirled around as I moved it forward.

"This belongs to your family," I said.

He stared at it for a moment and then moved forward, toward

me. I didn't have time to react or anticipate the movement as he approached, it was so fast. His figure became a blur of white and at first, I didn't know if he was going to hit or hug me. But then he extended his arms.

I had no chance to give him the hug he wanted. The moment of motherly love that he was searching for.

Because he passed right through me.

I gave out a startled cry as I felt an intense pressure move through my midsection, like I had put on a too-tight life vest. The feeling dissipated quickly and was gone, and so was he.

As was the locket. He had taken it.

Still sitting on the ground, I turned back to my family. They stared at me with a mixture of fear and awe. I had put a hand on the ground to push myself up and go to them when another figure appeared standing in front of me.

It was Patty. She looked down at me, wearing the same jeans and white striped T-shirt as in my earlier vision. Her hair was pushed forward on either shoulder, and her eyes were a light hazel. She gave me a slight nod and then put her hands to her stomach.

My eyes widened in understanding. There was a small bump under her shirt, one I hadn't seen before. I placed a hand where new life had taken hold in me.

She was pregnant. Four kids, not three, as everyone had thought. She was haunted that no one knew the full depth of her loss.

"I'm so sorry for what happened to you," I said to her as I looked up. "We know. You can be at peace now. We see you."

She gave me a long look before she nodded again. I felt a connection to her, as though if she had been my contemporary, we would have been friends. Maybe raised our babies together. But no, her baby never had a chance. None of them did. And they were trapped here, in the ruins of their once-happy home, forever witnessing the violation of the property and the awful whispers about what really happened to them. The worst kind of purgatory.

She smiled at me, a small smile of understanding and connection, and I saw the locket was around her neck. And then, she faded away.

I pushed myself up off the ground and turned to face my family. Reality had returned, with the sun shining again and the buzzing from the insects loud.

"Time to go home," I said to my family.

I couldn't wait to get back to my room and my bed, but after all we had gone through together, I knew what *home* actually meant. Us, together. It didn't matter where.

Here, with all four of my kids and my husband, alive and well, I was already home.

Chapter 38

I spy . . . our house," I said in a whisper.

"Home non-haunted home." Nick leaned back against the driver's seat and closed his eyes briefly.

We were in our driveway after five hours of driving back to Milwaukee. We had left the Vickery house and remained mostly silent on the way back to our house, processing what had happened. I kept glancing back at the kids to make sure they were okay. Or at least as okay as possible.

True to resilient kid form, they all moved on to complaining about missing power cords for their electronics and asking when we were going to stop for food.

All was right with the Somerset world.

It was the middle of the night by the time we pulled into our driveway, with Nick hitting the garage door button from the end of our street, eager to get inside and step away from the long, strange trip home. The kids threw themselves out of Tammy as soon as Nick put the car in Park. He and I sat together for a moment, alone.

He held out his hand limply, and I put mine inside. His fingers curled around my palm.

"Is it really over?" he said quietly, eyes still closed.

I nodded even though he couldn't see me. "It is. The Vickerys are at peace, and we're home. It's over. Except for one thing: Nick, are you ready to own property in Indiana?" I turned to him with a smile.

He rubbed his forehead. We had discussed this as we drove through Illinois—no state prizes. I'd told him I wanted to contact Jillian Samson in Tucson, Arizona, and talk about purchasing the property from her. She didn't even know the Vickerys—we did. Across time, space, and any semblance of reality, we knew them. And I wanted to clean it up and make sure they had a proper resting place, with headstones. He'd said he needed to think about it.

"Patty would want that," I added. "Something to acknowledge that they existed, that they mattered."

"I know. It's a great idea," Nick said into the darkness. He squeezed my hand.

I turned to face him. "Listen, this was a literal nightmare of a trip. It didn't go the way any of us could have imagined, but . . . thank you. Thank you for taking us on this trip. You always put me and the kids first, and want us to have everything and every experience. Together."

He opened one eye and slowly turned to face me. His face softened into a small smile, and he tightened his hand around mine. I rested the side of my head against the headrest, smiling back.

"No one is going to believe us," I whispered. "And how could they? I wouldn't believe it either."

"I guess it will be the Somerset family adventure for us to remember. That's all I wanted, anyway," he said. He exhaled loudly and ran a hand over his cheek. "Now we know we Somersets can do literally anything, at least."

I laughed and put my other hand on his, one on top and one on the bottom. "Oh yeah. Flat tires, weird motel rooms, bad fast food, ghosts, hauntings, creepy lockets. None of it is any match for us. Watch out, world."

"And the adventure isn't over." His gaze slowly slid down to my midsection.

I twisted my mouth into a half smile and widened my eyes. "Yeah, I'm going to need a few nights of sleep in my own bed before I can even think about what's next."

He pulled my hands forward, and I leaned in so our faces were close. "We got this. I love you."

I kissed him and put my forehead on his. "We always do. I love you, too."

"When should we tell the kids?" he said.

I exhaled. "Soon. But let's get a good night of sleep and feel more human first." I shook my head. "And hey, before I forget, I just want to say: I feel like we went through the storm and came out okay. God, it finally feels like the sun will shine again." I turned to him and gave him a cheesy smile. "I guess you're my sunshine."

A sliver of light appeared in the garage as Piper stuck her head out of the house and peered down the driveway.

"What are you guys doing? Stop being weird out there," she called. The garage returned to darkness as she closed the door behind her, no doubt adding seeing her parents cuddling in the driveway to her trauma list.

"Back atcha," Nick said with a laugh. "I will always be the sunshine to your rain."

I closed my eyes and shook my head, laughing. "That's not what I meant. But I'll take it, wedrio."

"Guess we better follow the pied Piper," Nick said as he unbuckled his seat belt. He reached for the door but stopped as I grabbed his biceps.

"Hey, I love you," I said.

"Love you more." He winked at me. "Well, not as much as I love the TripTik, but you get it."

"To the next adventure," I said with a smile. "I spy . . . a really weird future, but we get to do it together."

Epilogue

It's a boy! You have a son," Dr. Patel, my obstetrician, said from behind her mask.

I looked to Nick, who was next to my hospital bed, gripping my hand. Tears began to slide down both of our faces as the nurses placed our son on my chest.

I put a hand on his tiny back and closed my eyes.

"Oh my God," Nick said over and over as he kissed me on my sweaty forehead.

"A little boy," I said, and looked up at Nick, smiling through tears. I laughed when I saw he was crying harder than I was. He had been emotional at the births of our other kids, but something about this—our last, for sure no question about it, vasectomy already complete—cut any strings of restraint inside of him.

We'd made the decision not to find out the sex of the baby, figuring we should completely surrender and go with it. The kids had all placed bets, with Piper voting girl ("to secure the female spot in our house"), Leo voting boy ("to make things even"), and Sophie asking repeatedly if we could get a kitten instead.

The spoils would go to Leo.

"Let's get him cleaned up and we'll bring him right back, Mom." The nurse at my elbow reached for my son and scooped him off of me, whisking him away before I could even get a proper look at his face.

I wiped my forehead and looked at Nick, who grabbed my hand again. "So, are we going with Tate?"

Nick glanced over at where the nurses had him under one of those heat lamps in a plastic Tupperware-looking bed. "Tate," he said with a smile as he looked back to me, squeezing my hand.

Piper, Leo, Sophie, and Tate.

My chest tightened as a wave of gratitude came over me. We had survived. All of us. From ghosts to lockets to houses to hauntings, all the way to a surprise baby. We had done it, and pulled each other close rather than tearing each other apart.

"Here he is, Mom." The nurse reappeared with Tate bundled into a white hospital blanket with blue and pink stripes.

"Burrito baby," Nick said as she placed him in my arms, careful to avoid the IV line.

I looked down at my son, filled with love. His perfect eyebrows, eyelashes, little tuft of hair.

"Nick, look. He has a little mark," I said as I ran a finger over his impossibly smooth cheek.

"Stork bite," the nurse said from behind Nick. "We see them a lot. They usually go away after a few months."

"Nick?" I said, my voice lower.

My beautiful son had a birthmark on his left cheek. A small, strawberry-shaped mark.

"Nick," I said again as I stared at it.

It can't be. Stop. It's not the same.

But it was.

"Stork bite, like she said," Nick said, but I heard a waver in his voice.

Tate made a noise and opened his eyes, locking his gaze with mine. A jolt of primal emotion ran through me. An innate sense of love, a fierce protection instinct, and an overwhelming sense that we were back on the newborn roller coaster.

I couldn't believe that we were lucky enough to get to do this again.

I pulled Tate closer to my chest, our eye contact still unbroken. Nick placed his hand on the blanket, and we both understood.

I silently communicated to Tate that I would always protect him, always find a way to put my body in front of any danger to him, that I loved him more than he would ever know. And his dad would do the same, felt the same.

He blinked, tiny wet eyelashes moving up and down.

And then I heard his voice. In my head.

Hi again. I missed you, Mom.

I gasped for air, and the machines began to beep and alarms went off. The nurses were unconcerned and laughed while they shut them off, busying themselves with cleaning up the room.

Nick's hand on Tate stiffened as a silent understanding passed between us.

I looked up at him, and I saw everything behind his eyes.

This is our child. We will protect him no matter what. He's ours.

I nodded and looked back down at our baby.

"Welcome to the family," I whispered.

Acknowledgments

As a child in the '80s, classic vacation comedy movies were a viewing staple. From *National Lampoon's Vacation* to *The Great Outdoors*, I watched as families limped through summer bonding in the most disastrously hilarious of ways. So when I sat down to write this book, it wasn't difficult to explore the horror in road trips—ghosts or not. Between the long hours in the car and the many potential disasters, all the ingredients for mayhem are there. And that's before adding in any paranormal passengers. This book is an homage to the movies of my youth and to all of us parents who have ever had to use a rest-stop bathroom that made you want to dive into a barrel of hand sanitizer.

I have to thank a few folks who dared to travel on this journey with me—may your Check Engine light never illuminate and your tire pressure always be perfect:

Ryan, Paige, Jake, and Kevin: Thank you for all the trips and family vacations we've taken together and for always providing new material. While we haven't encountered a haunted amusement park or water park yet, I'm confident we would prevail like the Somersets.

Holly Root, super agent: Thank you for the many years of support and creative pivots we've had to do together in this crazy industry. It's been a wild ride, and I can't wait to see what's next.

Kate Dresser, unicorn editor: This book might be my favorite one that we've done together. I'm eternally grateful for your advice and guidance, and I always look forward to your feedback. Thank you for being so amazing! And thank you to Tarini Sipahimalani for your support and enthusiasm—working with both of you continues to be such a joy.

Shina Patel and Nicole Biton: Thank you for all your hard work to connect readers with my books. Working with everyone at Putnam has been so wonderful, and I'm beyond fortunate to have such great people on my team.

The KL crew and extended families: Thank you for providing me with enough road-trip memories to fill an entire series. I will never forget driving eighteen hours in a minivan with a combo TV/VCR, watching recorded airings of *The Price Is Right*, *General Hospital*, and *The Sally Jessy Raphael Show*. And yes, the Cracker Barrel scene is for all of you.

My friends: Thank you all for your amazing support. You all are spectacular, and I could not do this without any of you. You guys attended signings, sent supportive texts, and generally allowed me to be slightly unhinged as I worked through a deadline. First, I tormented the neighborhood with a demon. Next, I threw in some witchcraft. At least for this book our suburban enclave was safe. I can't promise anything for the next one.

All the readers, reviewers, booksellers, and Bookstagrammers who have supported me: Whenever I'm having a difficult or stressful day, it always seems that I receive a message of support.

It's an understatement to say that your thoughtful words and posts encourage me to keep writing and keep going when things get tough. I am forever grateful and can never repay your kindness.

And to Lucy: Thank you for being by my side (literally!) as I wrote this book. Rest easy, sweet girl.